CHEAP AMUSEMENTS

CHEAP AMUSEMENTS

A HAYDEN FULLER MYSTERY

GRANT TRACEY

Book Club Edition

Twelve Winters Press

Published by Twelve Winters Press, a literary publisher.

P. O. Box 414 • Sherman, Illinois 62684-0414 • twelvewinters.com

Cheap Amusements was first published by Twelve Winters Press in 2016. "Toronto, 1965: *Cheap Amusements'* Beat" was published by TWP in 2017. Chapter 1 of *A Fourth Face* was published by TWP in 2017. The Press plans to release the complete novel *A Fourth Face* in 2017. The character Hayden Fuller and the phrases "A Hayden Fuller Mystery" and "Hayden Fuller Mysteries" are the property of Grant Tracey. All rights reserved. The songs listed on pages ix and x remain the property of their individual copyright holders. Neither Grant Tracey nor Twelve Winters Press benefits financially from any purchases readers may make to listen to the suggested playlist.

Cover and interior page design by TWP Design.

Cover art copyright © 2016 Miles Wisniewski. Used by permission. All rights reserved.

Author photos copyright © 2015 Mitchell D. Strauss.

ISBN
978-0-9987057-0-5

Printed in the United States of America

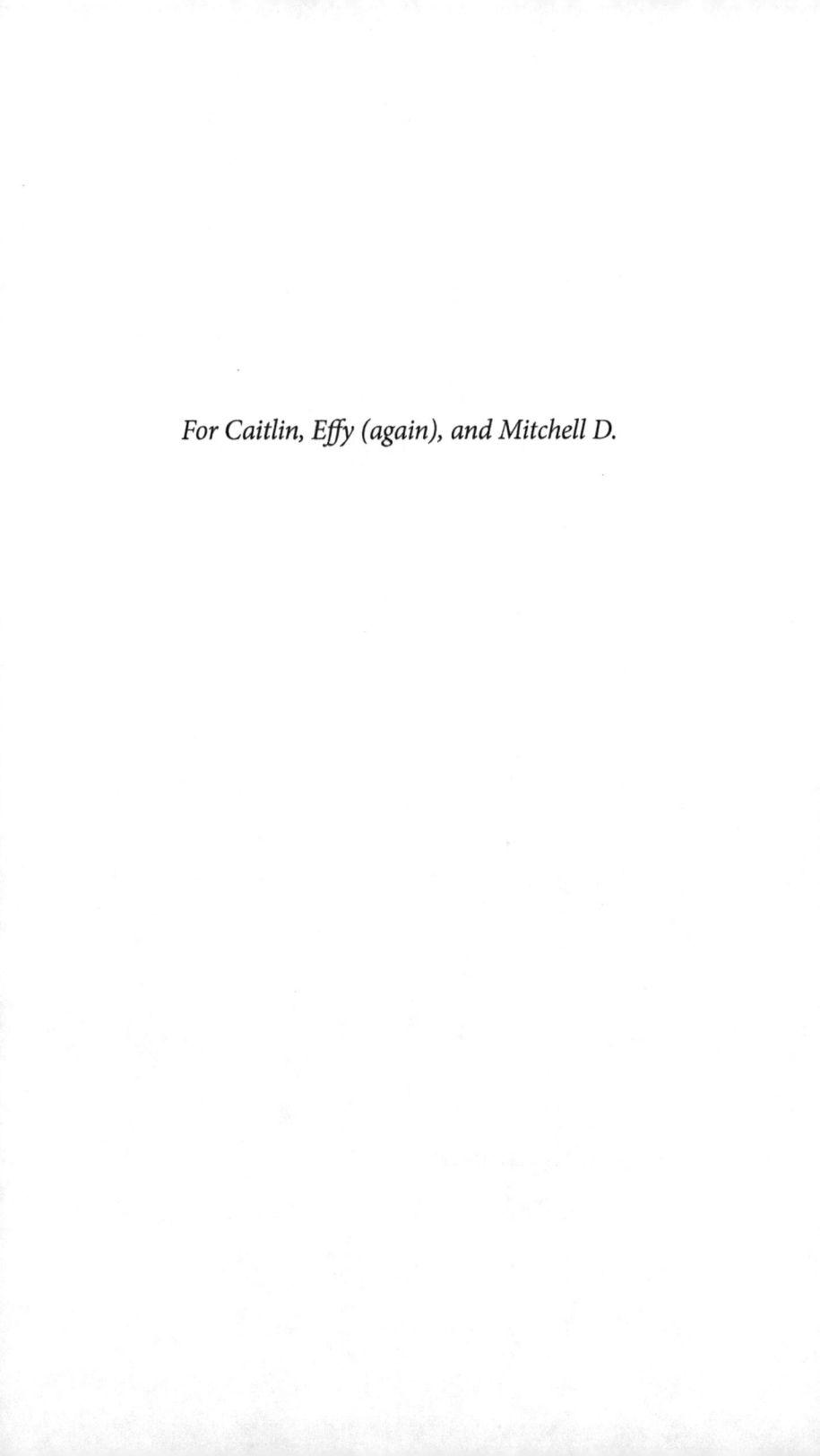

For Caitlin, Effy (again), and Mitchell D.

Contents

Author's Playlist of Jazz Selections

Grant Tracey invites you to listen to the following songs which he feels match the mood and content of the prologue and each of the chapters. They are readily available via various music archives.

Prologue
"Moanin'" by Art Blakey & the Jazz Messengers (*Moanin'*)

Chapter 1
"Cool Struttin'" by Sonny Clark (*Cool Struttin'*)

Chapter 2
"If I Were a Bell" by Miles Davis (*Relaxin' with the Miles Davis Quintet*)

Chapter 3
"Me 'N You" by Hank Mobley (*No Room for Squares*)

Chapter 4
"Take Five" by Dave Brubeck Quartet (*Time Out*)

Chapter 5
"Say You're Mine" by Donald Byrd (*Cat Walk*)

Chapter 6
"Broadway" by Dexter Gordon (*Our Man in Paris*)

Chapter 7
"Monk's Dream" by Thelonious Mon (*Monk's Dream*)

CHEAP AMUSEMENTS

93 Days Ago

The sky was black, clear, and speckled with dim stars, but it wasn't as cold as it should be for early December. Hayden Fuller was watching the sky, the tips of trees, the foamed frost of dark grass, ahead of him waiting, vaguely hoping. His breath twitched from his lips like small snakes. They had to find the girl.

The tip, a muffled voice, said the girl was holed up here. The voice called Hayden's office earlier that afternoon and Hayden wasn't sure if the tipster were a man or a woman. The one distinguishing feature to the cadence: the speaker said *again* like an American with the second syllable rhyming with Jen as opposed to the Canadian heavy emphasis on the second syllable "gain." Police Chief Sal Lambertino, who Hayden immediately called for backup, was chewing his lower lip and was worried. The picket fence of his beard had stiffened against his jawline. He let out a sharp gasp of air and huddled nearer a narrow slant of pine trees.

They had just passed a small grouping of cabins, empty, and there was one more cabin to go, a football field across from them, light flickering from one of the front windows. There were no human shadows in the cabin but the light danced as if there were a burning candle. Someone had to be close by. Where? Could be an ambush, the kidnapper lying fallow in the adjacent fields of foam, waiting for Hayden and Sal to cross the open expanse of tall grass and frozen cattails. "I don't like this—too much ground," Sal said.

"I'm not too crazy about it either." Hayden pulled his pork-pie down along the tip of his ears. He wished he had worn a toque. Sarah Kerr, the daughter of his client Mrs. Kerr, had been missing for two days. According to Mrs. Kerr, the girl had allegedly received a phone call from her guidance counselor telling her to meet him at the coffee shop at the corner of Eglinton and Yonge to discuss her senior thesis. "Be home soon, Mom" were the last words she said. The counselor hadn't made the call. He had been in a meeting with fellow Castle Frank faculty at the time it was placed. Lambertino told Hayden not to hold out much hope. The girl was probably dead. Might never be found, but he had a full force of men behind him, loaded down with weaponry.

The window light danced with the rhythm of thin scarves on a downhill skier.

Suddenly bright lights filled the spaces around Hayden and Sal. Mounted high in trees, the arc lamps cut diamonds in the snow. It was so bright that Hayden felt his face tightening into a squint. Machine gun fire blurted from across the way, nicking spots of bark from the pine trees. Hayden dropped so low that snow filled his lower lip. Sal was on the ground too. The constables behind them and the R.C.M.P. returned fire.

It was a sharp attack like the fine stick work of a jazz drummer. The melody across the way was a robust ack-ack-ack. "AK-47," Sal mumbled. "A commie gun."

In the brief respite between gun bursts, a car engine slowly cranked. Even though the weather was unseasonably warm for early December it was still cold enough to play havoc with a car battery. Hayden motioned to Sal to their right and mumbled "getaway." Sal nodded and asked for cover as the two men broke across the tall grass. The sky and the cabin against it shook as Hayden closed in on the car, a Rambler, with a shadow of a man behind the wheel. "I see him, there, there, behind the wheel." Hayden tried to get a shot off but hit the radiator. Steam hissed.

Sal opened up, spiderwebbing the windshield, the front end of the car drooping in sync with the man behind the wheel. Nothing was upright. Hardened leaves and bits of wood cracked under their shoes as they approached. Sal opened the door.

"What the hell?"

It wasn't a person. It was a bullet-riddled mannequin, a jacket around its shoulders. It didn't have a face.

"Fuck—"

And then they heard a second motor. A boat sludged across the slush of lake. It thumped up against chunks of ice, but it was definitely moving. It mustn't have far to go, Hayden figured, because there was no way it could get across a partially frozen lake.

The other police officers formed a curtain around the cabin and were already searching inside for the girl. "Captain—" one of them shouted.

Sal and Hayden rushed into the cabin, the fresh heat warming their faces. A carpet was kicked back from a trapdoor. They opened the door and followed the ladder to the cold, slapping water below. This was clearly the exit port. Sal's flashlight cut arc lines along the wood beams and hollow splashes of water. He shook his head, the flashlight creating rings a glass might make on a counter top. "We don't have anyone on the other side. Might as well radio ahead, but it's pretty pointless."

"He wanted us to come close without catching him. He wanted us to—" Hayden's stomach felt like it were full of rocks. "Let's check the cabin."

There wasn't much to see: a couch, three TV trays, a small transistor radio protected by a crotched leather case, primitive bunk beds with threadbare bedroll, a bookshelf loaded up with *National Geographic* magazines, and charred wood in a stove-top fireplace. The room was warm and the candle was burning dim, its flickers filling the room with Neolithic-looking shadows. In one corner was a huge Gladstone suitcase. It was heavy.

Hayden took another breath. He was afraid of what might be inside.

He was right to be afraid. Folded up was a naked blonde, a huge Christmas bow christening the top of her head. Her bloody parchment hair stuck to her shoulders, two bullet holes were behind her right ear. Sarah Kerr.

1

It was one of those days where everything is covered with layers of gauze, a kind of dusky twilight vibe, as if the world has stopped spinning and life's brightness is now layered in thin-veiled threads. I pushed back my porkpie, wiped tired eyes and swallowed, my voice catching. "So, how long she been missing?"

Another missing person case.

Like Sarah Kerr.

Guilt is a strange thing. Just when you think the responsibilities that failure brings have abated, you find yourself tossing in the wee small hours of the morning, agonizing over the case that got away.

Kim Stabulas studied the lines in the hardwood floor. They ran parallel but every once in a while a wobbly knot suggested that rhythmic order could be knocked off its axis. "Two days."

No ransom note, no phone calls, nothing. Cathy had been working at the family store, when she said she had to meet a girlfriend at the corner of Yonge and St. Clair. This was at 6 p.m. on Saturday.

Yonge and St. Clair.

Yonge and Eglinton, 95 days ago.

It was now Monday, the last day of March, late afternoon.

The Stabulas mom and pop grocery had been in the family for over thirty years and was just below her bedroom.

"Who's the girlfriend?"

"She didn't say." Nick Stabulas, Kim and Cathy's father, crowded over my shoulder. "She wasn't one to, you know—reveal private matters." He had a wide-set face, bushy eyebrows, and a solemn expression that resembled a man squinting through a bright fire. "She's very *proper*. Never stays out late. Never speaks badly of anyone. She just isn't that kind of girl, you understand?"

Kim nodded, half-heartedly. "A saint, my sister."

The tone was slightly ironic and coated with regrets. I wasn't quite sure who she was sad for: herself or her sister.

"Three days ago, Cathy met with her guidance counselor. Well, he used to be her guidance counselor—" Kim looked away, eyes skimming details in the room.

"As in high school guidance counselor?" Cathy graduated four, nearly five years ago. I pulled on the brim of my porkpie. "She's still seeing her high school guidance counselor?"

"I'm not crazy about it either, but ever since the girls' mother died Landover has been a care provider, trying to talk Cathy into going to college. She has the smarts for it, he says." Nick shrugged apathetically.

Kim shot sharp edges at her father. "Yeah. This was one of those meetings. That was on Friday."

"Who is this guy? Did you say Landover?"

"Yeah, Landover Leeds."

Landover Leeds. The same guy in the Sarah Kerr case. He was her guidance counselor too. He was in a meeting at the time of her abduction. Toxicology reports on Sarah came back clean, but there were traces of semen. She had been raped, strangled, and shot twice behind the right ear.

Cathy attended Castle Frank High School from 1956–60, Sarah attended from 1961–65.

"She didn't have many friends." Nick shrugged with his big shoulders. "It was probably Lisa who called. Lisa Steinmetz—"

I wrote the name down in my yellow note pad. I had the spelling right the first time.

Nick had given me photographs of Cathy yesterday and it was hard to tell her apart from Kim. She and her sister were Irish twins. Kim born in January 1941; Cathy eleven months later in December. Their faces and figures—long and lithe with athletic arms, modest breasts, and strong upper thighs—were very similar. Kim's hair, however, was sleek and black, like drawings in a four-color comic book. Cathy's hair was short, thicker and red, cut just below the ears, and even in still photographs you could tell that it bounced with a sassy energy. What was most striking about Cathy were her penetrating eyes, warm, with their dark black comfort. It was a mesmerizing yet odd combination for a woman in the predominately English, Irish, and Scottish confines of Toronto: red hair, black eyes.

I stared into the bedroom. It was very polite, neat: twin beds with cover corners folded over in precise triangles; a bookshelf crowded with tight upright books; a small coffee table, a lamp, and a dozen or so jazz records fanned by a modest hi-fi unit.

"I shared this room with her." Kim pointed at the two beds. "That's before I moved out on my own at seventeen.

Everything in here is hers, except a few clothes in the closet and that bed."

I made another note.

"She kept the bed, hoping I'd return, I guess."

There wasn't much else in the room but three Harold Barkley photographs torn from the *Star Weekly* hanging like pennants over the foot of her bed. I was in one of the photos, between the circles, wristing a shot over Terry Sawchuk's catch glove, one hole. Sawchuk, now a Leaf, was with Detroit at the time, and he looked like a display case mannequin as the puck tucked under the bar behind him. One and four holes (high catch glove and low stick side) were my favorite shots to make. I miss the game. Big time.

"Leafs fan?" I asked, pointing at the Barkleys.

"The biggest," her sister said.

"Twenty-two goals, your best season, 1958–59," Nick said, smiling.

I guess he was a big fan too.

On the dresser at the foot of Cathy's bed were a handful of hockey programs done up in blue Art Deco lines with Tim Horton or the Big Z, Hank Zakoic, gracing the cover. On the back of the programs were ads for Dominion's grocery stores: "Mainly Because of the Meat!"

"Aww—" Nick groaned. "Goddamn Dominion's." They were putting him out of business. Three years ago the big chain opened just two blocks away, reconfiguring Nick's customer base to grandmas and kids. He shook his head. "You can't live on the baboes and the kids, you understand?"

"Sure."

Cathy couldn't have just wandered off, you understand.

Ninety-five days ago, Sarah Kerr had received a phone call from someone pretending to be Landover Leeds. Meet me at the coffee shop on the corner of Yonge and Eglinton to discuss your senior thesis, the voice said. She went and her folded up body was found two days later in a suitcase in a cabin. She had been tattooed with cigarette burns and two bullets were placed behind the right ear.

"So Lisa Steinmetz, huh? It couldn't have been this Landover guy she went to see?"

"She wouldn't be involved with Landover or any guy over the phone. Like my father said, she was a quiet girl—" Kim shrugged.

Kim, by contrast, *was not* quiet. She wore a striking black-and-white jacket and medium skirt that vaguely resembled the vibrancy of a pop-art painting. The tight-sleeved jacket flared at the shoulders. The skirt was long with patches of white and black highlighting the curves of her hips and power of her thighs. She didn't quite fit in with her family. She was a realtor in a downtown office and had her own apartment. "You've seen her photographs. Does she look like the kind of girl that would run off with some guy?"

"I don't know." I shrugged.

I sure hoped that Cathy's fate wasn't like the girl's in the suitcase, and maybe I was doing too much thinking out loud, maybe it had something to do with all that gauze cluttering up the room and everything spinning askew, but when Nick's and Kim's eyes widened, I backpedaled and realized my thoughts were being spoken aloud. I do that sometimes. "I'm not trying to alarm anybody. I'm sorry. I just—I need something. A clue. A lead." I wiped the edges of my mouth. "You mind if I search her things?"

"No, no. Go ahead," Nick said.

I wondered if I could show her photographs to people.

Sure, they both said, and Nick pulled out a more recent one, a 3x5 from his wallet. It was slightly creased and taken two weeks ago. Cathy stood by the plate glass of the grocery store, head tilted, slightly shielding her eyes from the sun, a twist of a smile rising up from the corners of her mouth. It was as if she were retreating from something she really needed to share but was afraid to.

"Did she write a diary? Was she seeing anybody?"

"No. Like I said, she was a home girl, you know?" Stabulas rubbed at a bushy eyebrow and looked away. "She didn't date much. Worked in the store." He glanced over at Kim and I sensed disfavor at his older daughter's lifestyle and abandonment of old country ways.

"Tell me about Lisa Steinmetz—"

Lisa Steinmetz, a working girl. Not the sharpest knife in the drawer, Nick said. Occasionally, after the hockey game on Saturday nights, Lisa, Cathy and two others played bridge.

"Bridge?" That seemed just a little too English—not at all a Macedonian pastime.

"Lisa isn't Macedonian. German and English, I think," Kim said.

"She lives on her own." Nick again passed some kind of veiled judgment over female independence. She also didn't have a good relationship with her parents. "Her father used to hit her and drinks too much."

"She told you all this?"

"To me they talk, in the store," Nick said. "Lots of bad things in her home, you understand?" The heavy traces of his Eastern-European accent were more pronounced when he got excited. The rhythms gave him the dignity of experience.

"Yeah," Kim nodded, "Lisa's had it rough. And that's the extent of Cathy's social life. Bridge with a lost girl and hockey games in front of the TV on Saturday." Kim's lips were a terse line. "She also puts in long hours at the store."

Kim must have felt that her father hovered too much around Cathy's life, keeping her trapped in the home. As she spoke, she crossed her arms and shot him surly looks.

I wandered to the closet. Didn't find much of anything but simple, unflashy clothes: slacks and jeans and plain blouses and loose-fitting sweaters. On her tight bookshelf were novels by American and Canadian authors from John Steinbeck to Morley Callaghan. At the end of the shelf was a glass ball with a snow figure inside, a gentle reminder of childhood or a desire to hold onto a prior innocence.

"Oh, that's mine," Kim said. "That and the bed."

I nodded. I guess she was holding onto a part of her childhood too. I placed the glass ball back in front of the books and leafed through a dog-eared copy of Steinbeck's *East of Eden*.

"Cathy loved that book," Kim said. "Read it twice."

"Uh-huh."

The jazz records were classic hard bop, my favorites too: John Coltrane, Sonny Clark, Donald Byrd, and Hank Mobley. Scrapbooks were full of clippings from several Leafs games, including game one of the '63 finals in which I scored a goal and an assist. Cathy penciled across the headline in blue, "Way to go Fuller!"

It was weird. I suddenly felt like we had a personal connection. Just those four words and it was like we knew each other.

I never felt connected to Sarah. I never got to know her. She was an enigma and shortly after her murder I met with her mom once a week, pursuing new leads, asking for hints, anything. We don't get together much now.

But there was no diary. No sense of a sexual history. Not much to go on.

That was until we got to the dresser's bottom drawer. It wouldn't open.

The first two drawers were crowded with underwear and socks and T-shirts. But this drawer—

"I didn't know that drawer locked," Kim said.

Nick Stabulas pressed in closer. "Me neither."

I pulled on it harder, and then reached for my Buck knife. "Do you mind?" I don't know why I was asking for permission. Cathy wasn't a minor. I should be really asking her to look in her dresser, not her father, but for some reason I was asking him—Old World deference? I'm not sure.

He nodded and shrugged reluctantly. I jimmied it.

And the drawer stuttered and yawped like the very wood was crying.

On top was a Big Chief Tablet. "My writings" was scrawled about the Indian's head. Doodles of men's faces, crescent moons, a clown face in a homburg, and unbalanced stars (some of the points more open than others) filled the rest of the space.

The pages were slanted with left leaning prose. "She's a lefty?"

"Yes," Kim nodded. "So am I."

What were the odds?

I never did learn if Sarah was a lefty or righty. I never learned much about her at all. The suitcase she was found in was traced to Eaton's. It was a model that only they manufac-

tured, and nine were sold in the four months before her disappearance: five on credit, four by cash. All of the credit purchases checked out: the customers still had their suitcases. The salesclerks couldn't recall any of the other buyers but one, a man with a heavy lower lip and eyes too close together. The sales gal didn't like him because he kept calling her "luv," and she was pretty sure it was a put-on English accent to hide his real accent because the voice had too much bounce in it. "You should be a cop," I told her with a smile. "The guy was a real creep, Mr. Fuller. If he had a chance to he would've patted me on the fanny." He was a big man and his eyes were constantly removing her clothing. A real fucking creep, she said, covering her lower lip for swearing. Unfortunately, the lead about the creep led nowhere.

The Big Chief Tablet wasn't a diary. That was clear at first glance. It was fiction. Stories. In time, I would look these over. Maybe there was a narrative thread to follow.

Under the tablet were sheer nighties, frilly panties, bras without cups, a black leather strap with a ball to place in your mouth, latex gloves, whips, dildos, and other sexual toys that left me only speculating on how they might function.

Her father's eyebrows knitted together. "That's not hers." He shook his heavy head, his face and eyes darkening. She was always home. When would she have time for this? And why would she bring that filth into our home?

Kim smiled absently. "Maybe she wasn't only playing bridge on Saturdays—"

Nick slapped Kim, staggering her against Cathy's bed. It wasn't an open hand hit but it wasn't a full fist either. It was somewhere in-between. "You have a dirty mouth," he said. He raised his hand again. It was chunky like a cut of pork loin.

I grabbed him by the wrist, spun him, and pushed him back into a wooden chair that he knocked about. "Don't touch her again." The edges of my ears hurt and I felt my heart knocking in my throat.

"I don't believe it. This isn't her." Nick's fists rested atop his thighs. "And you should have more respect for your sister, you understand?" He pointed at Kim. And then he lit a cigarette, a heavy thick brand.

I didn't want to believe it about Cathy either, but I didn't know her or her third face. There's a face we show in public and one we show in private, but we also have a third face, the one that catches up with and scares us, the face that we didn't even know we were capable of until it appears in the rear-view mirror, hellhounds on our trail. But have we the guts to honestly acknowledge that face, or do we turn the mirror away?

I had experienced this face in hockey: bloody, brooding moments where I really wanted to hurt somebody or was so fixated on the game and excelling that I no longer knew or cared who I was. It was like I had become Art Blakey improvising on the skins and tins without any of the beauty.

Suddenly my head clouded with the spun gauze of dirty cotton candy. I could barely breathe. "I'll check with Lisa about the bridge thing."

Nick exhaled sharply off his cigarette.

I continued searching through the sex paraphernalia and found buried in the folds of a slinky nightie an 8x10 color photograph of Leafs president Steven Smith and Board of Governors member Calvin Bullard. Smith, the light in the room refracting off the lenses of his Lombardi glasses, had taken over ownership of the club in 1961 after his father, the Old Man, stepped down. The forty-something Smith was a playboy and often drank milk with his bourbon to soothe an ulcerous stomach. He sported a thin, Errol Flynn mustache.

"Pal Cal" was a buffoon, a fat, fast-talking guy who always had a king-size bag of chips in his hands and flecks of grease stains on the lapels of his double-breasted Brooks Brothers. His appetites ran toward curvy women and betting on the horses. After most road games he floundered in some downtown Boston-Chicago-Detroit-Montreal-New York pub. For home games, he knocked back brews in his Maple Leaf Gardens bunker, a haunt cut in the east end Blues of the building where he watched games with an unobstructed view.

In the photograph, both men had their arms around Cathy who looked slightly uncomfortable between them, pouring champagne into the lip of the Stanley Cup. She wore a velvety red dress that matched the color of her hair. The Greco-Roman architecture behind her and marble floors and Art Deco flourishes (parasol webbing on light fixtures) cued me that this particular snapshot was taken at the Royal York Hotel. The Leafs often stayed at the Westbury but we celebrated Stanley Cup victories at the Royal York. Smith's mustache, which he had only started sporting recently, dated the photo from '62 or '63. "I was at those parties, but I don't remember Cathy being there."

"Maybe you weren't. They won the cup last year too," Kim said.

My neck burned. I took off my porkpie, played with the short brim, and pushed it back on. I had been sent to the minors with 32 games remaining on the schedule and the Leafs went on to win the cup in seven over Detroit without me. I retired following the season. I didn't want to try to catch on with another pro team. I was a Leaf through and through. "Yeah. I missed that party didn't I?"

"Well apparently, she didn't." Kim fluffed up one of her puffed shoulders. "But what's the significance of the photo?" She touched the corners of her lips. "I mean, why else would she save this?"

In a locked drawer of all places—

"Good point." The photograph wasn't framed or hanging on a wall. Instead it was buried among a bunch of unmentionables.

I flipped the photograph over. A row of numbers: 44 20 0. 79 42 0. "What the hell is that?"

"It's not a phone number," Kim said. "Or Social Identification Number."

Nick inhaled his cigarette. It was two-thirds gone.

There was another row beneath the first one with more numbers: 79.5390 and 43.8430. And two words, "Canada's Bazaar." One final figure beneath all of that: "$568,000."

"Bazaar? What does that word even mean?"

Nick didn't say anything.

Kim reached for a dictionary on Cathy's bookshelf. "Market."

"Market? What kind of market? Do the numbers suggest a code of some kind? Market? And the figure price? Over half-a-million dollars. And then there's all the sex stuff—Market? Meat market?"

"That's not her," Nick trailed off, his voice losing energy, a tunnel of ash dipping from his cig. "It can't be, you understand?"

No, I didn't understand, not really, but what did I really

know about Cathy? What would my third face have to say to the other faces in the mirror closing in behind me?

2

Landover Leeds was one of those athletic fellas gone to seed. His upper arms were full and strong, but his belly, from excessive drinking, strained the fabric of his sweater vest. His face, heavy with booze fat, made his eyes look small. But his hair was big and thick and had a bent back wave in front that was searching for a surfboard.

"Thanks for seeing me," I said.

"No probs, pard." He smiled. His lingo was fast and loose and a product of this era. He was a fifty-something hipster who wanted to fit in with the kids he counseled. On the walls of his office were prints of trees and rivers and some kind of diploma from the "Mind Control Institute" in Flagstaff, Arizona. To the right of his desk was a bulky console with levers and a microphone.

I told him about Cathy having gone missing.

"Troubled girl." Ever since her mother died Cathy had been lost. In high school, she attended his therapy sessions. They had had some breakthroughs in which Cathy found peace and calm and a sense of coming to terms.

"I know you can't tell me about what was said in here, and I respect that, but I was just wondering like how troubled?"

"Like way-out troubled, bro. Nuff said."

My porkpie rested on my knee. I don't know why but I had removed it out of some old-fashioned sense of politeness. Landover had that vibe to him—old money, an Englishman whose ancestors probably went back to the Conquest of Quebec or the United Empire Loyalists and the War of 1812. "Uh-huh. What about Sarah, Sarah Kerr, you knew her too?"

"Oh, sad girl. Murdered. I had to answer a lot of police questions because my name was floated out there as the alleged contact person."

"It wasn't just floated. The girl told her mom just before she went missing that you had called."

"Well I didn't. I was in a meeting." He shrugged. "So whoever killed her knew me. Far-out, huh?"

I nodded.

"Look, I'll level with you, bro. I can't give you much skinny on Cathy, but—" Cathy needed to be free of her father, an old school fella; she needed to pursue a university degree and explore her creative side. She was a very gifted writer.

I nodded again.

"I believe in relaxation exercises to free the mind of all that white noise, you know? Judgment?—" He climbed out of his chair and showed me the gizmo to the right. "I don't know much about electronics. McClelland Stuart got this wired up and running for me—" He pushed sliders and flicked a master switch, that looked like it could send a plane off into the sky.

"McClelland?" The voice of the Toronto Maple Leafs since 1924, McClelland was a pioneer of early radio and one of the great ambassadors for the sport.

"He's an old friend, like Ancient Rome, man. We were in the Old Man's militia together, drinking buddies, 1940–1945.

Anyway—"

The electronic contraption was a jerry-rigged sound system. The student waited in the alcove—or what Landover called the Tangerine Room—headphones on, listening to soothing sounds of whales or birds or whatever. And then from his office Landover talked directly to the student, guiding her through the experience. He pointed at the next-door alcove. "You want to try it?" His eyebrows darted about, jigging to do a two-step, but his hair and kiss curl didn't move. They weren't in sync with the party.

"No thanks. Sounds a little too hey-wow for me."

"No, no." He held up a hand. "It works. It'll take you to a fifth dimension, man. Gets the students outside of their self-consciousness and loosens them up. They can face themselves."

"Relaxation exercises, huh?" I pointed at the diploma on the wall. "Is that what you learned at the Leonardo Da Silva Mind Control Institute?"

"It took me four summers in Flagstaff to get that degree." He smiled sheepishly. "Where would you like to go, if you could go anywhere in your imagination?"

"Outer space."

"Far out—" He paused, tapped his chin twice, and pointed at the toggles and sliders. "This takes you there. And I talk you through some exercises and you're with the stars, man, totally refreshed—"

"Totally." I smiled politely. "I don't mean to be indelicate, Mr. Leeds—but Cathy graduated four, nearly five years ago." I wiped the edges of my mouth. Light shone through his office window, leaving shadowed curtains between us. "Do you frequently maintain contact and advice sessions with students after they graduate?"

He sat down and placed his feet up on the desk, pushing his arms behind his head. Maybe I should put my hat back on. I did.

"Her father is Old World, man. Forget Ancient Rome, he's Stone Age. I'm trying to bring Cathy into the twentieth century, man, that's all." When he chuckled it was a little bit wet. "That girl shouldn't be tied up in the store and a sense of duty. She needs to get out and explore her own life." He shrugged. "I was just—a voice—trying to help her. Nothing more."

"Far out," I said.

He smiled.

I GET THESE HEADACHES. They start behind my eyes and then spread to my ears and the world winds up rotating about 25 degrees, not much, but enough to not spin the way it should, as events become dried-out swirls of spun cotton candy, and then I start saying things that I should keep inside (like about the girl in the damn suitcase). The headaches aren't that bad, more of a dull ache, but Dr. Abramowitz thinks they're from all the hits I took as a player—not just the dirty crosschecks to the head or Gordie Howe elbows along the glass, but the moment-to-moment, shoulder-to-shoulder bumping that occurs in the corners and at the front of the net. That "activity" (and he always refers to hockey as an activity with air quotes, like it's a bad thing or something to ever have laced up the skates, even though he admits to loving the game: "ballet on ice") caused bruising on my brain, spots of blood to appear and spread like lean fingers. So, whenever I feel off-kilter, I'm supposed to check in with doc. So here I was.

He's an older man in his late fifties, a chain smoker, with a stethoscope wrapped about his neck like a garter snake. His hair is a tight Brillo pad and he speaks with the cadence of a Borsch Belt comedian. His office is in the north-end suburbs, away from the Kensington Market where he grew up. Here marinara sauce is ketchup, local theatres show double-bills of B westerns, and strip malls sell flowers, one-hour dry cleaning, and donuts. Dr. Abramowitz's eyes have a wondrous mix of concern and the promise of letting you in on a really great joke. But like all comics, you can't trump him with any one-up jive. Don't even try. "You in a rush or something? What's with all the tapping?" He touched my leg, which even though I was propped on his examining table, was beating out a rhythm to an indistinct jazz score.

"Sorry. I don't have much time—I—" I had to find the girl.

"Make the time." He shook his head after looking into my pupils with the pencil light in his left hand. "You didn't do so well on the eye chart, Hayden." The smell of Juicy Fruit filled the air, masking the layer of cigarette breath. "The fourth row. You might as well have been reading Hebraic. I figured you'd have the chart memorized by now." He smiled, his eyes crescent moons.

Back in my playing days I *did* have that damn chart memorized so that I wouldn't miss a game.

"Concussions are serious business. The medical profession isn't paying enough attention to them, not yet anyway. The research lags behind the need." He thumped heavy hands on the sides of his lab coat. "But you, my friend. Slow down, kid."

"I only know one gear, doc—" And it was fifth. He knew about the missing girl, and the urgency and all. I couldn't ride the brake on this one. I had to approach it like a hockey game—crashing the boards, bumping the opposition, and running the goalie.

"This one won't wind up like the last one," he said, eyes full of empathy.

"I hope not. Ninety-six days ago. I count the days, doc."

"Sarah was it?"

"Yeah."

He shook his head and mumbled something about why some of our species crawled out of the mud and couldn't have just stayed there. "No new leads on that case?"

"None. A dead file, cold case."

He nodded again. "This one isn't going to end like that one, huh? I just feel it." He graced my shoulder gently with a heavy hand. "You'll find her."

"We'll see."

He smiled, a lopsided grin. "Feeling any nausea?"

No. Just the gauze, that cement head mixer feel of everything tilted, off axis.

He knew I took target practice twice a week at the local police station on Bay Street. Was I wearing my headphones?

I laughed. "They're not headphones, Doctor A. They're called ear plugs. And yes I wear them and additional over-the-ear protection too."

He nodded a third time.

I don't use a big gun. A .45 has a lot of kick. I carry a snub-nose .38. I know how to control the recoil to avoid any other damage.

"Good. That's good. Dizziness?"

"None."

"Dizziness." This time it wasn't a question.

"A little. When I bend over to tie my shoes."

He wrote something or other on his clipboard and mumbled something in Yiddish. "Bright lights a problem?"

"Only if it's the goddamn media wanting an interview."

"I'd laugh along with you Hayden, but this is some serious bullshit. Joke with your tailor, not me." He jotted down more numbers.

"Tailor? Do I look like I see a tailor? These threads came off the rack at Simpsons and Zellers."

"More jokes." He sighed. "Part of your dizziness might be anxiety over the Sarah case. And now this new case. And, I'm afraid the rest of your dizziness comes from the residual damage suffered from all the hits you've taken. I don't know what another serious hit might do to you."

"What are you saying?"

"I don't know. The headaches seem more frequent. More regular. That worries me." He glanced at his chart. Apparently, I now had more headaches a month than I did six months ago.

"Look, it's not like I'm going to jump out of rolling cars for fun. I mean—I'll be careful."

"In my right eye, you'll be careful. Always with the yakkety-yak jokes." He handed me some painkillers and told me to take life ten miles under the speed limit.

"That's good advice, Doc, but there's no highway signs where I'm going to be traveling."

ONE OF THE LAMPS stood in the far corner of the room, a hand on the hip, breasts sagging slightly, left leg flexed, dimples on knees and upper thighs. The shade on the lamp's head was pink and corrugated and resembled a fez.

The other lamp was to the left of Cal Bullard's desk, staring directly at me. Its aqua green hat was propped back with strands of blond hair twisting underneath like dying, yellow grass. Aqua Green's eyes gently pleaded, wanting the joke to stop. I nodded briefly, and then she looked off, through my shoulders. She was a shorter lamp than the other one.

Bullard grabbed a handful of potato chips and crunched, flecks fell on his desk blotter, the edges of his white shirt, and broad tie. He trapped a laugh along his upper lip. He rubbed his hands together and his eyes wrinkled as if he were our evening's impresario.

"So what did you want to see me about, again?" He cupped a hand by his ear, suggesting I needed to speak up. I was known as the Quiet Leaf during my playing days. "How many times you been slapped around, Fuller?"

I had had over twenty fights in my career, over fifty-five stitches across my face and hands, two missing teeth.

"'Cause you aren't listening. I told you, I know nothing about this missing girl. She probably went away on a toot. She'll be back." His eyes wrinkled again. "I'm also starting to wonder about your eyesight."

Steven Smith, the Old Man's son, leaned behind "Pal Cal" and laughed uncontrollably, stroking his Errol Flynn mustache as if it were its own on/off switch, regulating his moods and expressions. His slender white hands were so pale that they seemed to glow with phosphorous.

I glanced about the room. Over my shoulders were two brick buildings filling up the space of the oak door. Lou Fortunado, ex-Ranger, was one of them. He led the league in penalty minutes for 1958-1959. We had rumbled a couple of times and I followed our Captain's advice, "Get in as close as you can and grab on. A big guy on skates can't hit you if you get in close. Just don't let go." I never did let go, but that didn't stop Lou from nearly biting my ear off. Lou's black hair was slicked with enough pomade to be a fire hazard. "What's with all the Dippity doo, Lou? I hope nobody lights a match," I said.

He grunted.

Next to him, hands in the pockets of his coal gray suit and leaning with sulky languor was Building Number Two, "Cool" Athol Leighton, ex-Bruin, and all around badass. He once busted up a woman's face in a Chicago hotel fracas. The details were sketchy and because she was a hooker nothing much came of the matter, not even a league suspension. He settled with the woman out of court for $2,000. As she took the payoff, her face was akimbo, like a primitive Picasso portrait: one ear lower than the other, the nose too far left.

By contrast, Cool Athol's face looked as if it had been splashed with cologne, as sprigs of perpetual sweat popped around his eyes. The skin across his cheekbones was stretched taut. He looked like Jack Palance, circa 1953. The only missing items were a dandified black vest, twin six-guns, and Shane giving him hell. Athol's eyes floated around the room like hovering dragonflies. They couldn't land or fix on a damn thing.

"Hey fellas." I waved. "I hear Warner Brothers is looking for some extras for their next gangster film—Jimmy Cagney's making a comeback. A sequel to *White Heat*."

Simultaneously, their arms crossed with command presence.

"Funny." Athol's eyes jumped from me to Bullard's desk to the blue carpet speckled with bits of off-white.

"Yeah. A regular riot," Lou said.

"Oh, Jackie Gleason. Even better. Bang, zoom. Things are looking up, boys."

"Funny."

"I think you said that already. Can't we bring up the level of our conversation? See any good plays lately?"

"That's enough." Smith sat on the edge of Bullard's desk, one leg off the floor, his pants riding above his white socks. That killed me. I knew cops for seven years. The plainclothes detectives always wore suits with white socks. Smith was no cop. And his skin was so parchment thin I could see little rivers of vein pressing at the surface. But white socks. Really?

"They're only letting your sad attempts at comic banter ride because I haven't asked them to shut you up. So I'm being polite and now I'm asking. Shut up, wise guy." He pointed, his finger, a pale stiletto. And then he removed his glasses, wiped the lenses with a bit of cloth, and put them back on. They were brow line-style, like Vince Lombardi's, the bridge of the glasses low enough to show off Smith's eyebrows and neatly frame the eyes. But Smith's eyebrows were so faded that they resembled wet chalk lines.

"Come on, Steve." Bullard waved at the two lamps, his hands semaphore flags. "Let's keep things light. No need for overtures of violence. That's why these lamps are here." He giggled into his fleshy shoulder like a frat boy sneaking a cuddly girl into his dorm room at night.

I shrugged. "Cathy Stabulas. That's why I'm here."

"We already heard that melody," Smith said. "We don't know her. Get a new tune."

"Yeah. Never heard of that song," Bullard said, a little too quickly for my taste.

"Look at the fucking picture." I pointed with my porkpie.

"Language." Smith wagged another stiletto. His father, the Old Man, believed in decorum. Leafs season ticketholders, who sat in the Reds, Greens, or Blues, received an annual letter reminding them to wear a suit and tie to the games if they wanted to renew their season tickets. Hockey was a very upscale affair. My dad's seats were high in the Greys—that's where all the working people sat. None of us got an annual letter.

But fuck, there was nothing upscale about the son. Like Bullard, he was a good-time fella, a playboy. "I don't tolerate profanity," he said.

"Uh-huh." And what about the women in the goddamn room? This wasn't sublime, some kind of pop art collage; it was profane and crude, the kind of antics of a spoiled rich kid, like pulling up all the flowers in a neighbor's garden. The women stood still, forgotten traffic signals.

"Is it bright enough in here for you?" Bullard reached the lamp standing next to him and tweaked a breast. "You want me to turn up the light? I think this one has three settings." He tweaked her breast again.

"Where did you get these girls?"

They were Gardens page girls or ushers, directing customers to seats or selling concessions. Eighteen years old. And they were getting a fine bonus for this afternoon's entertainment. Smith held up a flash of phosphorous, reassuring me that yes, they were of age. He pushed his glasses back against the bridge of his nose.

Yes, this is 1965 and we are all a part of the go-go generation, the new permissive society, but come on, man, this was way too much. I didn't see fat-ass Bullard or Skull and Bones

Smith in long white go-go boots and pasties. And I expressed my feelings on this particular inconsistency. My censor was off and I said what I thought aloud.

"God, you're such a prude," Lou graveled behind me. "A regular crew-cut square."

My hair *was* shorn, buzzed. And if respecting the rights and dignity of others makes me a square, then give me my membership card. "Whattya going to do, crosscheck me in the back of the head when I can't see you, Lou-doo? That's how you played the game—"

"Keep talking, Crumpled Suit. You'll get yours."

"*Crumpled Suit.* I like that." I put my porkpie back on. Adjusted the brim. "That's a step up from Funny. Crumpled Suit. It has a certain gutter poetry. Crumpled Suit. I give it four smiley faces. Not quite five, but four."

The blonde looked at me pleadingly and her upper lip peeled back ever so slightly.

"And don't touch her again, Pal Cal. Nobody's paid enough for that bullshit." I smiled, a kind of sidewinder grin. "I mean it. Or I'll climb over this desk of yours and lay you out."

Bullard tried to laugh off my threat. "Boy, you were always so quiet as a player. I see retirement's done you some good. Made you more confident." He reached into his bag of chips and pulled out a handful that looked like it had an ear or two in it.

I pointed at the photograph. "She was at the Stanley Cup party two, three years ago. And now she's missing." I wondered if Cathy's drawer full of sex paraphernalia was tied into Smith and Bullard's choice of décor: human lamps.

"That's it. That's all the evidence you have tying us to this girl? A Stanley Cup party? Jesus Christ."

I made the sign of the cross and bowed my head penitently.

Smith was not amused. He leaned sharply forward with his shoulders. I don't know how he kept himself from falling off the desk.

Suddenly there were two gentle raps, and Brian "Spinner" Terrien, the Terrier to some, spun into the room. He was short, small across the shoulders, with tightly curled hair and eyes too close to the bridge of his nose. He weighed only 150 pounds and was probably too slight for the NHL, but he had this endless energy, like a spinning top, or a thousand firecrackers going off all at once. Pop, pop, pop!

He twitched his shoulders nervously, once, twice, and stretched a hand up over his head, an all-purpose greeting to everyone in the room without really landing on any one in particular. Spinner's pants were high-hipped, pleated, and dusky argyle socks completed the ensemble, granting him a perennially young-man-about-town appearance, or what they called in 1920s theatre, a juvenile role. All he needed was a tennis racket to fully look like a country-club regular. Brian was my age, twenty-nine, had been a call-up, eight or nine times when I was with the Leafs, but never stuck.

"Spinner, how the fuck are you?"

He nodded with appreciation. I was always good to the AHL guys. Many of my fellow Leafs shunned the call-ups because with only 120 jobs to go around in all of the NHL, they didn't want one of *those guys* encroaching upon their or a fellow veteran's roster spot. But Brian worked hard. He just didn't have the speed, toughness on his skates, or the hands around the net to last. He had a great first pass, however, which was very effective in getting the puck out of our zone.

I liked the cat.

Smith wagged a fist of recognition at Spinner and pushed a button at the edge of Bullard's desk. A wall panel slid open behind a bookcase. Beyond the threshold were blue, corrugated floor-length curtains, lots of chrome, and spotless white bar stools. Brian smiled at me, before slip spinning around the bookcase, and then, as quickly as it opened, the wall slid closed behind him.

Damn, the Gardens were full of secret, unchartered territories. You could hide a person inside this building pretty easily. Maybe Cathy was here. Somewhere?

Bullard, with Brian's entrance, now had enough time to look at the photograph and so did Smith. They both adjusted what they had to say. "All kinds of dolls go to our parties. So what?" Smith said.

"Uh-huh. And check out the numbers on back. Any ideas what those might mean?"

"They're not a girl's measurements, that's for sure. Or if they were, that doll would break your bloody back," Smith said.

"Yeah, can you imagine an ass like that? 43.8430? That's some ass." Bullard licked bits of chips off fingertips.

That just cracked Smith up and he twisted his mustache again. He was laughing so hard I thought his glasses were about to slip off.

"How do you like being retired, Fuller?" asked Lou in his dark, gravelly voice. It was rocks sliding along the bed of a dump truck.

"Did you say something, Lou? I thought maybe it was feeding time at the zoo."

He plodded in my direction, but was held back by Pal Cal's

upraised, stubby hand. "You never should have gone to the media with that Davis story last year. That's why you're no longer in the game," the man with the king-size potato chip bag said.

"Candy-ass traitor," Lou said.

"Yup, that's me, a regular candy ass." I shrugged. "Check my record, Lou-doo. I played in 458 consecutive games, three times as many as you. The only time you approached that kind of number was when you added up your penalty minutes in parts of three seasons."

He shuffled his feet and his hands hung in front of his thighs—an angry ape in repose.

"I was a regular iron man. Never missed a practice. Played with my ribs taped, my wrists sprained. Four or five times I suited up with concussions. I scored 107 goals in seven years. Won two Stanley Cups. But I'm a candy-ass, uh-huh, that's right."

"Nobody says you weren't tough Fuller, but you shouldn't have given Stana Younger that story."

"I didn't give her any fucking story." Now it was my turn to hold up a hand. "But enough about me. That was last year. New season, boys. What about the girl? Or that figure on the back, $568,000?"

Bullard grabbed the photo. That amount set something off. His calm jocularity momentarily grayed. He turned to the lamp in the far corner of the room. "Isn't it a beautiful color? I think the pink shade is the cup duh grassie."

Bullard was always an asshole of an Anglophile, and maybe that's why so many reporters excused his atrocious pronunciation of French surnames (for Bullard, Richard lost all the "ree" of the first syllable and simply became Richard, as in the Second or the Third; Plante lost the long "a" sound of New England's aunt and became a green leafy thing, a plant; and Gagne, lost the "gone" of the first syllable and the long "yay" sound of the second and became a word emphasizing somebody literally choking on his knee). He still flew the British flag alongside the Canadian one at Leafs games, pronounced "territory" "territree," and had a framed portrait adorning his living room of Teeder Kennedy in his Leaf's white-with-blue piping shaking hands with the Queen.

"I don't remember the girl at all," Smith said. "But the number. That's interesting."

"How so?"

"It's just interesting." He rubbed at his chin, his eyes wet flames.

"Okay, play coy. But I think you know this girl. And you know why she's missing. Or have an idea."

"How many girls did you meet at parties or lay at various hotels? Do you remember them all?" Smith worked a piece of lint off his pant leg. "She's just a girl."

"When I get to the truth, I'm opening you two up and you'll bleed slowly." I leered at Smith and Bullard.

"Come on. Don't be such a clam." Pal Cal grabbed another handful of chips and patted one of the lamps on the shoulder. "This is a visual gag. It's funny."

"Funny? You know what I also don't find so funny? You got two bouncers: one an ex-Ranger, the other, an ex-Bruin. You couldn't even buy local. There's no ex-Leafs you could have hired? That's what I call a real fucking traitor." I moved toward the lamp at the side of his desk and handed her two twenties. She told me her name was Dawn. "Give the other one to your friend," I whispered, nodding in the direction of the far corner. "And put some clothes on. You're better than this."

3

Minutes later I was on my way rinkside to watch the boys practice when I ran into McClelland Stuart, the voice of the Leafs and hockey. He had just climbed down from the Gondola, a broadcast perch, suspended fifty-six feet over the ice surface. He was short, jaunty, wearing a long black overcoat and a tight-fitting homburg. Even though all of the rinks were now heated, McClelland insisted on the overcoat—it was part of his image, fashion élan, and gentlemanly style.

"Fuller, glad to see you, boy." He was always jovial. I never saw him cross. "Seeing the brain trust?" He rolled his eyes, and his chipmunk cheeks shuddered. He had a hawk nose, and a slightly quavering voice that sounded vaguely adenoidal. But the fans loved him. I couldn't figure out how his nasal twang was a voice suited for radio but McClelland was famous all across Canada. His catchphrase, "He shoots, he scores," had become industry standard.

McClelland didn't care much for Bullard or Smith. He missed the Old Man and worried about the future of the Leafs with their patriarchal figurehead gone. "You can't have playboys running a hockey team. You need men of character."

I nodded.

"You know those two clowns almost traded away The Big Z for a cool million in '62?"

"Of course, everybody knows that."

"Well, I'll tell you what you don't know. We could have had Bobby Orr." He looked over both his shoulders, as if he were to let me in on some kind of top-level, RCMP secret. Bobby Orr, a phenom two years away from breaking into the league, should have been a Leaf instead of the property of the Bruins. In 1960, the twelve-year-old Orr wrote the Gardens telling them he wanted to play for the blue and white. Smith and Bullard wrote back, saying they don't look at twelve-year-old prospects. Talk to us again in a few years. The Next One was so put off by these two assholes and their lack of appreciation and attention that he went ahead and signed a contract with the Bruins. By the end of the decade, McClelland believed, "mark my words," the Leaf era of greatness will be over. "Bullard and Smith. All they care about is money." He listed what they made in concessions, and season ticket sales, radio and TV rights.

The figures were staggering.

I let out a sharp whistle. "$568,000? Does that mean anything to you?"

"How much?"

I repeated the number.

"No, not specifically. But I'm sure that amount can be found here. The Cashbox on Carlton Street, that's what Dick Bledsoe called this place. And it's true. That's all this is to those bozos. One giant cashbox." He laughed. In the past two years Smith and Bullard had watered down the syrup in the concession stand soft drinks to stretch their profits and dumped enough salt on the boxes of popcorn to force fans to drink the watered-down pop. "An S with a line through it. That should be the crest on the Leafs sweater."

Bledsoe was one of my favorite sports writers. He was funny, irreverent, and once wasn't allowed in the Gardens for two weeks after criticizing management for trading away Jim Thompson. Thompson was the Leaf representative during the Players Association fracas in the late '50s and wound up shipped off to Chicago. Bledsoe questioned the club's ethics and was barred from the Gardens. In response, he called it the "Cashbox on Carlton Street." The man has integrity.

McClelland had the same integrity. He loved old-time hockey, talking about old-time hockey, and dreaded the advent of expansion (rumors abounded that it would happen by 1967). McClelland argued that the game could only expand if the American hockey player got better. Right now there's nobody from the U.S. good enough to play this game except maybe Tommy Williams and he's just average.

"Frankie Brimsek was pretty good."

"Yeah." McClelland nodded. "Quickest glove I ever saw." He sighed. "Mr. Zero. Six shutouts in his first seven games. Nobody will ever top that."

"Yeah." I was too young to have experienced the Eveleth, Minnesota, native's arrival in Boston, but when McClelland spoke of the past you felt as if you were there with him, witnessing, reliving it all.

And then I told McClelland about the case I was working on. He listened with his head tilted. He recognized Cathy's photograph. "I remember that girl. She was in their offices. Three, four times at least in the last few weeks."

"Really? They said they didn't know her at all."

He tightened his overcoat, adjusted his homburg. "They know her." He had seen her maybe just two, three days ago. Maybe even yesterday.

"You sure?"

"Does Bobby Hull use a curved blade? Yes, I'm sure." And then he leaned in toward me. He smelled of Clorets. "Be careful, Hayden. These guys play for keeps."

"Dangerous?"

"Very."

They weren't just getting money from the popcorn and pop either. There were rumors of connections with gangsters, drug dealers, and gamblers. "They also might be skimming."

"Embezzlement?"

"Taxes, concessions. A lot of money's going in, but I don't see it all going out. It's in their pockets. Or the Bolemac Corporation's pockets." He turned up his collar.

"Bolemac?"

"Yeah. It's a concocted private company made up of Smith, Bullard and Toronto-area gangsters. Moving pots of money. Hiding it for investments." Bolemac does all the repairs at the Gardens and their contracts, the ones Smith and Bullard sign off on, are outlandish. 'Metal fastener, $200.' You know what a metal fastener is?"

"No."

"A screwdriver. A bloody screwdriver." He laughed. "You should see those contracts. I have. Be careful."

"I will." I nodded.

He smiled and said he was heading to Mainly Drew's, a tavern across Carlton Street for an open beef sandwich and a cup of tea.

McClelland, like me, didn't drink. Never touched the stuff.

And he hated to drive. Most play-by-play guys are kind of quirky and have their rituals and superstitions. McClelland wears the same blue and white tie whenever we play Montreal, because in 1963 he wore it and we won the series in five games.

But the driving thing was odd. It wasn't a mere superstition. The practice of hating to drive came from a dark, very real place that he refuses to talk about.

I vaguely know the story. Years ago he was a passenger in some kind of horrible auto accident and hasn't been able to get behind the wheel of a car since. He has to be chauffeured everywhere by friends or taxis, busses, and trains.

"The numbers on the backside mean anything to you?"

"Latitude and longitude lines, maybe?" McClelland fished up north during hockey's offseason. He had his own boat called the *Kid Line* and was kind of into nautical nuances. Timmins was a favorite get away and its longitude and latitude lines were close to those on the photograph paper. "Sounds like north land numbers to me."

"Latitude and longitude. Thanks, McClelland."

He beamed.

Sarah was killed up north, about 65 miles from the city, in a cabin, by a small lake, more like a reservoir.

"Still no inkling as to what $568,000 might mean?"

"No idea." But there were two safes inside the Gardens. And he had no doubt that one of them could hold that kind of money.

"Really?" An inside job? Somebody lifted money from a safe?

"Nothing's been reported."

"Yeah, right. And they don't know Cathy, either."

McClelland chuckled over that, his laughter deckled with edges of desire for more gossip. "Well, keep your stick on the ice." He smiled at himself for using that old expression, the same one that my father and probably his father before him said goodbye with.

"I will."

And then with a quick wave, McClelland jaunted off. He walked as if he were slightly prancing, like a small dog gently straining on a leash, his homburg shaking ever so.

I liked McClelland; he was charming, a man who enjoyed conspiring when he spoke, letting you in on secrets and a coveted space that just belonged to the two of you. But he was also a complex man, full of gray bigotry. One night, after a game in Chicago, we were in a bar, and I remember him saying, as if he were reading the evening's stat lines, "Boy, there sure are a lot of niggers in this place."

I SAT IN THE BLUES, feet up on the seat in front of me, watching the Leafs go through their paces.

Coach Hugh "Two-Fisted" Farrell, his voice echoing like stamping feet, had them skate through a repetition of two-on-ones. He was bald, with hair at the sides of his head like shorn hedges. His nose was long, his eyes intense blue marbles. "Faster to the puck. Hockey's a game of desire. It's a streetcar, boys, and you haven't caught it," he shouted.

He must've really liked that line because I heard it twice more in the span of ten minutes.

Next Coach scrimmaged them in royal blue versus gray mesh shirts. Small Bear, hair close-cropped, worked the corners, chipping pucks to the slot. His skating style was short, choppy, and deceptively quick. The Big Z was gliding down the wing. Local reporters often mistook his loping stride for laziness, but the Big Z was ready for the playoffs to start. He had scored 32 goals this year and twice his slapshots left Bower wincing in the net, forcing him from the crease to skate in small circles by the dashers.

Bower was in his late thirties and should probably have been wearing contacts and holding a walking cane instead of a goalie stick. I know for a fact that Bower can't pick up pucks by his skates. He loses sight of them there all the time. But contacts could fall out during a game and what would he do in a goalmouth scramble with one contact in and the other gone missing? He'd be seeing an avant-garde world through a dark glass.

Defenseman Tim Horton couldn't see either. He refused to play with glasses. We called him Mr. Magoo.

I loved those guys. Bower was just the nicest player, and Horton was so soft-spoken, never an unkind word for anyone. But he was a bit of a prankster and a strong son of a bitch. One time in a Montreal hotel, the pop machine ate his change and a pissed-off Horton hauled the whole damn thing into an elevator and sent it down to the main lobby.

And then there was Danny Davis, head high with arrogance, cutting tight little circles at center—never back-checking—waiting for the next breakout pass to fly with offensive fury at Sawchuk, the goalie at the far end.

I never cared much for Davis. He was a hedonist, a narcissist, and any other self-absorbed "ist" you want to throw in. He took Polaroids of topless girls, the mornings *after* he had slept with them. You had to stay "through the night" to get thus honored with your picture "taken," and then he'd flash them to us fellas on the chartered flights. I'd be in a poker game with the fella and suddenly in my hand were four cards and a Polaroid. I always suspected him of cheating. With his Polaroid distractions, he never lost at poker.

He was also the reason I was out of the league. Like Bledsoe being suspended in 1957 for questioning the league, you didn't question the integrity of the sport or its players in 1964. No reporters ever wrote about a player lacing up the skates hung over, or another player having an affair with a teammate's wife. At least no one had until Stana Younger.

Late in 1961, I got a Leica for Christmas from Stana. We had just started dating and were an item for the next three years. Anyway, I got pretty good at taking action shots. I pumped the *Star*'s Harold Barkley for technique tips and perfected his skill at mastering dim-lit photographs with an electronic flash. Eventually, in time, I had my own dark room and worked with infrared.

Some of the fellas even took to calling me the Kodak Kid and asking if I would snap glamour shots of their wives and girlfriends, all sexy and suggestive. I used filters and expensive umbrellas for bouncing the light and gave their sweethearts a sheen of stardust. All of this brought in a nice chunk of change. Kodak Kid.

Later, I bought a set of telephoto zoom lenses, pushing me closer to the action and after all that, one of my teammates, a defenseman who twice was hospitalized with nervous breakdowns and joined me in retirement after the 1964 season, hired me to spy on his wife whom he suspected of fooling around with a physician who lived next door (she was). The physician was a plastic surgeon and at parties made a habit of telling people what "work" they needed done. I fucking hated the guy. I wanted to "work" his face over with my fists.

So, I snapped three rolls of film—infrared photography—of him and his baggy ass in private *consort* with her and made an extra $300 for my services. Maybe it wasn't as good as selling donuts, like teammate Tim Horton was doing, but I was making enough to get a better hi-fi and more jazz records. So it wasn't until late into my final season that my fourth surveillance case became my final curtain.

And this brings us back to Davis, the guy with the Polaroids and extreme good fortune at poker.

In February of 1964, the Big Z was really down in the dumps. He was usually discussing some ballet he'd just seen or work of art he had admired (he was partial to A. J. Casson and the Group of Seven), but all season he wasn't talking at all. He was a recluse, holing up on the road in his hotel room with his turtle, Frankie.

Toronto is an Anglo city. Immigrants and their children struggle to be accepted. I'm a Jew; Zakoic's bloodlines hail from Croatia. I can't tell you how many times people would ask me where I'm from. Toronto, I'd say. No, but where are you *from*? They were like placing me outside the group of "regular" Canadians. Russia, I'd tell them. Russia. My parents came from Russia. Oh, you're a commie kike? Yeah, I'm a commie kike. Uh-huh. How'd you get the name Fuller? My parents changed it, that's how. Oh, that's cool. Yeah, thanks, that's cool, l'chaim.

Anyway, one night over a couple of beers, a disconsolate Big Z tells me that he suspected that his wife Susan (an Anglo girl) was sleeping with Davis, who had recently been acquired from the Rangers.

"Have you seen any Polaroids of her?"

"Don't be stupid. Of course not. You think Davis would

flash them around if he did sleep with her?"

She wasn't stupid either. Susan graduated with honors in philosophy from the University of Toronto. Big Z was sure that there'd been sexual hijinks. Susan and Davis were seen at some jazz clubs and Susan did tell *Maclean's* that she and Davis were good friends. He was a gourmet chef, or some such damn thing. Cooked up an awesome soufflé.

So I followed Chef Davis for two weeks. Taking pictures. He was seeing women at the ROM; at George's Restaurant on Queen Street; and at Mainly Drew's on Carlton. He had this ugly technique: he'd sport a pair of Ray-Bans, walk up to a woman at a bar, drop the shades ever so slightly, and shake his head with a dismissive no if they weren't pretty enough. If they were pretty enough, he'd raise an eyebrow and ask if they wanted to fuck. Seriously. Just like that. A lot of women said sure. I never photographed him with Susan. Was he just being extra careful? I followed and followed.

Discovered he wasn't having an affair with Susan; also discovered that he *was* sleeping with Sharon, the slim-shaped blonde of our captain Benjamin Small Bear. Small Bear, an aboriginal from St. James Bay, upon hearing of my report from Big Z, punched Davis's lights out in a locker room skirmish. Super-tuned his ass as Big Z later said.

Davis played that evening on *Hockey Night in Canada*'s telecast with two black eyes. Media speculated on his raccoon-like appearance. Ward Cornell wondered if Davis had fallen over a coffee table in his Scarborough home as had been reported by the *Star*.

No matter, Stana broke the true story in her column for the *Toronto Telegram*. Within minutes of that column's appearance, I was in Bullard's office and on my way to Rochester for *conduct detrimental to the team.* "Tawdry" I believe Smith garbled while rubbing clean his glasses and describing my moonlighting practices to the press. Or maybe it was "Lurid." He always had a way with words. I finished out the season in the AHL and promptly retired.

Stana apologized profusely after she heard of my dismissal from the club, but it didn't do any good. I was mad, unfairly so, but at the time there was no forgiveness in my heart. She didn't follow me to Rochester. Stana opted for advancing her career as a reporter. We were done. I still miss her.

But I miss the game more and that smell of the rink: a brisk cold chlorine slap mixed with the wet undersides of a hockey glove. I breathed it in, and then a puck zipped by my head, slapping off the seat next to me. I shifted and looked ice level.

There was Davis, forehead furrowed, gray eyes like gunmetal. He didn't move, just leaned at the blue line, fixated.

"Okay, okay. I promise." I raised my arms in surrender. "I won't put my feet on the furniture. No more."

Bower was smiling and gave a gentle wave with his blocker.

But not Davis. He did look kind of funny with his heavy eyebrows and hair neatly parted down the middle like Shemp Howard's, but there was nothing funny about the eyes. Absolutely nothing. They were full of burning leaves.

AFTER PRACTICE I strolled over to Mainly Drew's. I'm not quite sure why: maybe to touch base with old friends; maybe to get the feeling of being a hockey player back in my blood again; maybe to escape my feelings of loneliness. With my shoulders sore and a pain behind my eyes, I ducked in, feeling like that *Spy Who Came in from the Cold* guy. Shit, why did I leave the painkillers in my car?

Mainly Drew's is one of those typical taverns in Toronto, built with little architectural panache: lots of angles and squared lines that reflect the cold simplicity of Presbyterianism. I squinted my eyes, even in the dark glimmer of the tavern they hurt, and ducked under low hanging cedar beams. Steins graced the shelving behind the bar, and I wondered if I ought to be wearing a miner's hardhat with a glowing light.

That's how goddamn dark it was in there. A jazz combo played on a slightly raised stage in back of the bar. The alto-saxophonist was solid, taking us away from the shoreline on repeated, varied riffs, and then bringing us back. But I really liked the drummer. The cat was unobtrusive but driving the sound with rim knocks and the odd bright hits on his snare.

The afternoon editions had hit the street so I wasn't too surprised to see Stana sitting at her favorite table with one glass of Guinness. That's all she ever drank. Just one. She was cautious.

And despite the pain behind my eyes, I became aware of an additional feeling: my heart pounding in my shoulders at the sight of her. I gestured.

She invited me to sit across from her. When we dated we sat side-by-side like high-school kids. That seemed so long ago.

Stana looked great, skin fresh, bright, and freckled. She had light features, delicate bones, and her blue eyes, what she self-effacingly referred to as dishwater beautiful, always struck me with their love light. Stana took you in for who you are and listened with exacting concentration and brightness.

She was one of those people who were always present.

No shrouds of eye shadow, no fake lashes. She wore gray slacks, a beige blouse, and a pullover sweater, no sleeves. I ordered tonic water. "Any big-time news scoops?"

She smiled awkwardly, asked how I was, and said that Montreal was ready to take us in the semis. The Leafs were three-time defending champs, but slipping. Two years ago was our best season, maybe the best of any Leaf team in history. We were the Prince of Wales Trophy winners for our regular season record and won the cup in 10 games, demolishing Montreal in game 5 of the semi's, 5-0. The Habs wanted to get even. Last year we won game 7 on their ice, Davey Keon, our slick skating center, netting a hat trick. This year, Montreal was tougher, grittier with Ted Harris and John Ferguson entering their second seasons with the club.

I nodded at her assessments. "Trying to make me feel good?"

"No." She shrugged, her nose raised in the dark light. She was tall, angly, with square shoulders and freckles everywhere. Sometimes even her eyes looked freckled. "I just think the Leafs are ready to be knocked off."

"I like Ferguson. He's a cement head but not just a goon. He can put the puck in the net, unlike Fortunado and Leighton." I told her about my meeting with the two ex-NHL *pugilists* in Smith and Bullard's office. "That goddamn room is like a bunker. Secret passageways and everything." I looked at my fingers. "I feel like shit. You got any aspirin?"

"I always got aspirin." She reached into her purse, the size of a milk crate, and handed me two.

"Management doesn't give a shit. It's just about money for them. The Cashbox on Carlton Street."

She smiled. "You seeing anyone?"

I looked away. "No." I dry-swallowed the pills and rubbed my hands together. "You?"

"No." She looked away. "Any leads on the Sarah Kerr case?"

"No. You hear anything?"

"No."

I told her how for a while there I was staying in touch with the girl's mother, giving weekly updates, telling her nothing new, but the case was always open for me. *I didn't tell her about all the nightmares I'd been having about a voice in a suitcase screaming to be let out. Sometimes I was the one in the suitcase, screaming, but I had no mouth, the noise a squawk of black crows.* And then the widow Kerr said talking to me was too painful and I didn't have to keep calling out of some sense of penance or responsibility, just call if I have anything new. When she first hired me, she gave me a $200 retainer. Two days later, we found the body. I never cashed the check.

"They'll never find that girl's killer—" She shrugged. It was what she hated about life, how it was so transitory and some mysteries were never solved.

"The final showdown. At the cabin? It was so flashy. Like the killer was making a big splash of it all. Amusing himself with his bag of tricks: searchlights, a mannequin, and then a motorboat stuck in the middle of a partially frozen lake." I shook my head. Lambertino plans to drag the lake at the end of this month, once the water's warm enough.

"Maybe the killer never got on the boat."

"What?"

"Maybe it was just a diversion. Maybe he was watching you guys the whole time."

"Hey," the Big Z shouted in my direction. "Have a drink

with us, Hayden." He was huddled around Small Bear and Bower. Their beers had high heads on them. The Big Z was usually reclusive, alone with his turtle, but all that boisterous enthusiasm must mean but one thing: everything's great with Susan.

"How's Suse?"

"Awesome." He smiled broadly and flashed a thumb. Just last week, they had gone to McMichael's Art Gallery and at season's end were heading for a second honeymoon in Mexico.

"Fine. That sounds fine," I shouted back.

"Mexico? Do you remember our vacation there, two years ago?" Stana reached for my wrist.

How could I forget? We stayed in our motel room most of the time and when not making love ate tortillas, hiked, or lounged in the hot sun, she in a white bikini.

She squeezed my wrist. "I'm really sorry, if I had it to do all over again, I wouldn't have run the story about Davis and Small Bear and Sharon."

"Bullshit."

"What?"

"I'm not being mean. Just being honest. If you had to do it again, you would still run the story." I touched her chin. "It was news. And you should run it. You're a professional." I looked at the rings crowding her glass on the table. "You really think he might have been watching us, the killer? I mean, just lurking?"

She nodded and apologized again for our muddy past. "It was a private utterance, between the two of us. You told me over our pillows. I—I had no right—"

"Small Bear? Christ. How did he get that name? He's one

of the biggest wingers in the game. And strong—" I smiled at the irony life can give us.

"His name's Small Bear not Small Boy. A bear's pretty big, even a small one," she corrected, her eyes flashing with shifts of light.

"Good point." I tapped the tip of my porkpie. Small Bear was actually a pretty good name. Whenever Chief got coerced into a hockey fight, he bear-hugged his opponent, leaving the potential sparring partner gasping for breath, and ending any desire on the instigator's part to throw a haymaker. "You're a newspaper reporter. I was mad at first, but I respect it. It's who you are."

She smiled. "Thanks," she whispered.

She was a woman fighting for elbowroom in an all-male bullpen. She couldn't afford to be sentimental. Sentiment would mark her as a "woman," placing love ahead of her profession. Around the other fellas of the press, she had to be tough and she was.

I told her about the new case I was working. Showed her the photograph, the numbers on back, and how I didn't want the Sarah Kerr outcome again.

"Cathy Stabulas?"

"Yeah—you know her?"

She leaned forward. "Do I know her? We were working on a story when she went missing. All about the shenanigans Smith and Bullard were pulling. Yeah, I know her."

"Tell me more. What story?" My voice suddenly sounded like McClelland's: adenoidal, scratchy, and full of a desire for coveted gossip.

Cathy was about to blow the lid off the Leafs organization. Skimming, cheating, drugs, but more importantly gambling.

"She was going to give me a big story."

"Bolemac Corporation. Screwdrivers for $200—"

"Yeah." She was surprised by how much I knew.

"Was she working for you, undercover?"

"No. No." She looked down and spoke quietly, her fingers drawing lazy figure eights on the tabletop. "But what she saw sickened her."

"Saw? What do you mean? Where?"

"She'd gone to this club four or five times—very exclusive."

"How exclusive?"

"Very."

And then I asked if kinky sex were involved and told her about the drawer full of dildos and other toys and skimpy clothes in Cathy's room.

"That fits the profile of what she was telling me. But our focus was on illegal gambling mainly." Bullard and Smith were running some kind of exclusive gambling service. Very Q.T., high stakes, roulette wheels, poker, like right out of a goddamn 1940s film noir. "Hockey's a god here and in Montreal. The league, the media, will do anything to cover up this story, but I'm going to get to the bottom of it, and those two playboys are going to be spending time in the Don Jail." She shook her head with disapproval. "We had a couple of preliminary meetings, Cathy and I, and then she disappeared." She snapped her fingers for emphasis.

"Shit." That means she's either dead or in hiding. "Where's this goddamn club?"

Stana's eyes squinted and danced with freckles. "I don't know. It's so exclusive, only a handful of people are invited or even know its whereabouts. But I know the moniker, Coughlins."

"Coughlins?"

She pulled a napkin from the boxy dispenser and drew the club's logo in stuttering blue ink. The marquee featured a homburg with a clown's face underneath.

"McClelland wears homburgs."

And then I thought about the doodles on Cathy's Big Chief tablet. There was a clown face with a homburg. She *had* been there.

"So do a lot of men. My father—"

"But why a homburg? I mean I wear a porkpie."

"I've noticed. A porkpie looks good in Miami Beach. But in Toronto? It looks affected—"

"Really?" I pushed it back. "I think it sends a certain signal—private eye for hire. Cat who digs jazz."

"It looks like a boy trying to be a tough guy. A porkpie isn't upscale. A homburg. Now that's upscale."

I doffed my porkpie. "Tah-tah. Cheerio."

"Oh, stop."

"Can I interest you in some crumpets, guv'nor? Clotted cream?"

"That accent is worse than Dick Van Dyke's in *Mary Poppins.*"

That cracked me up. "That was pretty bad." I put my porkpie back on. "Van Dyke, not me. You know what I love about a porkpie? You can do so much business with it. When you're asking questions and need a rhetorical pause or a reflective moment, you can push your hat back or play with the brim—"

She nodded with appreciation. Cathy had given Stana a few details but the biggest part of the story, the full confession was to follow. That was to have been unveiled later next week.

"Fucking great."

"One other tidbit that I think you'll appreciate: Davis is a regular at Coughlins." The four times Cathy was there she saw him. Playing the wheel and poker. "He wasn't winning. He seemed to lose every time."

"Hmm. I thought poker was his game." At least that's what I remembered from his days on the Leafs chartered flights.

"I've called him repeatedly for clarification, but he won't answer my phone calls."

"That fucker." I pushed back my porkpie.

There was another girl involved. Lisa Steinmetz.

"Why that's Cathy's friend, the one she was supposed to see the night she disappeared."

"Cathy said Steinmetz got her into the club. I can't get Steinmetz to talk to me either. I don't think she trusts women."

"Uh-huh."

"You think she'll talk to you?"

I nodded.

"You want to work together on this?"

"What the fuck—" It was Davis. He strolled in our direction, black wool coat swaying behind him like a cape. He started rambling, questioning my motives for being at practice, and why was I hanging out at a favored haunt of the players? Davis's neatly centered hair wasn't as sharp as usual. Two or three strands appeared to have broken off and defected from the flow of the pack.

Zakoic and Bower and now Small Bear followed in the wake of Davis's black-coated prow. He was a tugboat that needed to be tow lined. Bower had a hand on Davis's shoulder.

"Get your hand off me, Johnny. This ain't your fight."

"There isn't going to be a fight, Danny," Bower said.

"Last I checked this is a public establishment and I'm allowed to do business here," I said. "With regards to the Leafs, I'm a stockholder. I have two or three shares of preferred stock."

"What?"

"Blue chip, I believe." I took off my hat, looked at the inside, enjoying the moment this pause was bringing.

Stana filled the gap. "Mr. Davis, would you care to make a statement about the missing whereabouts of Cathy Stabulas?"

She sure had a knack for calm utterances that were truly fiery salvos. I loved that about her. She had a way with irony too. I figured it was all the Jane Austen she read as an English major at the University of Toronto. She studied with Northrop Frye, a pretty big cat in the field. Later, she spent a year at Ryerson studying journalism. She was always smarter than me, and a smart-ass to boot.

God, how I hated playing *Scrabble* with her.

"And while you're at it," I leaned in Davis's direction, "Could I have your autograph? I'm such a fan—"

Okay, I'm a bit of a smart-ass too.

Davis didn't appreciate my zingers and shrugged off Johnny's pensive grip. Then, Davis shoved me and I shoved back, sliding my chair against his strong thighs. Before I could get up and push away from the table, Davis seized the back of my neck, squashing my head into the tabletop like a caved-in jack-o'-lantern. Wind chimes rattled behind my eyes, a light metallic tapping.

I tasted bits of salt and spilled vinegar.

Hockey players have strong legs and tuchuses—you need them, to push off and glide and accelerate quickly. So with my face tasting remnants of yesterday's fish and chips, I forced my chair back and to the left and went with the best of all cheap shots, the hockey slew foot. I twisted my right leg free, planted it behind Davis, and with a slow drag, as if I were wearing skates, nicked him behind the calves and an Achilles tendon, sending him thudding to the floor. He might have bounced a couple of times. He wasn't too happy about it.

He rubbed at the sides of his mouth, and then rummaged inside his coat pocket and came up with a blackjack that resembled a slick-heeled banana.

I pulled the snub-nosed .38 out of my side holster and directed it at him. "You have any other statements you'd care to make?"

"Come on, Hayden, put the gun away," said Johnny.

"You have a license for that?" asked Davis.

"Since when does a hockey player need a blackjack?" Stana said.

Big Z and Small Bear weren't asking a thing.

"Yeah, I have a license for this. It comes complete with operating instructions, coloring book, and a coupon for Tim Horton's donuts." I pushed the seat sideways until I was propped against a wall. The wind chimes forming at the edges of my consciousness were now a slow rushing waterfall. "Beat it."

Davis dropped his arms at his sides and buried the blackjack in his coat. "Stay out of my business."

"Your business has become my business, pally. Where's the girl?"

"I don't know what you're talking about."

"Uh-huh." I smiled. I have a feeling there was something slightly off about my lopsided grin because Stana suddenly looked away. "How's Coughlins?"

"You talk too much."

"When I get answers to my questions, I'm going to talk a lot, pal. And then you and Smith and Bullard are going down."

"The girl should keep her mouth shut." His lips tightened into a terse line. He turned to Stana. "And that's off the record, bitch." He did up his jacket and strolled head high to the opposite side of the bar with his fellow teammates in retreat.

"Yours in Polaroids, pal," I shouted.

"What?" Stana's face was creased with worry. The freckles around her eyes were no longer moving.

"Inside joke." I exhaled. Maybe it wasn't that funny.

"You scared me just now."

"What, the gun? I've never fired it at a person." I shrugged. *Well except for that one time, sixty-five miles north of the city, the Sarah Kerr case. And that was a fucking mannequin.* "Twice a week, pistol practice at the cop shop. Head shots." I practice a lot. I did as a player, firing pucks at the four corners of the net, and I do as a detective, honing in on a silhouetted target with a bull's-eye. It keeps me in control, even-keeled. And frankly I like it. It's the only time, besides when I'm skating, that I'm not thinking. I'm just being.

"But why head shots? Isn't there more to hit in the chest area—less chance of missing?"

"Yeah." I shrugged. But if you land the head shot just right, the shooter goes down like a marionette with broken strings.

"You know too much about this—"

"Sorry."

"And the look on your face when you pulled your gun. I've never seen that look before. Even when you were playing hockey, I never saw that look."

"What look?"

"A third face." I had told her about the concept years ago. "That face was ready to use that gun."

It was true. I re-holstered the weapon and took a deep breath. And then I pointed at the numbers. "Can you find out for me what those latitude and longitude lines precisely refer to? I mean, the exact spot of land—?"

She wrote the numbers on the napkin under the Coughlins logo.

"I help you, you help me. We find the girl. I get the story. Partners?" She reached for my hand across the table. Her fingers were slightly shaking.

"Partners," I said.

4

"Tell me about Coughlins."

"What?" Lisa Steinmetz slowly sipped a cola at the El Mocambo. Potted palm trees swayed in the bar's crisp breeze and the table in front of us was a cold block of polished granite. I thought my fingers were going to get freezer burn.

"Coughlins. I know about it. And Davis and you and Cathy."

That wasn't completely true. I knew a little about it.

Lisa's face was wide, nose fleshy, eyebrows so plucked and streamlined as to be almost invisible. She tapped the table with chunky fingers. Her body was curvy, not heavy, but her fingers were porcine, the three rings on her left hand looking pinched and uncomfortable. "I called Cathy that night because I needed to talk?"

I wasn't sure of the hesitancy to her voice. Did it reflect intimations of danger or was she just that unsure of herself and insecure? She often ended sentences with questions. This was where she worked, waitressing. You figured she'd be comfortable in this setting. She was on break.

"What were you going to talk about?"

"Girl stuff."

"Davis? Come on, be specific." I pushed back my porkpie, took a deep breath. "Look, I'm not trying to pry and be an asshole here—I respect privacy—but I need some answers, real answers. A girl's life is at stake. That's if she's still alive."

I had already lost another girl in a missing persons case and I wasn't willing to play this case at practice speed. This was the Stanley Cup Finals. "Talk—"

"I think she's alive." She looked away.

"Why? Why do you feel that way?"

"This arrived in the mail this morning." She reached into her purse and pulled out a folded 9x12 envelope, heavily creased. Inside it was a black-and-white photograph.

It was Cathy. Her hair, heavy Cleopatra bangs, was unwashed and lay limp against her head and the sides of her face. Her eyes were flat too, lacking fervor. Her shoulders were curled in, stooped, and there were some small wisps of hair on her bare breasts. Suddenly I couldn't breathe again and the world was full of dirty cotton candy gauze.

"Was there a note? Ransom? Blackmail?"

"Nothing, Hayden. Just the picture."

"Jesus Christ." Davis? Who else had a fetish for this shit? Goddamn Davis. Sure, it's not a Polaroid but it's the same M.O., the handling of the photographic equipment suggesting the same lack of professionalism. The subject of the photograph was slightly off-center, the image a bit hazy, but not so far off as to be considered artsy, like playing with the horizon line in a landscape. This was just mediocre. "You need to go to the police, the press, with this story."

"I can't." If she did, she'd be dead. These were powerful people. Even a Member of Parliament had been seen at Coughlins. She sighed and played with a thin necklace around her neck. The finish in places was chipped. "Okay, okay. What do you want to know?" She pushed strands of dusky blond hair over a shoulder.

"About Coughlins. What is it? How do I get in to find her?"

"You think she's there?"

"If she's alive, I think she's holed up there or in the Gardens."

I had spent a good part of the morning reading Cathy's Big Chief tablet. The language of her stories was enchanting, bright with feeling. The heroines of her fiction were afraid to take risks and say how they felt to men—instead, they said how they felt to us, her readers, via a kind of confessional mode, but they said little in the worlds they inhabited. Some of the women worked in grocery stores and answered questions about bargain prices and specials of the day; others traveled lonely but crowded subways, hoping to be noticed, to be spoken to. I wanted to take these characters home with me, and tell them they were loved.

"Did she have a secret life that you knew of, a third face?"

"A third face?"

I explained the concept.

"No. I mean we all have secrets, right? Like right now, I can tell that you're looking at me, checking me out. You're too polite to say anything or do anything about it, but you're looking. And that's okay?"

I shrugged. "I guess you get a lot of that in your line of work?"

"Tell me about it? I mean, if I want a good tip, I got to put up with my ass being patted, you know?"

"What did Cathy put up with? Weird things at the store? Her father?"

"He's a jerk."

"Yeah. I gathered that might be the case. I saw him wallop Kim. It was a hard hit."

"They don't get along. At all."

"Yeah."

She paused, leaned back, and smiled. "I trust you. You're sincere."

"Thanks."

"I bet you're a good kisser, too."

I didn't know what to say to that.

"Because it just wouldn't be about you. You care about the other person?"

I took off my porkpie, to anchor me. I was short on sleep and that gauze of haze was swirling around again. I had to find the girl.

"Look. I'm sorry, I was flirting."

"It's okay," I said.

I did find one odd bit of social commentary in Cathy's Big Chief tablet that I didn't share with Lisa. Cathy had torn a full-page ad from *Life* magazine and stapled it to a page in the journal, folding to make it fit. The bizarre image was for Chase & Sanborn coffee. It featured a man in a hard wooden chair, his back to us. He wore suspenders. A woman, in heels, one leg raised, her slip and petticoat showing around her knees, was on his lap and kicking up a fuss as his raised, open hand, readied to spank her for not taste testing the coffee before buying it. The copy said something silly like, "If your husband finds out—"

I thought the ad was kind of sexy to be honest. The petticoat reveal gave the whole piece a peek into the forbidden. I don't believe in hitting women. I've never, ever, hit a woman, but the ad was titillating like tan lines up against the parts of a woman's body that don't usually see the sun. Apparently Cathy would totally disagree with me and give me holy hell.

Her commentary on the Chase & Sanborn image was a knife's edge, there was nothing funny or cute or sexy to this campaign. She was *never* (underscore twice) going to drink Chase & Sanborn "ever again." The ad men who concocted this were just cruel and into "male domination."

Men are pigs.

She wrote that fifteen times, on separate lines (I counted).

This tirade was a stunning piece of cultural criticism amidst all of the fiction and creative imagination on display. It did reveal how put upon she felt as a woman. *Men are pigs.* The lines got heavier and heavier each time she wrote that.

"Like I said, that night I just needed to talk. I was having a hard time with my boyfriend, so I invited Cathy for a drink—" She looked around the room and rubbed her full chin against her left shoulder. "That's all. She didn't show."

"Didn't that make you curious?"

"Yeah, yeah, of course." She had a few drinks alone and called Stabulas's Grocery the next day but never heard back from her. "I figured she was busy?" She raised her thin eyebrows.

I nodded. "If you don't mind me saying, you don't look like the bridge type—"

"Bridge?"

"Yeah. You know the card game?"

"Bridge? I've never played bridge." She laughed, pulled back, and tightened the cardigan sweater around her shoulders.

"That's not what her father told me. You and Cathy—"

She crossed her arms. "I wouldn't trust a word her father says." She slumped forward, chewed at her lower lip, and blew hair out of her eyes.

Maybe it was Kim who mentioned bridge and not the father. Now I wasn't sure, but they both agreed to that story line. Bridge.

Maybe I should check my notes. Shit, I didn't write that detail down.

"You see how hard he works her? Ever since their mother died—Cathy's become a second *wife* almost?"

Mrs. Stabulas died nearly ten years ago and since then, according to Lisa, Cathy kept her father's books for the store, cooked his meals, cleaned, and was the primary care provider.

"If not bridge, then what? Was it Coughlins on Saturdays?"

"Always after the hockey telecasts." She smiled wanly. "She was a Leafs fan."

"I know. I've seen her room, the Barkley photographs—"

Lisa tightened the cardigan. "You care about her, don't you?"

"I don't know her, but, yeah, I do."

"I can see it in your eyes."

Maybe Lisa could see the loss of Sarah residing there too.

"Coughlins. I got her into Coughlins. Somebody got me in."

"Where is it?"

"It's in the Gardens. One of the upstairs offices."

"The one behind a sliding wall?"

She nodded. It was *that* exclusive. Her guidance counselor, Mr. Landover Leeds, invited Lisa in on the party during her senior year.

"Leeds? The guy with the Tangerine Room and relaxation bullshit?"

Leeds. There was a connection to Sarah too. Leeds.

"Yeah." Her face darkened. "Pompous ass."

"What do you know about mind control and the Leonardo Da Silva Institute? Leeds has a diploma from—"

"Leeds couldn't call the room a simple color like red or green, oh, no, he opts for tangerine, because it had a 'far-out vibe.'" Anyway, Mr. Leeds, at this one afternoon appointment, handed Lisa a card with a silhouette of the NBC peacock, you know, and the words, *worship the cock* written under it. That made Lisa laugh and because of that laugh Leeds knew she was good material for Coughlins. "It was a great place to meet hockey players."

"I had never heard of it."

"I met Danny Davis there and Spinner—"

"Spinner?"

She shrugged at the mention of his name and readjusted her cardigan. It was that cold in here.

"I know him. Nice guy—so you were underage when you were first at this club—?"

"Yeah. Don't be such a square. I've known about sex since I was fifteen? How old were you?"

I shrugged. Fourteen. A hockey bunny, a middle-aged mom, snuck into the dressing room after a morning shoot around, and we did it after everyone else had gone home. I still had my skates on. Lisa was just seventeen when her guidance counselor pimped her out. I was going to have to have a follow-up with this Leeds fella. How many other girls did he pipe into Coughlins with his pithy business card test? So "Cathy was a regular there?"

"I wouldn't say a regular. But I got her in. She went some Saturdays."

I showed her the photograph taken of Cathy and two of the Maple Leafs Board of Governors.

"Yeah. That's the Coughlins crowd."

"This is the Royal York."

"Yeah, but Smith and Bullard run Coughlins." They skimmed and took a cut. A big cut. "Man, there's nothing those guys won't stop at."

"Who are their partners? Who's fronting for them?"

"Migano."

"Babe Migano? The gangster?" The ex-Montrealer emigrated to Toronto in the post-war era and now flourished in drugs and the numbers racket. "Have you ever heard of the Bolemac Corporation?"

"Bolemac? No, I don't think so—"

Could Migano be helping to divert funds, divesting the Cashbox on Carlton Street to line all their pockets? "Bolemac does construction work at the Gardens. They ever talk to you about that?"

She bit her upper lip and shrugged. "Bolemac. Sounds like a comic book character. A bad guy of course. No. Don't know Bolemac."

"Thanks for filling me in on Coughlins." And Landover Leeds and his Tangerine Room and "Worship the Cock" charm. It was time for some follow-up conversations. "This problem you had with a fella? Is he a hockey player?"

"Yes." She shrugged. "Was?"

I let out a sharp whistle. How could I be a detective and not know about this exclusive club? During my last two seasons with the Leafs, I did four surveillance jobs, finding out whose hockey wives were fooling around with other fellas, but I knew nothing about Coughlins.

And Smith and Bullard sent me to the minors. Fucking hypocrites. *Conduct detrimental to the team.* Please. They're running a sleazy escort service, a couple of real swingers, and are in league with a gangster like Migano and his Bolemac front. "It's an escort service, right. High end?"

"I never got paid for sex. But sex is a part of it. The girls hope to land a rich man. And the drinks are expensive. And the guys pay a lot for drinks so you got to put out." She held up a hand. "I'm not proud of it." She looked around for the fourth time. "I'm getting out. I'm leaving town?"

She was just waiting on her ex-hockey player to come get her. She wouldn't give me his name. He had a final deal to close or something.

"Deal?"

She shook her head as if she couldn't say anymore.

"Is it Spinner? I saw him at the Gardens. It's Spinner, isn't it?"

She nodded.

Were they blackmailing Bullard and Smith? "Blackmail can get you killed—"

"We're not blackmailing anybody," she said, not too convincingly. "We're just getting paid for services—"

"What kind of services, Lisa?"

"Services. It's not exactly legal or else I'd tell you? I can't talk about it. It's not stolen jewelry or something—"

"Something else stolen? Say $568,000?"

"Shit no. Christ, you're bringing down my good mood." She blew heavy air between her lips. "You're a real downer, you know that?"

"I want to find a girl before time runs out. If that makes me a real drag then write that on my tombstone." I breathed heavily.

How the hell could Cathy be a part of all this? It didn't sound like the woman who wrote such sad, beautiful stories.

A friendship with Lisa would always be about Lisa. But maybe they had something else in common, some shared secret? Lisa was physically abused by a drunken father. Did Nick slap Cathy around too?

I flipped the photograph over and showed her the numbers on the reverse side. "These mean anything to you?"

"Bingo? Results from a bingo game?"

"It's longitude and latitude lines. I just wondered if—does *bazaar* ring any bells?"

"As in weird?"

I laughed.

"Cathy needed some escape. Don't be too hard on her." Lisa looked furtively around. "Did you know that three years ago Cathy bought herself a new car, a '62 Ford Falcon, a modest set of wheels, but her father didn't think a girl should have a new car so he made her sign it over to him? Can you believe that shit? Talk about Old World values. Nick took it from her."

"Did she get any money for it, did Nick pay for it?"

"You kidding? No. So Nick's driving around in her car. Well he was. He now has another car. Traded the Falcon in a few months ago to get a new set of wheels. In-fucking-credible." She shook her head.

I couldn't believe the way Lisa spoke, crude and brittle. She just didn't seem like the kind of girl Cathy would hang with. But what did I really know about Cathy, or Sarah for that matter.

"Maybe she just ran away, you know?"

"But you don't think so?"

"Check with Smith and Bullard?"

"I did already. Treated the whole thing as a joke. Had two women dolled up like human lampshades—"

"Naked?"

"Yeah, except for the fezzes on their heads."

"Hell, they're repeating themselves. They did that gag at the club?"

"What?"

"I was one of the lamps—wore a pink headdress—"

"Looked like a Fram oil filter—corrugated?"

"Yes?"

I wanted to believe Cathy just ran away from all the forced responsibility but knew that was no dice, not with that damn topless photograph.

I was thinking more and more that she was hidden somewhere in the Cashbox on Carlton Street. Maybe I was just hoping that she was. That was my only hope. "Did Cathy have encounters? Sexual encounters at this club? Weird, *bondage* encounters?"

Lisa laughed. That kind of stuff was available at Coughlins, but Cathy wasn't the type. "There's one woman who wears a dark mask. Nobody's seen her face. She's known as Starzz with two z's. She's wild. She'll do anything." She laughed again—a short angry burst. "I don't think Cathy was all that into sex?" She paused and laughed as she spoke. "I think she still might be a virgin—"

"Uh-huh."

Lisa pulled her shoulders back before smiling weakly and

looking one final time in the direction of the bartender and the street outside. It was turning gray with late afternoon drizzle. A chestnuts vendor was warming his hands over his pushcart. "I better get back to work. Things are picking up."

"Sure."

"There are some pretty crazy people who go to Coughlins. And I just hope—"

I nodded, thinking of that lower dresser drawer and the leather mouth strap with a ball.

"Wish me luck, huh?" Lisa now said. I had forgotten that she was still sitting there. Her face was pale in the green swatch of bar light and now her hair looked green too. "Spinner and I are going to head out west—start over—stay out of trouble."

She tapped the cold granite as if wishing herself luck or superstitiously trying to ward off evil spirits. "I guess, maybe the trouble's already started, huh? And it's following me?" Suddenly her eyes widened as if she were envisioning hellhounds on her trail and tongues of flame.

"Maybe," I said, looking away from the fire.

5

The sky outside my office window was gray and rain fell in penciled streaks. Stana and I sat on the floor poring over our notes. I was apologizing for forgetting that I had sent out my three office chairs to be refinished and they wouldn't be back until Friday.

"You always were disorganized."

"Hey, I've got a filing cabinet now." I pointed at the black cabinet and its four drawers. "Well, there are only five folders in there, but hey—"

"That's it. Five folders? No bottle of Canadian Club or a .45 with its shells rolling around?"

"That's only in the hardboiled novels."

"I thought you guys only existed in the hardboiled novels—"

I slyly nodded and shook my head. How many summer hours did I put in with the police force and at night classes at York University to acquire the training to get my license and become a peace officer? "Not anyone can hang up a shingle. The government monitors us detectives pretty closely."

"I know I was just joking." She leaned in and played with my shirt buttons.

I smoothed her hair. "So what do you think? This is it."
I stretched out my arms and she took in the office: a filing
cabinet; a wood desk with a lamp and a low-watt bulb; an
ashtray full of Wrigley foils in one corner (a black phone was
in the other); a blotter crowded with eccentric doodlings and
dates circled on a calendar; on a far wall a Matisse print of
what looked like a penguin on ice skates; on another wall an
Export "A" calendar featuring my first pro team, the '57-'58
Leafs; a hat rack, sporting my porkpie and blue wool coat
and Stana's black-and-white windbreaker; a bright basin with
separate hot and cold taps; hardwood floors; and a window,
with venetian blinds, overlooking Yonge Street.

"Spartan, but very, very disciplined. Like you were as a
player. I guess that's why you don't have a swivel chair like
most detectives. Instead hard wood chairs, three of them, all
getting re-finished—while we get splinters in our asses."

"Be nice—"

"That's okay." She wiped the corners of her mouth and
smiled, her eyes filling with light. We were sharing a greasy
box of poutine. "Not having any office chairs makes it kind
of romantic."

It was. "Yeah, all that's missing is a glare of sun, your white
bikini, and spicy burritos."

She leaned in and kissed me.

"The burritos weren't that good."

She laughed and touched my face. "For a guy who got over
fifty stitches in his playing career, how come your face isn't
all marked up?" She had once stepped into an elevator with
Small Bear and Sawchuk and there were zipper shadows everywhere.

"I always take my stitches out early, a few days before I

should and treat the wounds with cocoa butter. It works—"

"Cocoa butter." She smiled. "I'll remember that."

We went over our notes again and how Lisa said that Coughlins was the exclusive club hidden behind Smith and Bullard's sliding wall. Maybe Cathy's hidden in there. "So how do we get in the Gardens to look? We need evidence."

"We'll need more evidence so the cops can get a warrant," she said.

After I had talked to Lisa, Stana contacted Castle Frank's guidance counselor Landover Leeds at his home. She mentioned Cathy Stabulas's name, my ongoing investigation, and rumors of moral turpitude (his, not hers). Playing it cagey didn't get her anywhere so she gave out with three little words, "Worship the cock." And there was a long pause, and then an even longer pause. "Let's talk, but not my home." His voice snick-snicked like a pair of hockey skates. "My office." His office was on Front Street, across from Union Station. He couldn't get there until later tonight. Nine P.M. He still had to work out at the gym: pump iron, run laps, maybe hit the bag.

A regular Jack LaLanne he was.

Stana also mentioned the $568,000 figure written on the photo's flip. "We'll talk about that too, but not on the phone." We were to meet him in a few hours.

"A second office? I don't get it. Why's he need a second office?"

Stana shrugged and dipped her chin. "It is strange—"

"It's not like he's an artist or writer or something—"

"You know what else I found?" She tilted her head and raised an eyebrow.

I removed a spot of gravy from her upper lip. "What?"

In 1957–58, Landover held a special Thursday night counseling service for a group of nine high school girls experiencing some kind of trauma.

"Yeah, I know. Cathy was a part of that group. Cathy's Mom died in 1955—"

"Yes, Cathy was a part of the group, but so was Lisa Steinmetz."

I nodded and felt rocks breaking in my stomach. "Could he have been recruiting this group for Gardens' bunnies? Human lamps?"

"I don't know." Stana wore a white dress with spaghetti straps and a shiny black belt. Around her neck was a thin chain with an ankh. This was the most feminine looking I'd seen Stana in years. And I liked it.

She reached into a black milk crate of a handbag and unfurled a rolled-up piece of paper with nine names listed. She got them, after much prodding, from Castle Frank's school secretary. The only names I recognized were Lisa and Cathy. "We'll need to look into this," she said.

"Uh-huh."

"Oh, and the longitude and latitude lines?" She squinted her eyes and they danced with freckles. "Barrie, Ontario." The other series of longitude and latitude lines were close to Vaughan, Ontario, but she hadn't found the specific location yet. A field, apparently, in the middle of nowhere.

A field apparently in the middle of nowhere. That's where Sarah Kerr had been killed, in a cabin, near Vaughan. A coincidence? "It's just so random—" It can't be a coincidence.

"What about this case isn't random?" Stana shifted against the wall, pushing her back away with the side of a hand. Rain pinged against my office window and the penciled streaks were now a lot heavier, creating dancing coins on the window's ledge. The sky too had darkened from gray to charcoal black.

Stana wondered if Cathy might already be dead.

"She can't be dead. She just can't."

"What if Lisa were lying? The photograph angle just doesn't make any sense. Why would Davis send a photograph of a topless Cathy to Lisa?"

"To intimidate her?" I said.

"No. It's too easy and stupid. Davis is a lot of things but he's not stupid. Someone's setting him up."

"What?"

"Let's say Lisa's in on Cathy's murder or kidnapping. So to buy herself time and detract attention from herself out comes this convenient nudie. There's no note, no ransom, no nothing. Just a stupid picture. It's a stupid move. Davis won a scoring championship in 1957-58. He was Rookie of the Year in 1955. Stanley Cup champ last year. He's a winner. This is *not* a winner's play."

I dialed Steinmetz's number. The phone rang and rang and rang.

"What about the father? Could he have hurt Cathy?" Stana asked.

"He loves her. He was crushed when I opened that lower dresser drawer. He kept saying, 'That's not her. That's not her, you understand?'"

"Exactly. But what if he found out that *was* her, or at least a part of her? Could he have lived with that, reconciled that sexuality to his Old Country ways? Maybe he killed her? I mean, she told me some things in our interviews. He isn't a nice man. What if the kinky stuff drove him to murder? You saw the way he slapped Kim—"

"I did—"

"He took away Cathy's car—could he have taken away her life?"

"That's crazy." The rain now pounded and water trickled in through the window. "Absolutely crazy."

"There are patterns of behavior here." She laughed. "Sometimes you're so naive." She leaned forward and kissed my cheek.

"I always loved the smell of you." I touched her chin, and then slowly pulled her towards me and kissed her. She yielded pleasantly under my hold, tasted of salt and gravy, and then kissed back fervently and it was three years ago all over again. I breathed in the smell of her shampoo.

"I think the father's abusive. Kim got away. Cathy didn't."

I didn't want to believe it, but then I started thinking about the slap. *Men are pigs.*

"Do you think I'm pretty? I mean—"

"What?"

"I mean, I know we were an item, and Mexico and everything, it's just—" It had been a long time since she had been loved.

"You're very pretty," I said.

She looked away. She hadn't felt as accepted, as confident in her body, since the breakup. With me, she enjoyed how I lingered, watching her prepare for bed, slipping out of her bra and into her pajama top or getting dressed in the morning, putting on her bra, as if that were one of the grand privileges of being in an intimate relationship, to be allowed to look at the nakedness of one another and to be accepted for who and what you are.

I leaned in and kissed her nose. "And I still love the smell of your hair."

She playfully punched my shoulder.

FORTY-FIVE MINUTES LATER I was at Kim's upscale apartment. I figured I should do this interview solo. Stana was streetside, waiting in my '63 Ford Galaxie, the engine running so she could stay warm. With Kim, my words rushed along like a slinky skater on a breakaway.

"Slow down, slow down," she said.

I took a deep breath. When Kim sat in profile, head slightly tilted, she looked an awful lot like Cathy: high cheekbones, fleshy jaw, and a pointed chin. It was a strange feeling of *déjà vu* that caught my breath, like one of those dreams you have when you're falling from a high window. They *could* be mistaken for twins, not just Irish, born in the same year, but actual twins.

"So tell me about Coughlins." I reached for the plastic mug in front of me. It was full of pens: blue with yellow lettering, Kim's name and the company she represented: Ogilvie and Beggert, Real Estate.

"Coughlins?"

"Your sister wasn't playing bridge on Saturdays. She was going to Coughlins with Lisa."

"What is it, a pizza place?"

I told her: an exclusive club, escort service, right in the heart of the Cashbox on Carlton Street. The whole S&M scene is a part of the package too, including some masked dominatrix called Starzz.

"You think that could be Cathy?" she asked.

Maybe. *Men are pigs.* Maybe it was her way of getting revenge?

Kim smiled incredulously and turned away in her pink, puffy chair.

"She never took you?"

"No. We went out for pizza. That's it. Boy do I feel naive." She blew a ribbon of dark hair off her forehead and tucked her knees up to her chin. She wore tight Capri pants and a white blouse, unbuttoned so that her raised clavicles showed. It was one of her striking features and she knew it.

Kim's whole apartment was done up in 1955 Eisenhower-era modernity: low slung coffee tables, hammock-style chairs with triangular leggings; framed Renoir prints, and a fireplace nestled inside a rock wall. Her television set was new, white, solid state, and broadcast, no doubt, a color signal. Most of us were still watching baseball in black and white.

She pulled on her cigarette. It was king-size with lipstick on the filter. "I don't know anything about this. That's wild." She laughed, almost as if she were admiring her sister's boldness. "I bet Dad will get a kick out of this."

"Kick? Like the way your father hit you? I bet that wasn't the first time."

She looked away, at a far corner of the ceiling. "It wasn't. But never Cathy. He never hit her. He loved her. I was the nuisance. The daughter he didn't want. The one that didn't obey—"

"Could he have hurt Cathy? Her lower dresser drawer shows her own *unique* streak of rebellion—"

"He didn't know about that."

"What if he did? I mean, what if he had discovered her kinky past—is he capable of murder—?"

"We're all capable of murder." She returned her gaze as I pushed back my porkpie. Her eyes darkened. "But murder his daughter? No."

I asked about the car, if Cathy bought a car that she had to sign over to Nick. Kim sighed and said that story was indeed true. She now blew smoke in the far corner of the room.

I rolled one of her Ogilvie and Beggert pens between a finger and thumb.

"So what's your next move?"

"I'm meeting with Leeds in an hour or so and then Davis. Get some answers. I need evidence to get a police warrant to search for Cathy in the Gardens—if she's still alive."

"My father took everything from her. I got out so he couldn't do the same to me." Two months working at Dominion's as a checker and then real-estate training and suddenly Kim made more in three months than her father made all year. "That really killed him. A girl making more than a man." She blew more smoke, and her thin lips grimaced. "Fuck that."

I was surprised at how easily Kim shifted from cool, detached realtor to brassy hard-edged working gal, to sexy hostess, who kept offering me drinks from her wet bar and was surprised when I settled for tonic water.

My parents were alcoholics and I had a stomach full of their blue moods, anger and incoherence so I was an anomaly in my playing days: a hockey player who never drank Molsons. Ever.

When I was a kid, Dad locked me in our family car and visited the local tavern for an hour or so, tossing darts and drinking. On the ride home, I prayed and prayed that he kept the car between the white lines.

"What can you tell me about Spinner Terrien, Lisa's on-again, off-again boyfriend?"

"I don't know. Some ex-hockey player. Had a couple of brief stints in the pros. I heard he might be kind of funny." She held up a limp wrist. It looked like a dog's paw.

With only 120 spots in the pros there were a lot of players you could say had "brief stints." Hell, our goalie Johnny Bower didn't make the big time with the Leafs until he was 34. He was three-time MVP in the American Hockey League and had to wait his turn to stick with the six-team league. And if Spinner liked men or was bisexual that was his business. "Bolemac Corporation. Anything *funny* about that?" She was annoying me with her attitudes and a thin veneer of smart-ass crept into my questioning like vines of poison ivy.

"Excuse me?"

"Bolemac?"

"What's that? An expensive brand of Tupperware?"

I laughed. "No. A front, a construction company. Does work at the Gardens and may be a place to hide certain pots of money. Smith and Bullard are involved with it. So is a tough mobster, Babe Migano."

That made her sit up and straighten her shoulders.

"You recognize his name?"

"Who doesn't? He's big-time."

"He's a crook," I said.

"A woman doesn't always care about how a man makes his money. She cares about how he makes love." And from what she had heard from people at work and at parties, Migano was dynamite in bed.

"Great." I looked at my fingers and shook my head. Being great in the sack wasn't my strength. I was okay, but no MVP trophy winner. "What about counseling at the high school. Trauma counseling?"

"Oh, with Landover? Yeah, he tried to rope me into that. I wasn't too interested. Touchy-feely horseshit. Let's all hold hands and sing. Cathy went." She played with the bottom cuffs of her Capri slacks. "A lot."

"Did it help?"

"I thought the guy was kind of creepy and quit going after three or four sessions. Cathy stuck."

"I thought you described him previously as a helpful family *friend*—"

"I never quite said that—"

"Uh-huh." I told her about his calling card and *worship the cock*, and wondered if he had sprung that sales pitch on Cathy or Kim during one of their sessions.

"*Worship the cock*?" She laughed. "Doesn't he have it backwards? Women are the ones who give birth. The vagina, the womb?"

"How could you let this creep into your family."

"He was good for Cathy. He was trying to get her away from our father."

I rubbed an edge of my chin. "How often was he seeing Cathy?"

Kim looked away and filled her voice with fabric softener. "Not that often. Once a month maybe? To discuss her future."

What about the other girl, the one in the suitcase? How often did he see her?

"Landover was in a meeting the day she was abducted, remember?"

"Uh-huh. Convenient."

"*Worship the cock*. God, seriously? I think Freud's got it all wrong." The fabric softener edges returned to Kim's voice. "So does Landover apparently." She laughed and tucked her knees in closer to her chin.

She was confident in her position, eyebrows knitting with challenge as she tackled Freud's assumptions. No doubt, Kim could sell just about anything from her anti-Freud stance to products I should buy, like an Ogilvie and Beggert home.

I had read a couple of her ads in the Ogilvie and Beggert listings spread across the coffee table. Kim had a real talent for placing the reader in the heart of the scene and helping us feel the cozy comfort of the home on the market, even before experiencing the listing up close and personal. *Picture yourself next to a Bay window, as the sun dapples. . . .* Her prose was creative and inviting.

"It's all about enchantment," she said. "I'm the Hans Christian Andersen of Realtors."

"Speaking of fairy tales. This is a pretty expensive place." I looked behind her and felt underdressed in my porkpie. On the fireplace mantle were various Eskimo carvings, first editions, keys, and two cigars in cellophane. Cohiba. I recognized the brand. I smoked one myself after we won our second cup in '63. "How do you afford this?"

"I afford it. I *make* a lot of money."

I wondered who the man with the Cohiba was in her life and scanned the apartment for other indicators of his presence but all the chairs were pushed neatly against the dining table and no plates or abandoned bits of silverware were lying about. The careless presence of a man was absent.

Half a glass of what looked like flat Coke sat on the far edge of the mantle. The mouth of the glass had a lipstick stain matching the one on her cigarette filter.

She saw me spot the stains and lifted her cigarette. "You ever notice in the movies how you can never trust anyone with a cigarette holder?" She laughed. Three years ago, Kim smoked with one—it made the taste gentler, milder—but once she started selling homes, she quit the practice. Selling is about being open and attentive to the needs of buyers. A cigarette holder sends the wrong signal; it suggests not being quite Canadian, but foreign, continental.

She laughed again. "I also wear darker, conservative clothes now. Don't want to be too bright or show up the wives. You've got to keep the wives happy to close the sale. Men sign the check, but the women make the decisions. In my business it's A.B.C. Always Be Closing. That's the bottom line."

I nodded. There was a real no-frills, hard edge to her.

"And, get this, I wear men's deodorant. Can't have my perfume challenging what the women sport."

"That's strange." I laughed. "I swear I smelled Chanel No. 5. I—well, all good perfume smells like Chanel No. 5. It's the only perfume I know."

Kim took another puff off her cigarette. "Well, I'm not trying to sell a house right now."

"Oh." I looked down at the pen in my hand.

So she was wearing perfume.

"If you're interested, I'm interested." She leaned back in the puffy chair and smiled. Her upper lip was a little heavy. She wasn't just flirting with me like Lisa did. This was a real overture, a different kind of sales pitch. And she was a great-looking woman, but I was starting to be interested in Stana again.

"So how many houses do you sell a month?"

"Let's not talk business." She patted the spot on the couch next to the chair. "Sit here. I'll pour you another tonic water."

Her tone was a strange mixture of mockery and seduction.

I wasn't quite sure of just how deep the irony cut, but even with the high cheekbones, fleshy chin, and supple curves like Cathy's I didn't find her appealing. I like a more muted, subtle approach. Shirley MacLaine, Teresa Wright, they're more my kind of woman. Not Marilyn Monroe.

"Okay. I see that you're going to be shy." She leaned forward.

"Look, I—"

"Sex can be invigorating—"

That's what Davis used to say, while flashing around his Polaroids. "Sorry—"

"Well, it's seasonal. Not the sex, the house selling." She laughed again. "Lots of homes sell around the start and end of the school calendar and holidays, but I average nine to ten a month."

I whistled. "Wow. Ten percent commission on that?"

She nodded. Toronto was in a housing boom. "Look at Richmond Hill. Right now, it's cottage country." But in ten years it will be a thriving suburb, city. West, east, north, the sprawl is on. From here to Barrie the land boom is happening.

Barrie. She mentioned Barrie. Was that some kind of slip?

If I had the money to invest, she insisted, I ought to buy houses, and sell them in a year or two. I'd make a fortune off the equity. Better yet, buy land north of the city and sell to future investors. Now's the time to take the risks.

"I don't have any money." What I had as a hockey player— and that was never much—I spent. Seven years in the league, 458 consecutive games, and I averaged about $7500 a season.

"You sound bitter."

"Not really. I just didn't like the way it ended."

"Yeah." She knew about that. Most people did.

"You know your sister wrote to me, care of the Gardens, before I even took this case, 1964." I looked at my fingers. "After I got canned and sent to the minors, she writes telling me that I was on ice for more goals scored by my team as opposed to against my team than any other player on the club. Cathy said I was the league's top defensive forward and there ought to be an award for that. It's funny, I didn't think about that telegram and who wrote it until this morning—"

"So you have a prior history?" She smiled. "The two of you—"

"Well, I don't know—it's just a weird connection that's all—"

"You really do want to find her, don't you? You don't even know her but you care—"

"Yeah." I shrugged. I knew it wouldn't take away the pain of having lost Sarah 96 days ago, but it might help, it might give me a little closure, but something else was emerging from all this, something that surprised me: the Cathy on display in the Big Chief tablets, her sensitivity, her vulnerability, that part of her, for a girl I didn't even know, I was truly beginning to love, I think.

6

The rain hadn't let up. The driver-side wiper of my Galaxie needed to be replaced and instead of clear damp glass I was squinting through psychedelic scratches of rainbow streaks. In the shadows of Front Street, Leeds's office building was dark, and angry gargoyles were on two of its lintels. A heavy maple blocked most of the street's dim light, creating a greater aura of uncertainty. "What else can you tell me about this cat?" I asked Stana, as I pushed in the brake and clutch and threw the car into first, killing the engine.

Fifty years old; graduate of the University of Toronto, 1938; one year at the law school at Osgoode Hall; played varsity football, 1936–37; Olympic pole vaulter, 1936; guidance counselor for twenty-two years at Castle Frank. Ran for office twice, unsuccessfully, as a Conservative for an eastside Toronto riding.

"Good work."

"That's not all. In 1942, he was in a car accident and killed a kid. No charges. The kid stepped out from between two parked cars. Guess who was in the car with him?"

I squeezed my eyes and pulled up my collar anticipating a fight with the rain. The left side of my jaw felt tight and a headache was coming on again. I reached for painkillers in the glove box and dry swallowed.

"You get a lot of headaches?"

"Sometimes. They just come on."

She wondered if it were playing-related. I shrugged. Stana's chiropractor friend was convinced that hockey was the worst sport ever. "A national disgrace" he called it. Right up there with football and boxing. Bad for your back, your head.

"Remind me to never refer that fella to anybody. *National disgrace*. Please."

"Did you ever have any concussions?"

"Yeah, of course." I had had a few; saw stars now and then after giving or receiving a terrific body check. Big deal. "I think it's the rain. It does something to my sinuses." I wasn't about to tell her about my off-and-on meetings with Dr. Abramowitz or his warnings for me to percolate ten miles below the speed limit.

"Sinuses, right. Jesus Christ, Hayden. How often do you get headaches?"

"Now and then. Relax."

"I don't know why you players don't wear helmets."

"You don't want to be a candy ass, that's why."

Stana mumbled something about macho horseshit.

"Okay, Popeye. Let's get a move on. Oh, and who the fuck was in the car with Landover? You thought with all these headaches and concussions I'd forgotten, didn't you?"

"McClelland Stuart." They both had commissions in the Old Man's militia, 1940–45, located off Church Street. "You know in case we were attacked at home or something? Old Man Smith had all of the Leafs, its employees, and broadcasters sign on for military training."

"Really?" That was interesting. "How did Landover fit in? What did he do for the Leafs?"

Stana shrugged. "But he and McClelland *were* driving home together after one such training session."

"Crazy."

Minutes later, after walking under drooping branches and fighting off water dripping down my porkpie, we were climbing toward Leeds's second-floor office. The light in the hallway was dead and so was the light at the top of the stairs. Both of the light fixtures looked like dirty tulips, full of smudges and dry fly flecks.

There were no other signs of upscale pleasures than those two tulips. Walls needed to be replastered and the lobby's carpeting was so threadbare as to display the hardwood slats angling through. The carpet's once blue pattern was now covered over with dingy gray from the weight of heavy footsteps.

On the frosted glass to Leeds's office door was a decal in the lower left corner. A line drawing of a man with Einstein hair and outstretched arms bouncing aloft two globes, eastern and western hemispheres, like atomic fireballs. "Da Silva Mind Control Institute" circled about the image.

And then I smelled gunpowder.

So did Stana. It was sharp and pinched the air.

The door to Leeds's office wasn't locked. It had only been pushed to and we nudged it open all too gently. The room was very still. A radiator thinly clanked now and again and there were Neolithic shadows of trees on a window. The roller blind was snapped up tight. Every desk drawer was open and in patches of black silhouettes, I saw a body slumped in a chair.

"Don't turn on the light." I stopped Stana until I pulled

shut the blinds. "Now."

The small desk light splashed a cone of yellow across Leeds's face, his bulgy eyes open but strangely contented, as if in his last breathing moments he had resigned himself to death. A hand lay flat, palm up on his thigh, and there were powder marks on his shirt were the bullet entered. I pointed at the hole. "Look. Whoever did this got awfully close."

"A woman?"

"Maybe. Or a really good friend." I shrugged, covertly moving. "Someone he trusted. That smell is awfully fresh." I held an index finger to my lips, unholstered my snub-nosed .38, and quickly opened a narrow closet door. There was no one in there: just five pairs of shoes, one of them a set of woman's blue pumps. I picked them up. Four fedoras were ordered on the top shelf, all of their brims resting at the same point. On the rack were several coats and sweaters. Some of the sweaters had leather patches on the elbows.

"Is this Leeds?" she asked.

"Yup. Mr. Tangerine Room himself."

I sat on the front of the desk. On the blotter was a gym bag, with shorts and a T-shirt poking between the hard cut edges of the zipper. Across from Leeds was a polished wooden chair draped with a white towel. If this had just happened, why was there no commotion when we came in? Why didn't we hear feet trampling down stairs?

"Look at the shoes. The edges. They're wet," she said.

Small coins of water dripped from the low heel of one of the shoes. I snapped my fingers and ran back to the office's lone window, rolled up the blind, and raised the glass. Beyond the black fire escape, in a distant alley, was a woman running, her shoulders throwing her forward. Her body in the rain was a series of sharp angles caught in intermittent cones of streetlights. She wasn't wearing any shoes. "Goddamn it." And then, just as quickly, she was gone. Streaks of rain dimpled small puddles on the sidewalk.

I plunked the shoes on the desk. They were heavy. "Damn."

"You said that."

"No, I believe I said, 'God damn it.'"

Stana wondered if the assailant were a former student, a member of the special therapy sessions? Paying dividends? "Look at these drawers." Papers were strewn everywhere. One drawer was even upended and tossed at the foot of the corpse's office chair. A filing cabinet was toppled over, resting on its side.

Stana touched the corpse's neck. "The body is still warm."

"Right. But how warm and how long dead?"

Far from the fallen filing cabinet and fanned papers was a solitary cubicle, like the one in Leeds's Castle Frank office. It had rippled glass walls, a padded chair, headphones, and a reel-to-reel contraption with a jet engine's console that resembled the rig I saw in his Castle Frank digs. *Tangerine Room Two?* "Check this out." There were seven or eight tapes in the cubbyholes along the wall, featuring what appeared to be whale noises, loons on a still lake, and one session called "Mist over the Smokies, a Tennessee morning."

"He did relaxation sessions here?" Stana brushed up against my shoulder.

"Relaxation. Right." So he was a quack on the side, earning extra coin as some kind of mind healer, courtesy of Da Silva. I laughed briskly. In a far cubbyhole was a ledger with dates, numbers, and initials. It looked like hieroglyphics. *CS.* "If that's Cathy she was here four days ago."

"Four days ago? That was just before I was supposed to interview her."

"Leeds was running some kind of racket. But what?" I flipped the ledger's pages. In back, stuck in the ledger's creases, was a bright 5x7 photo: Landover in a turban, eyes brimming with comic mischief. Typed at the bottom, newspaper copy: "Appearing at Massey Hall, Lanzo the Great, Southern Ontario's Outrageous Hypnotist. Tickets $2, $2.50 at the door."

"Lanzo the Great?" Stana laughed, shoulders rising. "Lanzo the Great." She snapped her fingers. "Yes. I was at that show." She was just a girl; for her ninth birthday Dad took her to see the illusionist. "Lanzo, Landover, got people to bark like dogs. Dad said he couldn't be hypnotized, he had too strong a will, so at my urging he volunteered, and wound up putting on four jackets and some blankets because he was so cold—"

Power of suggestion. I wondered what he was suggesting in Tangerine Room Two? And for what purposes? What's his racket?

"Whoever got here wanted something specific. Something on paper." Stana turned back to the corpse.

"Not the ledger apparently—"

"Paper with linen in it?"

"$568,000?"

"Maybe." I tapped a finger at the edge of the desk. "Shit, shit, shit."

I dialed Lisa's number. She answered on the fourth ring. I told her that Leeds was dead.

"Wears a rug," Stana said.

"What?"

"Look at the weaves." She pointed. One set of lines waved left; another set of lines broke in a completely contrary direction.

"Wears a rug," I repeated to Lisa.

"He blamed God for his going bald. He mentioned that in our very first 'therapy' session," she said.

"Don't you see? His killing might mean you're in danger?" She didn't see the connection.

"Leeds is connected to Cathy's disappearance. You're connected to Cathy. You're also connected to Leeds. You might want to lay low. When are you getting out of town?"

She didn't say anything.

"Lisa?"

"Yeah. I got it." All of the bounce was now out of her voice. She sounded like she had fallen in a well. "Got it." She promised to leave town soon.

I gathered the "deal" hadn't gone down the way she expected. She didn't answer my questions about that.

I hung up and picked up the shoes. Spots of water stained along the sides like small lakes. "Boy, did this gal have big feet."

"Be nice."

"I'm just saying. These shoes are a ten or an eleven. Maybe even a fourteen." I shrugged and now it was my turn to mumble like a disgruntled Popeye, "My sister's feet expanded to an eight after her third child."

"I am's who's I am's," Stana said, talking out of the side of her mouth, scrunching shut one eye.

That cracked me up. "You know what's really sick, really random?" I pinched at the space between my eyebrows, trying to force the headache away. "We never even got to really talk to Leeds: one brief encounter with me, a phone call with you, and now the fella's dead. Gone. Like that. His life. Over."

"Lisa's a witness," Stana gently chided, reminding me. "Don't have her leave town."

"Her life might be in danger."

"Cathy's life is in bigger danger. We need Lisa around. Something about her story just doesn't add up—" She shook her head. "The whole Davis thing. It's a phony I tell you."

"Davis is a fucker—"

"Maybe. But that doesn't make him a killer or in on Cathy's gone missing."

"What about what he said at Drew's?"

"He was just barking. There was no real bite there. And you were the one who went all John Wayne with the gun and everything—"

She had me there.

Stana tapped the edge of her chin. "You know what would happen at this point in a hardboiled detective novel?"

"Do I really want to know?"

"Yes, you do. The detective would find an address written on the inside of the rolling papers the victim used for his cigarettes." She smiled, pleased with herself, her eyes dancing.

"That's just silly."

She reached for the corpse's toupee. "What if?"

"Wait. This is a crime scene. We don't want to contaminate—"

"Really, are you serious, says the man who sat atop Leeds's desk and lifted up a pair of shoes—"

"You got gloves—you had them on outside—"

She shrugged, slid them back on, and pulled off the toupee. The top of Leeds's head was stippled with swatches of sticky residue. Inside the hairpiece was a yellow-lined piece of paper taped to the cheesecloth.

"No fucking way."

Stana laughed. Scrawled across the paper were 402C and three additional numbers: 42, 23, and 7.

"402C? Some kind of safety deposit box, like at a bank?" I rubbed my chin again.

"Well, I don't think it's more of your ever-loving latitude and longitude lines—"

"Funny. Union Station's across the street. Maybe this is a number to a holding locker."

"Union Station doesn't have holding lockers with letters—"

"It doesn't?"

She dropped the toupee back onto Mr. Leeds. It didn't sit quite right. It now looked like a displaced whoopee cushion. I tried to adjust it but only made matters worse.

Stana moved to the far chair and snapped out a towel. "He said he had to go to the gym. To work out." She pointed at the unzipped bag. "There's his stuff." She studied the stretched towel. "Property of Hart House" was written in indelible marker on a small swatch of sewn-in fabric. She folded the towel back over the chair.

"I think we just found the thread," she said, pointing to the ink.

IT DIDN'T TAKE us long to get to Hart House: Spadina to Harbord, and then I parked on Haskins. After walking through slanting rain we stood in front of one of the nation's oldest student centers. Built in 1919, the architectural style was Gothic, capturing the dark mood of the country after the

Great War. The windows were large, the exteriors round, one might even say downright stout, and the whole ensemble was cluttered with arches and vaults.

"Okay, you can quit making with the tour guide's report," I said. "Next you'll be talking about how it's wider than it is high—"

"No, I was going to say the building's contours are jagged." Stana blushed slightly and rubbed the back of a hand under her nose. In her third and fourth years at the university she led tours for prospective students and their parents. "The hardest thing was walking backwards and not tripping over anyone."

Hart House was immense and imposing. It looked like a giant Folgers can with added Gothic ornamentation.

Minutes later we were in the gym and its dusky brick walls and arched windows. We crossed a polished track and ducked down below the Art Deco swimming area with its light fixtures and marble tiling straight out of an Astaire-Rogers 1930s musical. Lockers were in back.

Some were floor length, some half-length. All were black with dented metal and slits at the top. 402C was a half locker at the end of a row, along a long wooden bench. Two discarded towels draped the bench that nobody stood by. Voices and shallow splashes echoed from the pool.

Inside the locker was a huge manila envelope with string slipped around a fastener in back. A dusty can of 8mm film was in the far corner of the locker. Probably about ten minutes of film.

The can barely fit into Stana's handbag. I don't know what else she had in there. A car's master cylinder?

"I don't have a film projector."

"I do. My parents do," she offered. I liked her parents. Her father worked at the T.T.C. and her mother was a retired schoolteacher. They were honest, direct, didn't stand on ceremony, and hated entitlement.

We breathed heavily. And I kissed her. I had to do something, affirm our existence against all this mess. My shoulders hurt with the weight of time.

I felt that the window on finding Cathy was closing. It had closed on Sarah 96 days ago.

She locked 402C.

I looked about again.

The envelope felt heavy, as if it were full of sand.

We slid away the towels, sat on the bench, and she smiled gently, pushing her lips together and made a big show of putting on her winter gloves. "Happy now?"

"Delighted."

She unfastened the bundle.

It was cramped with 8x10 photographs, five or so. All of the subjects were women. Naked. Medium shots: waist up and gritty grime haloed each image. "Looks like these were taken with a Speed Graphic, an f/16 setting, and shutter speed of around 200. Just guessing by the depth of field. Looks like about ten feet is in focus."

"Really, Hayden? Depth of field? Who cares?"

"Sorry, I was just showing off." I shrugged.

"A Speed Graphic? That's an old press camera, isn't it?"

"Uh-huh."

The fourth photograph featured Lisa Steinmetz. Her hair was darker than the dingy blond she now sports, her face much thinner. She was looking left, hoping to find an illusory moment of escape. Her eyes were vague, distracted, as if the cheesecake intentions weren't her idea. I'm pretty sure they weren't.

And then I noticed why the eyes were so distracted: they were caught in some kind of in-between space, as if the actions performed weren't of her own free will.

"Look at the background." Stana pointed.

Main lobby, Maple Leaf Gardens, Steinmetz parked in front of a photo of the 1947–48 Stanley Cup champs. I wondered what Syl Apps, Turk Broda, and Teeder Kennedy thought of Lisa's ass being thus arrayed before their likenesses.

On the back of the photograph was scrawled: "LS. 4/14/59. MLG."

Stana couldn't figure out the point of the photograph. It wasn't erotic, she said. It had a punishing quality to it.

"Oh, I don't know, some guys are into punishment pictures. Like spanking a woman. Not that I'm into that, but for some guys that's a real turn-on. I think these photos are a depressed fella's idea of French postcards. I really do."

"You think these are sexy?"

"Well, yeah. I mean, yeah. I mean theoretically." Shit, I was about to get smacked in the shoulder again.

"These pictures are *dirty*."

"The craftsmanship displayed here is terrible—"

Now Stana *did* punch my shoulder. "Do you think Leeds took the photos?"

The fifth photograph: Sarah Kerr. Her blonde-white hair fell atop her shoulders like heavy snow. It was flat and the eyes were dull too, like she was under a spell. There was a mole between her small breasts. On back: "SK. MLG. 4/22/62."

I could never forget that date. On April 22, 1962, we won our first cup, 2-1 over the Blackhawks at Chicago Stadium on a late third-period goal by Dick Duff. And then there was that picture of Cathy, the one I found in her lower desk drawer: the Royal York with Bullard and Smith draping all over her like festive bunting. That was April 22nd, too, or most likely early on the morning of the 23rd after drinks and more drinks. She was at the Gardens the same time that Sarah was. And then I snapped my fingers. "1962, that's three years ago. Sarah was only 17 when she was murdered. That puts her at fourteen in this picture."

"What?" Stana grabbed a hold of it. "Kiddie porn?"

"Yeah." And Lisa Steinmetz, 1959. That puts her at 16 or 17.

"That photograph that Lisa showed you, the one allegedly sent from Davis. Was it recent or was it taken on this date too, 1962?"

I don't know. I didn't know Cathy that well. I wasn't looking at the earlier photo close enough. *What else in this case wasn't I seeing?*

Stana's eyes furrowed. Lisa was lying. That photograph she sprung on me wasn't taken recently but was a relic from that Gardens party. "I bet you anything it's three years old."

It would be so easy to fool me, but now that I think about it, Cathy did look younger, the face more full with adolescent baby fat. I pulled out the folded print Lisa gave me the other day.

Davis had nothing to do with this, Stana mumbled. Lisa was trying to divert attention away from her to him. What's she hiding, why is she sending you on a false trail? "I don't think you can believe a word from Lisa—"

I shook my head. "This is three years old. Look at her hair. Bangs. She wears her hair out now. Fuck." I hated being a sucker. What was Lisa hiding? Who was she working for? "We've got to talk to her."

"We will."

"I told her to leave town—"

"We'll find her." Stana squeezed my hand. "We will. But first let's check out this film."

Her parents loved sharing home movies of Stana. When she was born, her father Clint got bit by the hobby and photographed everything from Stana's first bath, to *Early Morning outing at Jean Sibelius Square.* "By the time I entered second grade, Dad had tired of his hobby. So I guess, nothing's happened in my life since then." She smiled.

I kissed her nose.

Her parents' home was in the city's east end, Scarborough, off Eglinton, in a modest fourth-floor apartment.

I shuffled through the five photographs. They were all dated between 1958 and 1963. "Shit, I wonder if all of these girls were in that very first therapy session at Castle Frank."

"Probably," Stana said.

"The Tangerine Room. Landover Leeds," I mumbled. Lanzo the fucking Great. "Hey. I know this one too." DS, 3/12/63, MLG. Aqua green eyes, blonde. She was one of the human lamps in Bullard and Smith's office. In the photograph her eyes looked directly through the camera, unaware of any lingering stare on the other end. "She was wearing a pink fez." I had no idea what name was behind the initials. DS.

"He shoots, he scores," Stana mumbled under her breath, and then reached into her handbag, finding the list of nine names. She crosschecked the list against the 8x10's. Three of the nine girls from the 1958 therapy sessions were present in the envelope's pack of five, circa 1958–63. "Almost half of

these young women are underage. You *still* think the photos
are sexy?"

"No."

Stana shook her head and chewed at her upper lip. "Bullard and Smith. Fucking pimps," she said.

STANA'S MOM Rene was kind and didn't pry. She had
never once passed judgment on our having lived together
and she loved my sense of humor and the way I played hockey. She said I had integrity, didn't cheat anyone, skated every
shift hard, back-checked, fore-checked, and scored when my
team really needed it: in the close games, not the blowouts.
She followed the team religiously and the day I got shipped to
the minors a bit of her died. She got so mad at the Leafs that
she almost became a Habs fan.

Rene wore a pink pajama top with big white buttons and
her gray hair parachuted about her forehead and full face.
Her eyes lingered with pleasantries, like she were about to
share her favorite cookie recipes.

Her husband, Clint, loved to tell jokes and he was a die-
hard Leafs fan too. He preferred listening to the radio play-
by-play of McClelland Stuart over the television commentary of McClelland's son Bill, so, the nights Clint didn't work,
he synched his radio to the television's pictures.

The nights he did work, the Wednesdays and Saturdays of
Toronto's home games, the TTC ride to the College stop was
a congested mess, full of elbows, bad smells, and tidbits of
knowledge from the subways of hockey "general managers,"
suggesting trading away this guy or that guy for this one or
that. The arrogance.

As far as Clint was concerned, Coach and GM Hugh "Two

Fisted" Farrell knew what he's doing. Shut up, the rest of you, and let Farrell run the Leafs organization and me run this goddamn train.

"So we can't see this film, huh?" Clint's cigarette bounced on his lower lip, his T-shirt half-tucked in, half-tucked out, a suspender off a shoulder.

"No," I said. "For your own safety. The less who know, the better." I had already mentioned the photographs to them, including the topless ones of Cathy, the missing girl. *And Sarah, the girl I lost 96 days ago.* "I don't know what we're in store for."

"You think the films might be *suggestive*?" Clint looked over at Stana.

"Don't worry. I've deputized her a junior G-man. She can handle it," I said.

Clint wondered if we should be handing this stuff over to the police.

"Soon. I promise." But I wanted to look at it first and find enough evidence so that the cops could get a warrant and hopefully locate Cathy.

Rene hugged my left shoulder. "It's so good to see you, Hayden," and then she looked over in her husband's direction and then at Stana. Rene's eyes held a hopeful twinkle.

"You guys too. I missed you," I said.

Their apartment was on the frugal side of modest: a kitchen you could only stand in; a dining area with a small round table and three chrome-backed chairs (four wouldn't fit); a living room with a long coffee table, TV, radio, and a balcony off to the right. On the balcony were two lawn chairs and a small hibachi grill (not really much space for a block party). In back were a bathroom and two bedrooms. The hallway

that led to the bathroom was squeezed with books and records. Clint liked Frank Sinatra and Johnny Cash.

"Well, we missed you, son." Clint seemed an inch shorter than I remembered and his shoulders sagged a little. He
didn't have any plans to retire, but Rene thought he should
once he reached thirty years with the TTC. "That's just two
years away."

Stana wondered what the hell they were doing still awake.
"It's not late."

"It's almost midnight, Ma."

"Well, it's the weekend." They had been reading the latest Ed McBain when we arrived. They loved reading murder
mysteries together. Instead of watching late night with Johnny
Carson, they often fell asleep to an 87th Precinct novel. They
took turns reading to each other and enjoyed the sounds of
each other's voice. Rene was really good at taking on all the
different roles, Clint said. "Should've been an actress."

"Oh, get out." Rene playfully smacked Clint on the shoulder.

"That's where you get it from," I pointed at Stana, and then
rubbed my shoulder in sympathy with Clint.

They all laughed. There was something so gentle and romantic about the love that Clint and Rene had for each other.

"Can we get you anything before you start—you know—
movie watching?"

"No, we're—uh—"

I cut Stana off. "Actually I'm kind of hungry. How about an
egg sandwich—?"

Stana slugged me in the shoulder. "Hayden—"

"See what I mean?"

Rene laughed, her nose scrunching. "With some Tabasco, Hayden?" Rene's eyes glinted. She pushed strands of gray hair behind an ear.

"Yes. And maybe some green olives on the side? And chips or Cheezies?"

"Sure." She padded to the kitchen. She moved about a room lightly.

"You are shameless," Stana said.

"You want anything, hon?" Rene shouted from the kitchen. Her voice however wasn't light. All those years of teaching second grade taught her to project.

"No." Stana paused, tapping her chin. "Okay. Fried baloney. No bread. No Tabasco. And definitely no green olives."

"Check," Mom shouted, the frying pan already spattering with a frying egg.

IT TOOK AWHILE to thread the film. It was delicate and broke a couple of times, but once we had it through the gate, it clacked and burped along the projector's tracking, catching and bouncing now and then. The images were relatively clear, but the camera was stationary, people moving in and out of the frame and it was pretty obvious due to lighting inconsistencies that the ten-minute roll was spliced together from several different parties. The exposures weren't consistent.

Corrugated curtains and the chrome finish to the wet bar and chairs suggested without a doubt that this was the space in the Gardens behind Smith and Bullard's office, the one you could only access through a button at the side of Pal Cal's desk, the one Spinner Terrien slipped into after a perfunctory wave. Spinner wasn't in any of the images. Neither was McClelland Stuart, the voice of Hockey Canada.

But Davis was there. He played cards or stood by a roulette wheel, watching, his face, especially his chin, shiny with sweat. Who knew how much money he was losing each night. But with hands hidden deep in his pockets he didn't appear ready, anytime soon, to donate to the March of Dimes.

"We got 'em," I said. "Running a common gaming house. That's enough for a warrant."

"Yeah," Stana said.

Smith and Bullard, however, were having a good time, engrossed in their own narcissistic panache and pseudo bon-vivant charm. They were chatting, highballs in hand, liquor splashing over the lips of their tear-shaped glasses. The two playboys sported homburgs and Bullard had a huge bag of chips in his right hand. He liked to eat with his left—probably to keep the dice clean. Smith moved his shoulders as he laughed.

At least I think he was laughing. The images were soundless.

Sometimes a naked woman could be spotted in the background, sitting on a couch, quietly smoking with long white gloves, nothing else on her person. Once in a while a naked woman danced off in a corner like a lethargic go-go dancer desperate for more bennies.

Kim Stabulas was never naked, but she was sitting on the arm of a chair in one brief stretch of film. She wore all black, including razor-edge stilettos and gloves that shined as if they were buffed with wax. She smoked a cigarette off a long slender holder. Her eyes were heavily made up, as were her lush lips. A white-haired sable collared her neck.

Babe Migano, the ex-Montreal mobster, smoked a cigar the size of a .45, and was by her feet on the floor. He was a big man and I was surprised that one of the kingpins of crime would sit by anybody's feet, let alone a woman's. His face was very prosperous, full of success and contentment. He never rolled dice nor worked the wheel. He was an observer and occasionally he and Davis would have a brief conversation, Davis leaning in with his head, the top of his hair uneven and needing more Brylcreem.

"She lied to us, too," I said.

"What?"

"Kim. She knew about Coughlins." I laughed bitterly. "She told me she thought it was a pizza joint. Do you see any fucking anchovies in the room?"

This is dynamite, Stana said. "A grand jury will be looking into this." Check out the homburgs. What a perfect set-up for an exclusive club. Hold the party right in the Gardens pad. Who would know? An exclusive group of 10 or 15 guests could quietly party down after a hockey game or arrive in a limo at the Church Street entrance and nobody would be the wiser. "Our good friend Lisa's there too, I see."

I nodded. Lisa wore a black, low-cut gown. Her chin seemed perpetually tucked in, as if she were afraid of leading with it too much. Her body was displayed boldly, but her deportment—short, halting steps, slightly wobbling on heels—and overall fashion unease suggested a woman who didn't quite belong. She looked like a working girl, more comfortable waiting tables.

Migano's aloofness was one of choice.

"Who's operating the camera?" Stana asked.

"It's stationary." Could be on a tripod. Could be set up in a secret location, behind a two-way mirror. Few of these people knew they were being filmed. "They're too carefree, lacking in self-consciousness. None of them *look* into the camera.

Usually a camera draws attention. Check out the guy obliviously picking his nose."

"Oh, my god. He represents my riding—"

"An M.P.?"

"Two term."

After a few more spliced chunks, and the film shaking, there was one odd forty-five second riff of Landover Leeds in dark dress pants, pleated, and a heavy sweater with patches at the elbows. He sat in a leather chair and a tall woman, full of lithe curves and sharp angles, sauntered toward him, her thin hips swaying.

She climbed onto his lap and thrust up, down, and around and he mewled, at least he looked to be mewling, head tilted up, parted lips uttering pleasing sounds at the ceiling. The woman rolled her shoulders and arched her back like a cat. I think she was mewling too.

"Starzz. That must be Starzz. The woman in the mask Lisa told us about," Stana said.

"Really?"

"Look at the *mask*."

I hadn't noticed the *mask*.

Bullard and Smith, smiling, stood by the woman in the black dress. Flecks of chips fell to the carpet. Smith at some point applauded, took off his glasses, cleaned them, and then applauded some more. Davis was looking off at someone, probably Lisa or another well-endowed woman, outside the frame.

"I think they call that lap dancing," Stana said.

"Looks like fun, with the right girl."

I was surprised that Stana hadn't punched me. "Maybe later. At least a shower," she said.

"I can't see the woman's face."

"I'm telling you, she's wearing a mask."

And then I saw it. The mask was huge, with triangles around both eyes and feathers on the forehead. When Starzz arched back her head I could see the expressive playfulness behind the performance. The outfit would be perfect for Mardi Gras. "If I had beads, I'd throw them at her."

Really? Stana thought the whole act was too much.

We watched until the remaining lap dance footage bled into black leader.

And then we were quiet. The room. I stared at the bits of cold egg and baloney left on the plates Rene had served up.

There wasn't a TV on anywhere. I wondered if her parents had gone to bed.

I touched Stana's chin and lifted her face and studied the freckles that forever seemed to be dancing. "I'm sorry about last year. How I just shut you out—didn't return your calls, didn't—"

Suddenly my mouth was dry and my eyes burned.

"We've both made mistakes. Me at the newspaper—"

"We'll both try to do better." I crossed my heart and like a ten-year-old kid took her pinky, attaching it to mine. "Pinky promise." That made her laugh.

We had made out on this very bed many a time over the years, keeping the noise down so that her parents wouldn't hear.

Stana must have been sharing my memories, because she was now leaning in, her nose catching my upper lip, while we both readjusted and kissed, and fell back on the bed. I pushed hair from her forehead and kissed her harder and then kissed her nose and both eyelids. "I love you," I said.

She tapped my chin three times. "Who do you think is the girl in the mask?"

I shrugged. "I'm kind of glad McClelland Stuart wasn't at these parties, living the life of the hipster libertine. I kind of like him—"

She sat up with her elbows. McClelland was a smart businessman. Owned his own radio station, CKMS, and had a lot of other investment interests including housing, land development, and sought to buy a piece of a CFL team. "But he's no saint." He was having an affair with his radio station manager.

"But he's married."

"Oh, sure. But when did that ever mean anything?"

"True." I shrugged. *Men are pigs.*

"But the press just keeps quiet about it. It's hockey." She smiled thinly. "Excessive drinking? Wife beating? When does the press ever cover that? There's that star for the Blackhawks, fifty-goals-a-year-guy, who punches out his wife. Nobody touches that story. Nobody. Why?"

"Maybe it should be quiet?" My stomach was full of rocks. "What?"

"Hockey provides young boys with dreams—"

"And what about young girls, and the women getting hurt?"

"You got me there—"

"McClelland has an ego and a need to feed it. His radio station? CKMS 1480. The last two call letters? Those are his initials: McClelland Stuart. 1480 on your dial."

I didn't know what to say, so I looked back at the remains of a sandwich and cold egg. "Let's call the police. Call in Leeds's murder. And get a warrant and kick Bullard and

Smith's asses."

"Let's. But first—" She held a hand to her lips, my lips, and locked the door.

And we were quiet once again like we were four years ago, the first time we made love in her parents' apartment.

7

It wasn't a very good day, not for Pal Cal Bullard and Steven Smith. Not for the Toronto Maple Leafs. Not for the city. The Leafs had lost game one of the playoffs at the Forum in Montreal, 3-2. Jean Béliveau fed Bobby Rousseau a slinky pass, and the fast, shifty winger split the Leafs D before beating Bower.

The Toronto hockey club played a thug fest last night, more intent on bashing the Canadiens than working the puck. Horton, of donuts fame, took a five-minute major and the Big Z hit Terry Harper high and hard, giving the Habs rearguard a gash that required six stitches. "If you can't beat 'em on the ice, beat 'em in the back alley," the Old Man proselytized about the game back in the 1940s. I'd rather win on the ice, but, hey, that's just me.

For the city, their team's upper management was now under police suspicion and a warrant had been issued. "I'm lucky to still be standing," I said, my forehead pinching with a raised eyebrow. "I thought I was going to break an ankle over all this damn police tape."

That cracked me up and I bent over laughing at my own joke. I mean there was black and gold tape by the lobby, the main office, and Smith's office. X's were everywhere, man. My tone may have been light, but underneath the zingers gnawed a fear that time was not on our side.

Where was Cathy? I had hoped this bust would lead us directly to her or to a big enough clue to point me toward a resolution, but the longer this case went the more surprises and absurd twists confounded me.

"Smart-ass." Smith's tie and upper shirt buttons were loose, his hair dripping with alcohol sweat, his eyes unrecognizable behind flashes of light filling the lenses of his Lombardis, like sunspots.

For Pal Cal and Smith their office was full of police, reporters and photographers. Bledsoe was jotting down notes likes a jazz pianist, his fingers jittering. Stana crowded by a Laurinda Mays and a Dawn Stoukas—the human lamps from the other day.

Stana was stunning in dark slacks and a bright pink top, giving off a professional but warm appearance. She asked questions of the girls, on the side. Nick Stabulas, his eyebrows pushed together like the blade of a fat machete, was forced back by two constables, large patches of sweat under the arms of his off-white shirt and grocery store apron. The apron was soiled with food stains and splats of blood.

Chief of Police Sal Lambertino, my old pal who regularly received comp tickets from yours truly during my playing days, was conducting the investigation. He had a heavy jaw hidden behind the fence of a Hemingway fisherman's beard. His eyes were hard little stones. And when he spoke, it was his way, man, that's it, nothing else. I liked that about him. Direct.

"Yup. That's me, Smitty my boy. A regular smart-ass. And

these gentleman have, I believe, a warrant for your arrest." I introduced Sal and the five or six constables hunched around his shoulders. They all wore black hats with a thick red band. Their hats resembled a series of stop signs. The symbolism seemed appropriate.

Bullard reached into his bag for the biggest chunk of chips he could find. He looked disappointed.

"That's warrant, Smith. Not Wharram. Kenny Wharram? He plays for the Blackhawks. With Bobby Hull and Stan Mikita?" I laughed.

Sal shook his head, giving me the not-so-subtle high sign to scale things back a bit.

"We've done nothing wrong." Smith reached for a stout-shaped glass of milk with a chaser, in a smaller glass, parked inside of it. He sipped from the combination. "Nothing."

"Where's my daughter?" Nick strained, shifting his upper body away from the cops surrounding him, shouldering to get through the pack.

I was surprised that Kim wasn't here.

"Can he drink in here?" I turned to Lambertino.

He shrugged. "Sure. Let it go."

But I was enjoying it too much.

"I own the building, smart-ass," Smith said. "And you'll have a statement from my lawyer in the morning. This is all a misunderstanding—"

"What can you tell us about the Bolemac Corporation and hiding pots of money?" Stana asked, one hand on her hip, the other pointing her pencil like a thin microphone.

"I'm surprised you have the effrontery to ask me such a question, Miss."

"Well that's just me. I worry my *pretty little head* about

such matters." Stana tapped her pencil against her lips and flicked red hair behind an ear. It was a gesture she had inherited from her mom, an eerie, yet attractive echo.

"I know nothing about Bolemac—"

"Didn't they re-design this office?" I glanced around. "Put in that secret sliding door behind you and the accompanying wet bar?"

Smith sighed heavily.

The arrogance of these assholes. Like a stripper removing a long glove, Smith teasingly showed me the secret sliding door and back room the other day. Did he and Bullard not think I'd follow up on that goddamn clue?

Bullard flecked specks of salt from his fingers. "It's a construction firm. What more do you need to know?"

"It's a construction firm that you own with your friend Babe Migano," Stana corrected, her eyes narrowing, the freckles about her face much brighter than the ones dancing on her upper arms.

That got the attention of all the reporters in the room. Everyone jotted words now. Migano was a gambling kingpin in the greater Toronto area. In recent years he had shifted much of his assets into a series of five-star restaurants, including White Heat, a place on Mt. Pleasant near my old ethnic neighborhood, named rather cheekily after the Babe's favorite gangster film with Jimmy the C. *Made it ma.*

"I resent the implications. We are not in league with gangsters. The Leafs have never—"

And then Smith, sipping *colored* milk, started in with something about no comment and contacting his lawyers (who suddenly had become more than one). I couldn't *wait* to read the statement in tomorrow's editions.

Stana, pushing hair over the other shoulder, worked on getting follow-up statements from Laurinda and Dawn. They were seated in blue chairs with silver chrome. Their posture and actions were identical, like the Doublemint twins: shoulders back, left leg crossed over right.

No, they hadn't felt totally mistreated for being human lamps. Right leg over left. Yes, it was degrading, but they got paid well, and Mr. Smith and Mr. Bullard made no sexual advances. *What about touching your breasts? Like the other day? Right here?* They shrugged, together, left leg over right. "He didn't mean anything by it," one of the two said after a long awkward pause. *What about the photographs of you naked in the Gardens lobby?* I don't remember anything about that, Dawn said. Seriously. Me neither, echoed Laurinda. It was like I was there but it's hazy. *"How old were you when you were in this haze?"* Seventeen. Right leg now over left.

"Underage—" I smiled my lopsided lupine look at Smith. I had flashed that grin a lot while skating truculently to the penalty box.

I still had no idea what Smith's eyes were doing. The sunspots across his lenses resembled soft yolks wobbling inside of poached eggs.

But his voice had climbed a ladder. He was shouting, and it was breaking up like radio static. The two activities aren't related: the girls' topless photographs and the everyday business goings on of the Gardens. Apples and oranges. Yes, the pictures were taken here, but we're not responsible for the pictures. "We, the Maple Leaf organization, don't sanction those pictures." He emphasized organization in all of its syllabic glory, slowly, like a 33 1/3 LP on 16, to make his point, whatever that point was.

"Uh-huh," Bledsoe said.

"Uh-huh," I echoed. "What about Sarah Kerr, the girl that was murdered 97 days ago. Remember? The body in the suitcase?"

The room quieted, Bullard's hands quit rummaging for potato chips. Smith pushed himself upright, his lips a tense line.

"She was in one of the pictures. Topless. Fourteen years old." I pressed.

"Like I said," Smith nearly whispered. "Apples and oranges. We had nothing to do with—"

"Bullshit," Stana said.

"Answer the question," Bledsoe demanded.

"You want me to take your press pass away again, Dick?" Smith threatened. "And I can take yours away right now, Miss Younger."

"It won't be the first time," she said, winking at Bledsoe.

"I can get you a bail bondsman, Smitty," Dick quipped back. "Or a tailor who specializes in Brooks Brothers prison wear." Bledsoe's hat was nudged rakishly to the side and resembled a cap worn by a jester, cavorting about a stage, ridiculing Lear for his blind admiration for the fawning Goneril and Regan. Bledsoe's hair, streaks of which curled up and over the hat's felt brim, was gray, his green eyes mischief-riddled. But his eyebrows were the real gas. They wanted to do things on their own, like applaud over his wicked witticisms. "This is the hell of circus show. All you need is an organ grinder and a monkey on your shoulder, Steve."

That cracked everybody up.

Lambertino smiled at me. I guess he liked Bledsoe's column too.

"This is a campaign of slander and misrepresentation," Smith intoned, his voice dropping back to its more regular rhythms, his knifing hands blurs of phosphorous. "I don't acknowledge this witch hunt. We've done nothing wrong and I don't understand why we're being arrested on such flimsy evidence."

"Let's just say, it's unlucky for you that the judge who signed off on this is a Habs fan." Now Lambertino was cracking wise. It was good to see.

I turned to the girls as Smith continued a litany of double-speak and denial. Apples and Oranges. Oranges and apples. Lions and tigers and bears, oh my.

Dawn's and Laurinda's legs were still crossed, and hands poised like tiny shelves propping up each chin. "Mister Smith might have a point," Laurinda said while Dawn nodded. "He was never present when the photos were taken—at least I don't remember him being there—do you?"

"No," Dawn echoed.

"He's 'Mister' now? You don't remember anything about the shoots?" I said.

"I remember Landover, I think—" Laurinda said.

"Was he wearing a turban? Was he made-up to look like his alter-ego, Lanzo the Great?"

"Lanzo the What?"

"Smith wasn't there, ever? Really?"

She looked away.

"Who *was* there?" Stana's face tightened, her freckled eyes flashing.

"Like I said, Landover Leeds, the guy in today's newspaper who was found dead on Front Street. He was the photographer."

"Why would you ever agree to this? To appear topless, to—"

"I didn't agree to it—it just happened—I don't even—" Dawn said.

"It's like you were hypnotized."

The Tangerine Room wasn't just for relaxation but mind control too. So was the second "room" in his office. In the 1940s, doctors used a little something labeled narcosynthesis, a kind of hypnosis as a curative power, releasing the deepest traumas of combat-fatigued veterans, helping them on the road to healing. But what if doctors used those curative powers to manipulate and abuse impressionable and traumatized young women? What if the Tangerine Room with its levers and headphones and Leeds talking to the girls ever so quietly, discreetly, were but a ruse to drip venom in their ears, a regular Claudius poisoning Hamlet's father, subliminal poison underneath the whale cries and breaking waves?

"Yeah, like I was hypnotized." Laurinda nodded. So did Dawn.

"Where's my daughter," Nick interjected, shoving closer to Smith. "Let's stop all the goddamn talk and boiler-plated bullshit and find her, you understand—" His face had reddened and for the first time I noticed his nose wasn't straight—it looked like it had been busted in a fist fight and it didn't quite mesh with all the square lines to his face.

"We have people looking right now," Sal informed him. "Settle down." There was a police posse searching the entire Gardens for the girl. All levels. Sal's voice was firm. Nick had better settle down or else he was going to get slapped with some cuffs.

Nick chewed his upper lip and the determined line of

his eyebrows became an even heavier machete. The image fit him: everything he said hacked and chopped and lacked subtlety or nuance.

Dawn said that they never agreed to the photographs. They were taking group therapy to liberate themselves from their low self-images, but this was never part of the package plan.

So Cathy wound up hypnotized too to appear nude. What about Sarah, *the girl I found in a suitcase?*

According to Dawn, Sarah always wanted to belong to their group. She was just a middle-schooler back then, always studying at the high school's library (because it had a better collection of resources), getting top grades, winning essay contests, and planning to become a doctor, but there was this side to her that wanted to be free of her mother's pressure. Kind of wild, you know? Like, there are stage moms, Dawn said, who force their kids into showbiz and then there are school moms who always want their kids to get A's and excel at learning. Sarah's mom was one of those. A crazy, demanding school mom. "We even suspected she helped write some of Sarah's award-winning essays. Like for Kiwanis Club and stuff? Anyway, Sarah was pushing back. Against all of it, you know—teachers, preachers, mama? She wanted to be sixteen, when she was twelve. You follow me? With the boys?"

I nodded. "Did she do drugs?"

"No, nothing like that," Laurinda said. "Just boys. A lot of boys."

And what about Cathy's lower dresser drawer and the leather mouth strap with a ball?

"I don't know. I don't remember Cathy at all," the two girls uttered in overlapping dialogue. Was she even at the Gardens? They remembered her from Leeds's therapy class. She was the eccentric chick, a little weird, always reading her own poetry about staring into the abyss of Lake Ontario. "All of her poems ended with her at a lake."

"I want my daughter back." Nick and his words slithered down a dark hole. To tell you the truth, I kind of wished he'd stay in those sunken ruins and leave the stage—his act was wearing thin. There was something totally phony about the whole bit, the overheated father, the rush of angst to bring matters to justice. It was no Academy Award competitor. It was low-fi, acting at its worst.

Smith took another drink of doctored milk and wiped the back of his mouth.

Dawn held out her hands as way of apology. The girls in Leeds's therapy sessions were all suffering from some kind of body self-consciousness. "I always thought my hands were too big. Anyway—"

"What was Sarah's hang-up?" I asked.

"She thought she was too skinny," Dawn said.

"Yeah. She hated being willowy. That's the word she always used to describe herself, willowy," Laurinda said.

"Willowy, huh?" But they couldn't remember anything else or how they all wound up posing nude. Collective amnesia. *Narcosynthesis. Lanzo the Not So Great.*

"Were drugs involved, any drugs?" Stana tapped her chin.

"Bennies maybe," Dawn said with an absent shrug. "I don't remember much in the way of drugs—" It wasn't prevalent, apparently.

What was prevalent was Leeds and his reassuring "relaxation." He may have convinced them that they were all beautiful and pointed a way for them to conquer their fears by becoming less inhibited, less clothed. And what did he get out of the pictures—kickbacks on kiddie porn, sales to minors, middle-aged men, and members of Parliament?

"That may be true," Dawn said. "But I never saw the photos before. You'd think I'd have seen them at school or something. If Landover was selling the work, it must've been a pretty discreet clientele."

"Coughlins Club discreet? What did your fellow classmates know about that outfit? Not much," Stana said.

Dawn nodded. "Landover wanted us to free ourselves from judgment, but I don't remember any suggestions to free myself of my clothes—" They both laughed, left leg over right.

Like I said, subliminal messages, that's how. Given commands that you follow without even knowing you're following them. Think of it as a form of exploitation, mind control, chipping away your free will.

One of the girls laughed, "Mind control?" The other said, "Say what?"

He had some kind of diploma from some kind of institute in New Mexico, I said.

"Flagstaff, Arizona," Stana corrected, pushing pensive fingers and shrugging into a half-smile. "Come on, girls. Think. Think hard."

There was another guy, Dawn vaguely recalled. Burly, but she couldn't recollect his face. He sounded kind of English, but a phony kind of English. Too much "luv" and "mate" tossed about like tips at a diner's club.

Smith spewed more gobbledygook, a combination of legalese and self-entitled posturing. Bledsoe quit writing. "Are the Leafs going to win tomorrow night with all these distractions?"

"Damn right we're going to win. The boys owe it to this city—"

Right. Owe it to the city. More like the boys owe it to me to get my sorry face off the front page of three dailies.

"A burly fella, huh?"

"Yeah, he was big," Dawn said. "And he smelled of coffee, cigarettes, and licorice." But that was all she could remember.

"Where's my daughter—" Nick broke free of the two constables and jumped the desk, side-rolling across it, seizing Smith by the lapels and throttle swinging, one hand on Smith's turkey neck, the other slapping free the glasses.

Bullard, chips falling on the floor like bits of broken stone, cleared out of the way.

Nick's second punch landed on Smith's mouth, bloodying it.

"Why you big hypocritical phony," Smith shot back, shoving and kneeing Nick in the groin, bending him, and then kneeing him again on the chin, sending him sprawling against the desk, knocking about a chair. Constables pulled the two apart, catching errant fingers and separated fists about their faces.

"Goddamn it," Lambertino shouted. "Arrest that man." He pointed at Nick who was immediately cuffed.

"If she's dead, I'll kill you, you understand," Nick promised Smith, his voice traced with hard frost.

"Get him out of here."

Two constables escorted Nick from the office and down the stairs. He was speaking loudly in Macedonian.

I don't think he was reminding them of his in-store special: buy three get one can of peas free.

Stana tapped her foot, twitched her nose, and her eyes

creased with mild amusement. She thought there was something phony about the whole scene too.

I shrugged. "The guy's no Marlon Brando."

"He's not even Shemp Howard."

That cracked me up. Shemp was my favorite Stooge.

Smith readjusted his tie and wiped blood from his mouth
with the tight triangle corner of a hanky. His eyes were red-
rimmed from fighting and all the hard drinking he had been
doing. He checked his glasses. The frames weren't bent and
he put them back on, masking the raw exhaustion of his eyes.

"Okay, now for the cup duh grassy," I smiled in Bullard's
direction. "There's a button on this desk. Voila." I pressed it
and the bookcase behind Smith slid open.

We crossed the threshold. Blue corrugated curtains
gleamed even in the dim light. I turned to Bullard and
tweaked his nose. "Doesn't the light in here have three settings?" I tweaked his schnozzle twice more. Dawn laughed.
"Oh, there we go."

Lambertino had turned on the actual lights. "Settle down,
cowboy," he whisper-mumbled.

I turned to Bullard. "Where are your goons, Fortunado
and Leighton? I was looking forward to some verbal sparring—or at least discussing the Dow Jones—"

"They'll meet up with you again," he vowed. "Maybe soon-
er than you think—"

"Great. I'll make sure to wear my interview tie."

The constables searched the room. Half-empty liquor
glasses cluttered the wet bar and newspapers and magazines
were fanned about, but it was fairly clean. A copy of Steinbeck's *Of Mice and Men* was on one of the coffee tables.

"Where did you get this?"

"I read," Smith said.

"Yeah. You read. Tell me about this book—" Cathy read Steinbeck, a lot of Steinbeck. *East of Eden* twice, according to her sister.

"A classic." And then Smith recounted the plot. I wondered if he had gotten a full report on the slender novel from Cathy. His summation showed no savvy for the beauty of Steinbeck's prose and craft. It was all this happened and then that happened and then, teacher, this happened.

"Uh-huh." I pointed to where the wheel was usually set up for roulette.

Bledsoe nodded. "I figured Bullard for craps myself." That got a few twitters from his fellow reporters.

"Gentlemen, ladies. Let's conduct ourselves with decorum." Sal held up a hand. "We are talking about an institution here. I don't like these guys either, but this is the Toronto Maple Leafs."

He had us there. The room quieted. I took off my porkpie and dropped my head, in observation of a moment of silence.

"Fuck you, Hayden," Smith said. "We don't gamble here. This isn't a common gaming house," he assured us. "I have friends over. We play some small ante poker. That's all. Some like to spin the wheel. Small stakes. Some of you, I'm sure, get together with friends for a friendly game."

"And drinking—" Sal removed his hat and clutched his sandy hair. "With underage girls?" He pushed the cap back in place and threw his hands on his hips. "I don't think many of us get together and do that." He rubbed at tired eyes. "We have it all on film."

"It's just a party, an after hours party." Smith raised a phosphorous hand. "Very exclusive. The guests arrive in stretch limos. But there's no hanky-panky."

"Naked girls? A woman in black dancing on the decedent's lap? That's not hanky-panky?" Sal was now giving Smith the stink eye. It was a good bit. I could see it on Wayne and Shuster. I bet he also did an awesome double take and a wicked slow burn.

"It gets a little wild, but I assure you the women are all of age—"

"Not the women in those photographs—" I said.

"As you undoubtedly have already heard. Landover took those photographs. I had nothing to do with that. Apples and oranges. Unfortunately, it happened here at the Gardens. I will have my people look into that. I promise."

"Apples and oranges," Bullard echoed. "Apples and oranges."

Just how was Landover not affiliated with the club? He was part of the Old Man's militia, 1940-45. Trained with McClelland Stuart and Syl Apps and all those boys.

"I know nothing of that," Bullard said.

"How did he get access to the Gardens?" Stana asked. "After-hours access?"

"Ask McClelland if they were such grand pals." Smith held up his chin. It was a real regal pose, a striking look that ought to be on a damn postage stamp or something. "God, that guy McClelland thinks he runs the Gardens. Saying how high the gondola should be off the ice. Inviting friends in. He's just a broadcaster—'he shoots, he scores.' Come up with some new catch-phrases for crissakes."

"Is McClelland involved?" Bledsoe asked.

"I'll let you draw your own inferences."

Talk about passing the buck. "This is a side issue," I said.

"Talk to McClelland," Smith reiterated, for all the reporters to hear. They were frenetically jotting it all down, heads tilted with feverish intensity.

"That spot right there, by the wet bar, Sal, that's where all the images were taken on the 8mm film." I glanced over my shoulder and snapped my fingers. "Which means the camera has to have been set up over here." The wall behind me was uncluttered: a couple of paintings and a gilt-edged wall mirror. I checked along the edgings and found another switch. I pressed it and the mirror's glass slid down, revealing a Bell and Howell camera.

"Two-way glass." Sal studied the camera. The casings on the front were smudged with a host of fingerprints that shined like melted caramel. "Get this dusted. Now we've got photographs of naked girls taken in the lobby of the Gardens and secret 8mm film shot in the very office of the president and his second in command." He pushed back his cap and rubbed his forehead again. "Game, set, match, Mr. Smith."

"They're not related. Apples and oranges," Bullard said.

"Oh, will you shut the fuck up," Smith said.

Bullard reached for another chunk of chips.

"GET IN THE CAR." The voice was dark gravel. Fortunado had a hand in the pocket of his tan overcoat. "The boss wants to see you." His lean eyes were the color of crisp bacon.

"The boss? He went thataway. Hi ho, Silver." I pointed at the contrail of police cars that had just left the Gardens. Smith, Bullard, Lambertino, a bevy of photographers, reporters and various hangers-on were tooling to the cop shop, just a few stops west at College and Bay. "Away!"

"We're free agents. It's a different boss, Crumpled Suit."

"Uh-huh."

Lou-doo's face was patchy shadows. The sky was the blue of faded jeans, but Fortunado would forever exist in shadows. Even his voice sounded like a dark, demimonde whisper.

Next to him, brightly gleaming in a camel-haired coat and tight Oliver Hardy bowler was Athol Leighton, chin tucked in, readying to take a punch and kick back twice as hard. The skin on his face was stretched Saran Wrap. His lips were pressed as if he were fighting indigestion. "You heard him. Get."

"Hey—" Stana, thinking quickly, created a diversion, bumping Fortunado. Lou-doo shoved back, straight-arming her like an open-field running back, and then I shouldered him, jumping in tight, tying up his arms, and chopping down on the gun hidden in the hand in his pocket. Lou-doo screamed and slipped, stumbled, and stomped my toes—his feet were huge. The cat could float across Lake Ontario on those HMS's.

As Stana staggered behind me and righted herself, I head-butted Lou to the ground. He landed on his elbows and bounced a little. My gun was now un-holstered and in my hand.

"With your history of concussions, I don't think that head-butt was such a shit-hot idea," Stana said.

"Will you relax?"

I wondered what Dr. Abramowitz would say. *Slow down, kid.*

"Well, let's go to this powwow. I assume it was to be a friendly conversation?"

Cool Athol nodded and wiped back a belch. "Jesus Christ, Lou. I can't take you anywhere."

I asked for Lou's gun. He reached in and pointed the checkered grip toward me. I handed the .45 and my snub-nosed .38 to Stana. "Go to the paper. Type up your story." I motioned Stana away. The evening editions would hit the streets in a few hours. And what a story: Bullard and Smith arrested. The Gardens affiliated with underage drinking, gambling, and a high-end escort service. What did all of this have to do with the missing Cathy Stabulas and the murder of Sarah Kerr? The headlines would be screaming to know, tonight, in their 26-point font.

And maybe I would finally get some damn answers.

"We don't want the girl, right?" Lou-doo dusted off his elbows.

"You're not in a position to ask, pal," I said. "Get going, Stana. I'll be all right. I'll call."

"Boss just said Fuller. The girl can go." Leighton tipped his hat, acting as if they were still the ones in charge and were doing us a favor. He pushed back his dandy of a bowler.

"You'll be okay?" Stana's eyes were wet.

"I'll be okay. I'll call when I'm done talking to Mister Big." I placed exaggerated air quotes around the name.

"You two can arrange your social calendar later." Fortunado shoved me toward a large yellow Buick. The glare hurt my eyes. Hell, it looked like it jumped off the pages of the Dick Tracy color comics.

My head was thudding, dark clouds forming behind my eyes. Stana was right about the head-butt. Stupid move, Hayden Ira Fuller.

The heavies, as they deposited me in the back seat, were surprisingly gentle, removing my porkpie and ducking my head so I wouldn't catch it on the car's metal frame. Lou got behind the wheel. Cool Athol sat by my shoulder. He popped a Tums and then another.

Cool Athol wasn't looking too cool right about now. "Bad clams?"

"Shut up."

"Well, don't tell me where I'm going, fellas. Surprise me."

They both shook their heads. Lou threw the big car in gear and gently nudged away from the curb. "You know, you're not nearly as funny as you think you are, pally," he said over his shoulder.

I never said I was Lenny Bruce but hey, bubeleh, I get by.

BABE MIGANO'S stone home in Etobicoke was huge, spacious, with a slow-pitched slanted ceiling, and dark cedar wood trim. A fireplace smoldered and I wondered where to leave my poles and ski boots.

"Funny," Lou mumbled.

A swank cedar door, larger than usual, opened. Migano sauntered toward me. He was a big man, 240, 250, and moved like an upright cheetah, padding softly with clear, calculated steps. Light glinted off his shoulders as if he were a backlit movie star. "My study." He gestured behind him.

Babe's teeth were straight and even, and there wasn't a mark on his face. He was no Al Capone.

He smoked from a holder. On the lapel of his bathrobe was a pink rose. His face was more Irish puck than Italian, like Jackie Gleason if the Great One were like sixty pounds lighter. His hair was sleeked back and his skin had that raw glare of a close shave with a hard razor. Nobody's face looked like that nowadays. He *did* belong in a movie: *On the Waterfront* or *The Hustler*.

"I hope my boys weren't rough on you?" He smiled and straightened his cuffs.

"Oh, no. We went over what tie I should wear for the interview, skinny or regular-sized. Skinny seemed a more natural choice." I flipped the tie's triangular corner up and then back down.

"You got balls—"

"Thanks. I joke, but I'm really worried about Cathy Stabulas—Is she even still alive?" I shrugged and looked at my tie. Had all my work been for nothing? Sometimes I felt clouded by defeat, that I wasn't any closer to finding her today than I was when I started.

"How would I know?"

"You hear things."

"I didn't hear she was dead."

I nodded. "Fair enough." I smiled awkwardly. "Landover Leeds?"

"He got what he had coming. Exploiting young women—"

"Yeah, and a bunch of hypnosis right out of *Flash Gordon*. Any ideas who greased him?"

Migano shrugged. "Small change—I don't bother myself with small change—"

"What about Sarah Kerr?" I felt my face tightening. "She's not small change."

"The girl in the suitcase?"

"Yeah. Ninety-seven days ago she was murdered." I shrugged. "Found some nudies of her done at the Gardens. Seems to be a tie-in with Smith, Bullard, Landover and Cathy. I'm not sure how, but—"

"This is a business visit, Mr. Fuller. Nothing else. I assure you." He glanced at the far corner before dropping his eyes back on me. "I want to hire you."

He pointed me to a leather chair. On the desk between us was a drink, two fingers of scotch. My drink was tonic water with a small plate of rugelach.

Migano had done his homework. "Most people don't know I'm Jewish."

"I respect Jews. They had to fight for their piece of the pie. Like us wops. The cake eaters aren't going to give it to us. And when we first came to this country we had to climb the crooked rungs on the ladder to success."

It was the *only* way to get ahead for many from the Old Country. I sipped tonic water.

"My dad was in construction and had ties to the mob." He sighed and gestured with his hand, making a lazy figure eight. "Ran some liquor back in the day."

"Cake eaters? That's what my dad called the Anglos because they didn't put olive oil on anything."

"Right." He paused, taking a slow sip of scotch. "Didn't want it dripping off their chins. Wanted everything dry. Pizza practically with no sauce." He shook his head and the figure eights were now much wider, like the turn and banking of a Boeing 707. "Leafs got a chance against Montreal?"

"We got money players, but I don't know. The run might be done—"

"What about this Davis fuck?"

"What about him? He can score goals but he doesn't back check."

"I think he stole my money."

"$568,000?"

Migano was impressed with how I knew the exact amount missing. The money was kept in a safe at the Gardens. It was

Migano's take from the Bolemac Corporation's handling of various accounts such as Coughlins (the hidden room behind the bookshelf).

Someone stole the money out of a Gardens safe before the funds were transferred to him.

"They always keep that amount on hand at the Gardens safe? That's a lot of chump change."

"Yeah. There was always some excuse to not get the money to me." He gestured away an imaginary fly. "And then the money, it got got. I think it was Davis." He took another puff off his cigarette. "I got it on good authority that he was in league with Lisa Steinmetz and Spinner Terrien."

I nodded. "How good of authority?"

"Real good. This person's on the inside. In my pocket. Aces."

On the wall behind him were black-framed photographs of Coney Island. I recognized some of the iconic images: people crowded around the human roulette wheel as it spun and twisted you off its perch, crashing into walls below. Next to the wheel was another image from the '40s, men and women stumbling through the turning walls of the Barrel of Fun. A plump girl, face and body pressing the floor, had a guy straddling her, trying to help her up, or possibly thinking of joining her in her fall from dignity.

"Coney Island? I'm sorry I was distracted—"

"No, no. I loved Coney Island." Before arriving in Montreal his parents raised Babe in the mean streets of New York, Lower East Side, naming him after the Yankees all-star right fielder, the Sultan of Swat, and Migano and his family visited Coney every summer. "Cheap amusements. That's what us immigrants called it. Cheap amusements. Didn't cost much.

Nickels, dimes, but it gave us hope."

"Cheap amusements," I mumbled to myself. That's what this case is, a series of false starts and turns, lies and double-crosses, and somebody was behind the curtain like the goddamn Wizard of Oz laughing over this shit, amused at my folly.

It wasn't the beach and the sun that made Coney such an attraction, Babe said. It was all about the rides. Some of them were kind of sexy, like the Barrel of Fun, where a guy could fall all over his girl, touching her ever so discreetly as they righted themselves and tried to stand. "I performed that maneuver. Even at nine."

"I bet it worked for you—"

"Oh, yeah." He shrugged proudly. "One of my best."

I never had fun at amusement parks. Everybody seems to be trying too hard to have a good time. There was a mass-produced plastic feeling to the way people played and laughed. "Cheap amusements? Not for me really." I glanced at my fingers. "But I played hockey. That's an amusement for millions in Canada. Maybe it's cheap too. I don't know."

"It's a way of life in Canada, pal. Nothing cheap about hockey. It's an honest game."

"Yeah." I smiled. "Thanks."

"So, you really don't like amusement parks?"

"They're not for me, no—"

He pondered that as if my opinion were worth considering. "Too old-fashioned?"

"No. Just too busy. I like things quiet now and then."

He shook his head. "Rollercoasters, on the other hand, that was all action, man, taking you somewhere."

He pointed at a much larger image over his right shoulder.

"The Cyclone. It had an 85-foot drop at a 60-degree angle. My stomach would be in my throat." He laughed. "I guess we all long for some return to our youth and Coney's mine." Both of his parents had died recently: one from cancer, the other from an embolism following back surgery. "My best times with them were at Coney."

"I hear you. My dad never did much with me, flew kites now and then, and listened to hockey on the radio, McClelland Stuart. Pop took me to my first game when I was four. I've been in love with it ever since—"

"I'd whack Davis. It would make it all easier." He shrugged. "But I want to wait until the playoffs are over." He laughed. "I'm kidding. Well, kind of kidding—" He laughed again.

I liked him. He was honest. "So you want me to find the money?"

"Yes, I want you to track Davis. That's all. I want *my money*. I need it. Davis had accrued quite a few gambling debts at Coughlins and at other, how shall I put it, Mr. Fuller, *underground* casinos. That's his motivation. I want my money, *all of my money*."

I could work his case in. "I have to find the Stabulas girl but this relates."

Just to my left the bright neon splash of the Wonder Wheel grabbed me, forcing me to look upon it. It was a yellow or gold Ferris wheel with rocking cars that nudged upright, touching the sky.

"I didn't take that girl. I know of your case and I know what you're trying to do. For your sake I hope you find her. I assure you, I had nothing to do with her going missing."

I believed him.

"And I didn't kill the other one."

"No, I didn't figure that for your style. It was too flashy, loud. An AK-47 and gunfire in the middle of a field lit up by search lights?"

He held up a hand, closed his eyes as if praying, and leaned back and said he didn't mess with women, ever. And he certainly would never fold one up in a suitcase. "That's just—wrong. Look at my business—" Construction, restaurants, gambling. "Sure I peddle H, but I have never touched prostitution. I got too much respect for women."

He leaned forward and spoke eloquently to the issue of how women were of a higher spiritual form. "Us guys will fuck anything. Women—they're nobler. Adam and Eve is such bullshit. Eve never reached for the apple. The guy did and then blamed her. Like I said, guys will do anything. Eve's the good one. And anyone who hits a woman is dead." He snapped his fingers twice, as if double-tapping a wife-beater behind the left ear. "Dead. That's my promise." He pointed with his cigarette holder.

If he respected women so much why did he have Cool Athol as one of his security detail, that creep punched the lights out on a Chicago prostitute, redesigning her face.

"He's married to one of my nieces."

I nodded, unaware that my previous comment had been spoken aloud. I guess my headache was getting pretty fucking bad. "So, Coughlins. That's not your outfit?"

"I get kickbacks for it. I put up the initial investment, but I don't party with them. That's Sicko Smith and Pal Cal's idea of a good time."

But I'd seen him on the 8mm film—him and Kim.

"The human lamps—you seen that bit?"

"Oh, yeah. Please. Infantile. They're a couple of arrested

adolescents who never grew up." He smiled. "Spoiled rich boys, yacht-club set. They play tennis, for chrissakes. I mean what does a business man like me really want?"

You mean a gangster. "More?"

"Well, yeah. But we want respect and acceptance." He poured himself another finger of scotch. "We want to be *legitimate*. I remember the signs. So do you. No dogs or—"

"Jews allowed. Yeah. I saw those goddamn signs." As a skinny kid in the early 1940s, joining my father for outings along Balmy Beach, and parts of Toronto East and the lakeshore, I saw them, boy did I see them. "No Jews allowed." We went to the beach anyway. My father would fight them if they tried to remove us.

"I want to shake things up, baby. Eventually, I'm going to leave that entire drug shit behind and make my money in more of the real chips, legit ventures. Like the restaurants and nightclubs—" He pinched his lips together. "You know what Wop means? Without papers. Well, I'm a Canadian citizen. I got my papers. I want in on the club, the action, the legitimate action."

Amen, I wanted to say, amen to that, as the immigrants on Coney's Parachute Jump fell through the sky, buffeted up by lean wires and promises of a better life.

8

First there was a question about academics, and then the photographs.

I hated asking, but I had to.

I had been listening to jazz, waiting on a phone call from Stana to touch base on her findings, when Mrs. Kerr arrived, sat across from me, her eyes slowly darkening as I told her my recent findings, all about Coughlins, the Gardens, Landover Leeds's murder and the topless photograph of her daughter. She said she didn't believe any of it, of course, not a word, but I didn't believe her—not the way her hands were about to snap the brass clasp off her purse.

When I first took the case I had been led to believe that Sarah was just a studious gal who stayed home nights, applying herself, expanding her intellect, learning Latin outside of school via a correspondence course just for kicks, adding one more language to her mastery of French and Spanish. She was about to be the recipient of an Ontario Scholarship. Now, 98 days since her murder, a different Sarah was emerging. One who was boy crazy at twelve.

"Did she not like herself much?" I told her what Dawn said. Willowy.

"No." Her mother looked away. "She wasn't interested in boys."

"That's not answering my question. Did she not like her looks?"

"Most girls struggle with their looks."

"Did she go out nights?"

"No."

"Could she have gone out without you knowing it?" Because I know she went *out* nights. They had lived on the ground floor of an apartment complex. Sarah's bedroom was also her study. "How do you account for the photograph? I'm not trying to hurt you. I want to avenge her murder."

Surely a "school mother," as Dawn put it, a woman who cared about her daughter excelling at academics, would have checked up on her late at night and peered into her bedroom, making sure she was sleeping. It only made sense. Mrs. Kerr had a hovering personality and would have known if Sarah went sometimes AWOL. "Come on, Mrs. Kerr. Level with me."

"I trusted my daughter."

"I know you loved her, but did you trust her? I mean *really* trust her."

The grip tightened. Yes, Mrs. Kerr had noticed that Sarah was missing some nights. They even talked about it, had a terrific row or two, and yet Sarah, to prove her loyalty to her mother, worked harder, got better grades, won more contests.

"Any boyfriends you know of?"

She shook her head.

"An adult boyfriend? *Think*. I think she knew her killer. I think the story she gave about meeting her counselor to discuss her thesis was a lie to cover herself. She went to a rendezvous point with a man she knew. To have sex. He killed her."

Her eyes watered and I handed her a Kleenex and then the whole box. She was so upset that she was choking as she spoke. Sarah *was* sexually active. Mrs. Kerr nodded, the squeezed handbag now resembling a collapsed lung. Their family doctor had told Mrs. Kerr that her daughter was no longer a virgin. "But I know nothing of any specific man or Coughlins."

"Did you trust Landover Leeds with your daughter?"

"Yes. At the time." Sarah wasn't doing any of the therapy sessions that Mrs. Kerr knew of, and Mr. Leeds was always directing Sarah to new contests to apply to and encouraging her to become a medical doctor. "He believed in her. Or so he said."

"Uh-huh. What about Dawn Stoukas, Laurinda Mays, or Cathy Stabulas? What can you tell me about her relationships with them?"

Dawn was the heavyset gal always trying to get Sarah to wear lipstick and eye shadow. She didn't know Laurinda, but Cathy came by the house now and then. When Sarah was younger, Cathy "babysat for me. Especially the nights I went curling. I also shopped at her father's store."

"You knew Cathy—"

"I never liked her father. He was a little too pushy, micro-managing Cathy all the time."

I smiled my lopsided grin. "How often did Cathy see Sarah?"

"Once, twice a week. She was really encouraging her to go to U of T."

They knew each other. Could Cathy have introduced Sarah

to Coughlins?

"I told you I know nothing about Coughlins." She dabbed at her eyes with a Kleenex. "And Cathy wasn't that kind of girl. She was a sweetheart to Sarah. Caring. A role model. A real sweetheart."

I wondered if there was anything else she could think of or had in her possession that might help me with this case. She pondered and said no, everything had been turned over to the police. There were no diaries. Nothing.

"The police have everything?"

"More or less." She crumpled up the Kleenex and dropped it on the blotter. Oh, she said, after the police confiscated Sarah's things, Cathy visited one more time and left with a bundle of additional stuff.

"What kind of stuff?"

"Clothes, photos, knick-knacks—I don't know. Stuff the police didn't take."

"Stuff that they missed or didn't take?"

"I never thought of that distinction—"

"Stuff that was hidden?"

"Maybe. I really didn't check. It could have been anything. I just told Cathy to take whatever."

Take whatever. A leather strap or a ball to place in your mouth?

AFTERWARD, I dialed Stana at the *Toronto Telegram*.

"You were supposed to call me yesterday." Her voice wasn't quite as annoyed as she put on.

"I did. I called."

But it was so short, the conversation. I was supposed to call later, to talk longer.

My head ached with the punctuated stringy pops of Black Cat firecrackers. Goddamn Leighton with his clumsy gun-toting sidekick Fortunado. This morning, as I laced up my hard-soled shoes, I lost my balance. The glare of the sun nettled my eyes. Office lights were off, blinds drawn. I was a regular vampire.

"Well, that's a switch. The guy complaining of a headache."

"Yeah. It was pretty good last time," I said. "Not the headache, I mean the—Right?"

"It was sweet."

Sweet? "Yeah."

"You *do* sound *groggy*. What did I tell you about that damn head-butt?"

"I know, I know. I should wear a helmet the next time I get in a street fight—"

That made her laugh and I imagined her shaking her head at what she called "my insouciance." Like I said, I hated playing *Scrabble* with her. "Anything new on the Cathy front?"

"Yes. Landover and Da Silva Mind Control? The Flagstaff group?"

"Yes?"

"It's an Esalen-type outfit," she said, specializing in helping people find ways to be more present in life. Through relaxation techniques, clients learn how to stay in the moment and discover the deeper truths hidden inside all of us—

"Far out," I said.

"No, really. It's a legitimate outfit. Nothing to do with hypnosis."

"Uh-huh. But you could use it as a cocktail mixer. Throw in some subliminal suggestions, and suddenly women are taking off their clothes—"

"Apparently so," she agreed, "but Da Silva's all right."

"Did you enroll?"

"Shut up."

"What else you got?"

Stana rattled off a short list of highly credible suspects: Leeds, the counselor; Lisa Steinmetz, the friend; Nick Stabulas, the father; Kim Stabulas, the sister.

"Her sister?"

"Why not? She was on that 8mm film. Coughlins. She lied to us. Big time."

I let out a hard whistle. "Yeah—"

"Her dad's still in jail by the way."

"Really?" That was interesting. Smith and Bullard were released on their own recognizance, but nobody posted Stabulas's bail. His friends or associates were letting him cool off. Or, maybe they were afraid of being seen springing him by the Fourth Estate and subsequently getting their photos splashed in the dailies. Maybe they were just vindictive assholes. How high was bail set?

She gave me the figure. It was pretty high for a working man.

"Hmm." I rubbed my tired eyes.

"By the way, Lisa has cleared out."

"I sort of figured on that."

Stana, under the guise of a public health official, had broken into Lisa's flat in the Kensington Market. Everything from the pad was gone, except twelve empty bottles of vodka on a small, stained table. The trim on the table's edges was peeled away and pock-mocked cigarette burns cratered the tabletop.

"Why all these details? Just tell me the story. Get to the

point."

"There *is* a point. She was living in a dive, that's *the point.*" Fingerprint stains were on the wood trim and smudging up the wall's switch plates. Thin sheets covered bedroom windows. "I don't think she had a lot of money. She was desperate for a better life, a life $568,000 could get her."

Lisa had also been a no-show at the El Mocambo. She was scheduled to work yesterday. No sign of Spinner either.

"They better be careful. Migano doesn't fuck around. Not with his money."

"Yeah." She paused. "And I'm not done. I got one more little bit of info." She had done some other checking on Leeds: the car crash that killed the nine-year-old girl back in 1942, the crash in which Leeds was driving and McClelland Stuart was a passenger? There was something off about the whole damn thing. She had been going over the original police report and the two follow-up newspaper articles. Things didn't jibe. Leeds's statements weren't consistent and some aspects were *too* consistent. On the report and in the articles, several details about the victim were too precise: the hat she wore was black with two red stripes; snow tented on both of her shoulders; and the cars she stepped between were big and bulky. But the detail that really mattered: how long was the interval between the girl's emergence from between the cars and her getting hit, that was sketchy, listed on the police report as a jagged flash of lightning to an interval of two or three seconds in the newspaper reports.

"Mac and Leeds where at a scene of an accident together, Hayden." Think about it, did this connect in any way with the topless girls appearing before a Speed Graphic camera?

Shit, Smith implicated McClelland in his closing rant at

the Gardens earlier yesterday. It was clear that the brain trust didn't like the man who had been broadcasting hockey since 1924, but who had what over whom?

"I think we better talk to McClelland Stuart," I said and dry swallowed a painkiller.

"I think we better," Stana said. "I already got us an appointment."

I TWISTED THE LAMP on the restaurant table away from me. It was a small lamp but the arc's glow cut like a Coast Guard searchlight. I blinked my eyes. The lids and lashes were sticky, bitten by specks of soggy cereal. I better see Dr. A soon.

McClelland Stuart, his apple cheeks puffy, his eyes sore with strain, smiled awkwardly while wiping gravy from the cramped corners of his mouth. He was eating a hot open-face sandwich and was in a hurry. The team and its support staff were readying to board the 11:30 P.M. train to Montreal. It departed in forty-seven minutes.

"I'm glad you took the time to see us," Stana said. "We appreciate it."

"I didn't have much of a choice, did I?" He shrugged, and then whispered in a low adenoidal whine, "It was my own fault." He nodded his head stiffly, the whites of his eyes pronounced like those on a jaunty dog, straining at a leash. His homburg sat next to him. He always removed his hat in the presence of a woman. I, on the other hand, not so chivalrous, I guess.

"So you know about the car?" McClelland answered our questions, nodding, looking as if he were about to be attacked by a pack of bigger dogs.

Stana adjusted the tablemat across from her, sipped her Coke, eyes dancing like diamond-backed snakes. "Yes. *You* didn't have much choice, did you?"

Her voice was new to me, jagged, broken. I'm not sure I liked it.

She reached into a purse that had rings for its handles. She slid Photostats from two 1942 newspaper articles toward McClelland. "The stories don't match, Leeds's details are off, out of sync with yours." She shrugged with her eyes. Important details, like how the girl was hit, inconsequential details like the make and design of the two cars she emerged from were too precise. "But as I told you on the phone, nothing has to come of this. Nothing."

"Right." He looked away, at the lamp, my tired face, back to the lamp. I think it hurt his eyes too.

Stana curved in with her shoulders. She wore a black blouse and dark slacks and an orange and black cardigan. It was the closest ensemble she had to 1940s Joan Crawford. She looked tough but still feminine. "It wasn't Leeds driving the car. It was you—"

He wiped the cramped edges of his mouth and his whole being appeared to be leaving the room, like air withering from a crumpling balloon. "How did you find out?"

"I have my sources."

This was the first I had heard of this. Her damn sources were Miss Instinct and Miss Educated Guesses. She was right about Lisa's lies and maybe Nick and Kim's, and now the Voice of Canada's.

"Let us reset the scene. You were at Old Man Smith's militia with Leeds. It had been a hard session. You had to clean your Enfield or—"

"Climb the rope. I hated climbing the rope."

"Right, climb the rope."

He laughed nervously. "I loved boxing. I could knock people flat, but I hated climbing the goddamn rope."

"So to vent, let off steam, afterward you went to a local pub—"

"I had some drinks," McClelland acknowledged. "Three, four. Maybe more." He reached for his milk and slowly sipped. White waves painted the inside of the glass, and then slid back down as he returned the drink to his plate's side. The gravy on top of his lumpy remains of Texas-style toast appeared to be hardening like cooling lava.

He hadn't had a drink since that night. But on that night nearly twenty-five years ago, he was on his way to the Gardens to do the evening's broadcast, when a girl flashed out from between two parked cars. "It was like a knife of lightning. She was bent low, chasing something, a ball, a toy, I never found out what—and she just was there, jagged lines in the night—"

Suddenly the car made a sickening double thump as the front end crumpled and the girl got tangled up in the under-carriage. "I'm pretty sure I wasn't drunk. Maybe buzzed, but I was afraid to take a chance, to own up to it."

"Buzzed, drunk, they're the same thing, McClelland," Stana said.

"Yeah, yeah," he acknowledged. At that time, 1942, he had a big endorsement deal with York Peanut Butter and Bee Hive Corn Syrup. Sponsors were unheard of for sportscasters.

So, Leeds, who wasn't driving and only had a beer or two, says to Stuart, let's keep the Voice of Canada safe from scandal, and volunteers to take the fall, telling the police he was the one behind the wheel.

McClelland wiped his chin, his mouth cramping, emotion flashing across his eyes. "How did you find out?"

"That doesn't matter. What matters now is what am I going to do about it?"

"You're not going to run the story? Tell my listeners—"

"Can you imagine your final broadcast from high above the gondola? 'Hello, Canada. In 1942 I, McClelland Stuart, caused the death of a young child because I had been drinking too much—'" She let out a deep sigh. "No. No. I don't see it playing out that way—"

Stana could be ruthless in pursuit of a story. She had sold out Sharon, Small Bear, me, and now Stuart. The "truth" was *everything* to her. Dusky cotton candy fuddled my head.

"What do you want?" He couldn't look at either of us.

I wanted him to put his homburg back on and look dignified.

"The truth," she said. "The answer to some questions so that we can get to the missing girl before it's too late."

Who would benefit from Cathy's gone missing? Who was she about to pull the plug on?

"I don't know," McClelland whispered, chin on chest. That night Leeds took the fall. Leeds *was* sober. Two beers, that's all. Under the legal limit.

The glass in the long windows behind us was stained with darting cherubs and splashing water fountains. The contrast in moods was striking. A loudspeaker listed a train number and said, "Boarding now for Montreal, Trois-Rivieres, and Quebec City."

McCelland eyed his homburg, stood, and slipped into his long overcoat with buttons that resembled anchors on a small boat. One of his arms got stuck in a sleeve. He struggled and elbowed on through. He looked like a little kid anxious for recess to start.

"But at what cost, McClelland?" Stana's eyes darted about, landing, holding his gaze, not allowing a furtive glance away.

"What cost?" For years, Leeds collected kickbacks. He got a percentage of all of Stuart's business investments. "Just one percent but it adds up."

"Sure it does," I said, my hands crossed, the pain behind my eyes hammock-shaped clouds, balancing above the horizon line, ready to drop.

"I got him access to the Gardens for his—"

"Photography sessions? Did you know about Coughlins or the photographs?"

"Yes, no. I mean—Leeds told me he was doing therapy there. It made the girls feel important to have their sessions at such a hallowed place, the Gardens."

"Was he doing Tangerine Room treatments there?"

"Tangerine Room?" McClelland looked down at his shoes, pensively. "You mean with the tape recordings and the—"

"—Relaxation exercises."

"Yes." He nodded his head slowly. "He was." Leeds had mentioned performing Tangerine Room activities at the Gardens and removing the girls' inhibitions, making them more confident. McClelland shook his head and played with the lip of his glass. "I wanted to believe him, that he was really helping them, so I chose to believe him, but deep down a voice kept telling me it wasn't right. The girls alone with him—there—"

"Something was creepy about it all—" Stana echoed, closing off his thoughts.

"Right. And because I chose not to mind what was going on, I'm responsible." He sat back down.

"Yes you were," Stana reminded him, her eyes roping him in. "So we're going to make some things right." She nodded. "Right here, right now."

Slowly his head nodded in rhythm with hers. He sat down.

"Leeds was blackmailing you and you let him into your investments. But the primary investment firm you worked with was Bolemac, right? The alleged construction company that was actually a subsidiary of Smith and Bullard?" Stana flipped through her notebook. The curled-over pages resembled a large sand dune.

He pushed his plate farther away and took another sip of milk, longer this time.

"What about the $568,000?" I jumped in. "The money Migano wants me to recover for him?"

"Migano needs it to keep up his end." He put on his homburg, buttoned his overcoat. Smith, Bullard and Migano were investing in land, north of the city. That's what those longitude and latitude lines were all about, south of Bradford in Vaughan, Ontario. Three-hundred and forty acres of land. They're going to build on it: houses, a whole city or suburb.

I let out a sharp whistle and played with the brim of my porkpie. "That's a lot of land."

"A new housing development. It'll be worth a fortune."

That's where Sarah was killed, 98 days ago. On that expanse of land and the abandoned log cabins.

This business arrangement between Migano on one end and Smith on the other was supposed to be pretty much evenly divided, but Migano's now short and Smith wants to take on more of the principal, a bigger percentage for bigger profits.

"Did Leeds steal the money? The $568,000?"

"Yes. Probably with the help of Steinmetz and Terrien." He stood up. "I got to go. The train—"

"For who? Who did Leeds steal for? Smith?"

"Migano most likely." McClelland blinked his eyes. "He was the one short." You can check the records at City Hall. By the end of this month Migano was supposed to meet his end, otherwise Smith was going to buy up the open shares and the land balance would no longer be equal between them. "Migano stole it from the Gardens."

"He tells the story differently," I said. "He says someone, Davis, stole it. It was Babe's money, his part of the Bolemac arrangement. Kept in a Gardens wall safe."

"Davis." Stuart laughed. Davis was a gambler, a womanizer, but he was no criminal. "A liar, but no criminal. Migano stole the money. I'm pretty sure."

"That's Smith's story?" Stana said.

"Yes."

"Told over a game of golf at the links or hanging with his cronies knocking back Molsons?"

"He's not my friend." A trace of resentment glided behind McClelland's words. "We don't socialize. It's business." The effervescent pop to his world was gone. "I got to go." He was itching to catch his train.

"Well, I don't believe Smith's story," Stana said. "I don't trust that chauvinist pig."

"Me neither. Although I think he looks a little bit more like a possum caught in car headlights than a pig."

She hit me in the shoulder.

"But let's say Stuart's version of the events is right—for

argument's sake, Stana. That makes Leeds the middleman. He collected the money from Terrien and Steinmetz to hand over to Migano. And then he got *got*."

Someone's doing a double-cross. Who? Smith? Migano himself? And what about the woman with the heavy feet running away, the one I saw in slants of rain and conical light, the one known simply as Starzz? "That's Starzz with two z's, by the way, McClelland."

They announced boarding for Montreal again.

"I don't know Starzz," McClelland said. "Never heard of her." He stood up.

"Oh, come on. You're telling me you've never been to Coughlins, you've never—"

"I never go. I never drink anymore, either." He looked at his watch. It was a Lucerne with a Leafs crest emblazoned inside the crystal. "I better get going. You're not covering the game tomorrow night, Miss Younger?"

"No, I have a bigger story to follow."

He smiled awkwardly, looking a little nonplussed. For McClelland Stuart hockey was his escape, nothing was bigger. Hockey was Canada. "Davis had a thing for Starzz, or so I hear. You might ask him about her."

I nodded.

He glanced down at his check, adding up the amount, calculating the tip.

I took the slip from him and agreed to pay for it. It was the least I could do.

He appeared pleased, his eyes shiny coins. I had heard that he was a very frugal fella and there were many jokes at his expense over what a cheapo McClelland Stuart was. "Thanks," he said. "Well, keep your stick on the ice."

I laughed out of courtesy, his farewell greeting not quite as bouncy as at our earlier meeting. Traces of sad resignation filled in the edges of his words like a heavy, black curtain.

I wondered if Hamlet were about to stab Polonius. I *felt* like Hamlet, the little shit.

"The story of that night, 1942, remains with *us*," Stana promised. "Buried."

He nodded ever so slightly, eyes brimming. "There's one other thing," he said.

Stana and I leaned closer.

"There was a third person in that car." He wiped his chin and let out a short sigh, like air still leaking out of that withering balloon. "Nick Stabulas."

9

Nick wasn't too happy to see me. He didn't even get up to shake my hand. He was lying on his cot, still waiting to be bailed out, arms folded under his heavy head. He failed to answer question after question with anything but a perfunctory grunt or a disengaged nod of no, no, and more no's. What does Cathy's drawer of "toys" have to do with the nude photographs? Did Cathy know Laurinda and Dawn? Did you know them? What was your relationship with Leeds? How well did you know Sarah? She visited with Cathy, the grocery, your home. What was the connection between your daughter and Sarah? Nick's upper lip curled tighter under his front teeth, and I kept firing away, his eyes resembling dark lentils.

The jail cell was in the very old part of the building. The floors were thin slats of dirty hardwood. Concrete walls were chipped and scored and pocked. It had rained a lot the last couple of days and stains the shape of the Great Lakes ran along the wall closest to the outside. The room smelled of mildew and piss.

"This isn't about me. Find the girl." Nick's "you understand" was gone, so was the lilt. His argot now mirrored the streets of Toronto rather than the fields of Macedonia.

"Oh, so you quit acting. That's nice." I was trying to nudge him, push him to talk, my face taking on its lopsided lupine grin.

Beyond the high cell window, the sky was dark gray and the jail bars bounced shadowed piping across the lower end of his bed.

"Excuse me?"

"The Old World accent, the down-home charm. It's missing." In its place was a flat series of kidney punches. "You're no longer the male Anna Magnani, you understand, attempting to speak English, you understand."

He didn't like that too much. His bushy eyebrows knitted together, like a heavy snake waiting in tall grass.

"The question in this case? Why was Cathy kidnapped or killed. She knows something. What? And who's at risk? Maybe Cathy's disappearance is some kind of payback, payback against you—and maybe her disappearance has something to do with a girl found dead in a suitcase—"

"What?" He propped up on his elbows, a part of a leg crossed over a raised knee. "Smith's the one you want to find—he's the one responsible."

"What can you tell me about Sarah?"

He sighed and shrugged, his eyebrows a heavy machete. "She was a mousy kind of girl. Never said much."

"Uh-huh. It's not Smith, asshole. It's *you who's responsible.* I saw the way you hit Kim." He had no respect for women. And now McClelland has connected Nick to the car accident. You know Leeds. Leeds took photos of underage girls. Had them under hypnosis. "Maybe someone's punishing Cathy for something you did, I don't know, maybe something involving underage girls?"

"That's a lot of somethings. Hypnosis, really?"

"Sarah was only fourteen when her photo was taken, fucko."

He got off the bed and stood by my feet.

"Don't take a swing at me, Nick. I'm not Smith." I ground a fist into a palm. "Fifty-five stitches." I pointed at my face. I knew my way around.

He exhaled sharply, turned his back, and walked to the jail window. You couldn't see a thing but sky. "I didn't take any photos," he mumbled.

"You like licorice—" I said. It wasn't a question.

"What?"

"Just connecting some dots, Nick. Loose ends, you understand?"

"You are a smart-ass."

I repeated what I learned from McClelland, how Nick was a passenger in the car the night the nine-year-old got killed and I knew of the hold Leeds had over the Voice of Canada, and wondered what shared hold did Nick have—he too must have cashed in.

"I didn't cash in. I didn't—" He couldn't. Nick loved hockey. It was his way into the "Canadian cultural mosaic."

"Where did you learn that phrase?"

He said nothing.

"Uh-huh. What can you tell me about Dawn Stoukas or Laurinda Mays? They described a burly fella, who liked licorice—"

"Don't know them."

"They were friends of Landover Leeds—" Look, Landover got a hold of something and used it as leverage on McClelland, forcing his way into the Gardens. Leeds started taking dirty pictures of girls, under-aged, and I think you were in on it, Nick, a couple of Old Man's Militia pals. "You were there during the photo shoots. You were Leeds's second."

"That's ridiculous." He turned from the window, his face a nasty vicious leer. His third face could hurt a whole family.

"And that fight at the Gardens? That was a total phony." Why else would Smith call you a hypocrite? "Because he knew you had something on McClelland." Laurinda and Dawn had vague recollections, too, of a second person being present at their shoots. I had thought it was Smith. "But it was you, big man." They describe the person as bulky, but because of the mind control, they can't put a face to the form. "How's your English accent, guv'ner?"

"That's bullshit."

"Nick, you were so worried about them making you that you needed to make with a scene, a diversion, and suddenly *la voila* you make with the fancy roll across a desk and a half-ass fist fight that was about as real as a Whipper Billy Watson wrestling match at the Gardens."

"Fuck you. Guard!" His voice was flat and narrow. "Get this asshole out of here."

"Are you blackmailing Stuart? You were in the car the night of the accident. You are, aren't you? That's how you're staying afloat—you told me about the competition, Dominion's, wiping you out—"

The guards escorted me from his cell.

On my exit, I asked if I could bring him anything next time. "Red licorice? Black? Cherry Nibs, or uh Goodies?"

"You take chances," he said.

"Goodies it is," I said. "Cheers."

WHEN I WALKED INTO Nick's Grocery Kim was behind the counter. That surprised me. Stana was surprised too. She gave me a look of genuine amusement, her mouth parting slightly, eyes brightening.

Ninety-nine days since I found the girl in the suitcase. Was I any closer to finding Cathy?

Stana and I hadn't shared much in the car ride over from the Don Jail. I was annoyed with how she treated such a dignified man like McClelland Stuart. Maybe I'm a little soft.

Maybe Kim's a little soft too. I knew she was quite a wheel at Ogilvie and Beggert and that she and her father had had a falling out when she was a teenager, and yet here she was, paying penance, manning the store, a pencil behind her ear, dark hair pulled back in a ponytail.

"Nick's still in jail, huh?" I said.

"He didn't want my money." Kim glanced away. A thin pulse flashed along her jawline.

The pain was palpable. Kim was the neglected bad girl, the lost, forgotten daughter.

Sun, falling, filtered through the plate-glass window behind her, leaving a box of shadow in front of the counter. The counter shimmered with faint stains from past coffee cups and pop bottles.

Stana bit her upper lip. "I'm sorry," she said sincerely. "Busy?"

"Not really." With the children of Macedonian immigrants moving to the suburbs, neighborhood mom-and-pop stores like this one, she said, were suffering. I smiled slightly, having said something similar to her recalcitrant father just minutes ago. "Sure there are a few customers," and they kept her father barely afloat, "but all those damn discount stores selling canned and boxed goods at a fraction of the cost—sometimes taking a loss just to squeeze us out."

"Fuck the big chains," I said.

Old World loyalty didn't go very far, Kim noted. Some baboes, shawled and shuffling, tugging their portable pull carts on wheels, buy two- to three-days' worth of milk, bread, and the evening paper, but that was about all the business she had to handle. And of course there were the kids, buying candy or hockey cards or comic books. They were always polite.

She shrugged and straightened the three major dailies on the blue shelves behind her. The comics on the twirling pencil-lined rack were all leaning forward, the tops yellowed.

I picked up the afternoon editions of Stana's competitors.

The latest spin from Smith's camp was printed in the *Star*. This was all a misunderstanding, the Leafs CEO had said, his finger wagging in a medium close-up shot. These are two unrelated events that unfortunately appear connected. Lucky for all of us, Smitty dropped Pal Cal's apples and oranges refrain.

Smith reassured the public that he was innocent of all malfeasance and in a few days the real story would come to light. This whole epic exaggeration was but the concocted petty results of an overzealous female reporter trying to make a splash in a male world and an ex-hockey player with an ax to grind against the organization that let him go for moral turpitude. "Wow," I said, holding the folded paper in my hands. "There he goes again with the big words. I'm waiting for him to call the whole thing *lurid*."

Stana pointed a lean finger about three paragraphs down in the next column.

"Oh, well, there you go. Says right here: 'Lurid coverage.

Yellow journalism at its finest.'"

The paper further reported what we already knew: Smith and Bullard were out on their own recognizance; Stabulas was still in the holding tank, proud and pouting.

I rubbed the edges of my forehead where my hat rested. My eyes weren't as sore as when we had met McClelland, but I was hiding in the perforated shadows, away from the sun. I tapped the papers on the edge of the counter top, next to the Beech-Nut chewing gum and Tums.

"Where's your sister?" Stana's eyes narrowed on Kim.

"No idea."

"I think you do. She's been in contact with you, hasn't she? You're too calm for someone whose sister is missing—"

Stana was all instincts. Maybe she should put on a homburg and learn a little dignity.

"Maybe I just don't like her that much? Ever think of that? Daddy's girl. Love of his life." Kim rubbed her chin.

I reached for and held it. "Don't play the hard-boiled dame. It doesn't fit you." I knew that under the mask of smoldering eyes was a sensitive, vulnerable woman. I let go her chin and she looked away, eyes watering. She wasn't wearing perfume, I couldn't smell Chanel, not a thing.

"I swear I know nothing of her disappearance."

"Lisa Steinmetz, then," Stana said. "It must be her. She and Spinner."

I snapped my fingers. "Of course." Was Cathy involved in the missing money? Did she help Lisa and Spinner lift it from the Gardens' vaults? Did she abscond with it? Was she involved in the double-cross? Maybe she was going to head out west with them.

Two young boys, nine and seven probably, came in wear-

ing heavy spring jackets and toques, wanting milk and popcorn in a box. A line drawing of a jolly circus elephant was
on the box cover looking like it enjoyed popcorn too. The
younger kid with a brighter toque bought two packs of hockey cards. "Hey—" He turned to me. "Aren't you?"

"I used to be," I said.

The kids left and a bell faintly rang.

The street outside looked like a hard disc. I rubbed my
chin. "Why did you lie to us, Kim? About Coughlins. You've
been there."

She played with her necklace, touched her collarbones,
and smiled wanly. Sure she'd gone a few times, as a guest of
Babe Migano's, but she didn't want Ogilvie and Beggert to
know about it. Those visits were a part of a wilder past and
now that she was a fast-rising star in real estate such associ-
ations could ruin her reputation and destroy her chance to
climb into upper management. "That's why. Maybe my sister
just wanted to get away. I know I wanted to. Christ, my father's not an easy man. Look, there was never a ransom note,
nothing threatening."

"Too much has happened since then," I said. "Way too
much. This whole thing feels threatening and I'm scared of
losing her, like I lost another one 99 days ago."

Look, I told her, there had been a man murdered in his
office chair; an unveiling of an escort service, nude photographs, and the sexual exploitation of underage girls; a movie
camera in Smith's office; and a land grab involving the Greater Toronto Area's number-one mobster, Babe Migano; and a
possible tie in with the Sarah Kerr killing. "Tell me about that
relationship. I hear that your sister saw Sarah once or twice
a week—"

"Yeah." Not much more to tell than that. Cathy was a mentor for the girl, proofed some of her award-winning essays, encouraged her to study pre-med at U of T, and gave the girl money every once in a while so she wouldn't have to work at Becker's to support her mom. Sarah was all about her studies—

"Is that what she was all about? I hear she was boy crazy at twelve. Never quite happy in her willowy body, but wanting to explore pleasure."

"I never saw that. Never. She was—"

"Mousy?" *That's what Nick said and I didn't believe him.*

"No. I wouldn't call her mousy. She was focused on school, but reserved in other ways."

"I think she might have also been a guest at Coughlins. A regular. You ever see her there?"

"No."

"Your own sister?"

"No."

I rubbed the corners of my mouth and gave a lopsided grin, my lupine look. "What was your role at Coughlins?"

"Role?"

"You're on the film—"

"I told you, I went as a guest of Mr. Migano's. He asked me on a date. I'm all right looking, you know."

"Uh-huh. You'll forgive me if I don't quite believe you. I mean you *are* good-looking—"

"Thank you."

"However, before you said, and I quote, that you suspected Coughlins was a pizza joint and Bolemac an expensive brand of Tupperware—"

"Very expensive," Stana jumped in. "I checked with City

Hall. Government lot line numbers. You represent Bolemac. You've helped Migano buy land in Vaughan. It's your name under the Ogilvie and Beggert banner."

"It was a business transaction."

"Uh-huh."

"Bolemac has done major construction at the Gardens, at Smiths, and at your apartment, Miss Stabulas, in the North End. You're up to this to your dark eyes." Stana pushed against the edge of the counter.

"Uh-huh," Kim said, throwing my self-reliant refrain right back at us.

"Very good," I said. "That was good. Nice intonation. Rhythm."

The bell dinged and an old woman with a shawl on her shoulders, a cart by her left hand, and stockings wrinkled at the ankles, asked if there were any day-old donuts she could take home. There were: three for the price of one. Kim bundled them together in wax paper and placed them in a bag. The woman squeezed some fruit and bread and paid for the donuts and left.

I wondered why'd she have the cart with her if all she was getting were donuts? Some people have strange rituals or habits that can't be forgotten. It's another kind of cheap amusement I guess. Like me during my playing days, with all my damn superstitions: left skate and left glove first, and always the last player on the ice, the last to tap Bower's goalie pads before the opening faceoff, and the last to head into the dressing room for intermission. Cheap amusements.

"You and Migano look cozy on the film." I reminded her of the couch in Smith's office and Migano nestled by her feet.

"I help with his business interests and assets—"

"That's all—?"

"That's my business."

"What was Leeds to the family?"

"Leeds, the counselor?" She looked up at the tin ceiling. It was covered with riveted bumps. One of the tiles was loose and hung down like a flag. "I told you about him. A quack."

"Yeah, a quack, but—" Stana reached into her purse, the one with the rings for handles that resembled ten-pound weights on a barbell. She pulled out the photograph, Cathy nude, the eyes distant and sad.

Kim winced at the photograph as if she were looking at a Weegee crime scene photograph of a fallen gangster covered in a police sheet. "How'd you get this?"

"Lisa Steinmetz. She said it was sent to her in the mail."

Kim bit the inside of her lip. "Cathy's like twenty here. She looks stoned. Out of it."

I pushed back the porkpie, and then dropped my hands to my hips. "And she may have been hypnotized or under some subliminal spell—"

"Subliminal?"

"You ever hear of Leeds's Tangerine Room?"

"And that bogus relaxation shit? I never—volunteered—" She paused and her face lightened, the eyes were less heavy. "Yeah—control." She nodded and pressed her lips together. "But why?"

"Why, indeed," I said.

Nick knew Leeds. Did Leeds have a family connection?

Kim traced a small shimmer ring on the counter in front of her. The shadow carpet was gone. The sky outside: dark. The pavement: a wet lake. "Okay. I saw him now and then." At Christmas he'd give the girls dolls or clothes. "Always brought dad a fruitcake." She never liked the guy. A total phony. A hedonist. For him, the good life was wine, a good-looking woman, and a fast car. "I overheard him telling dad about the girls he balled or fucked in the ass. The pig."

Men are pigs.

"What about your sister? Did she like the cat?"

"Cathy trusted him." She was seeing him for therapy and career guidance, but Kim never knew about the photographs. "He took them, the photos?"

I nodded. And somebody else was witness to it, another man. Dawn hinted there was a second man behind the camera on occasion.

"Not my father. Is that what you're intimating—"

"Is that what you thought I was intimating? I'm curious. Why did you think that?"

She pushed off from the counter and bit her lower lip. "I didn't think that. It's just—" She paused and played with a raised clavicle.

I looked away at the long row of canned goods along a far wall. Some of the goods had fly matter kissing their lids.

Cathy and her father kept secrets from Kim. The two of them went to hockey games together, listened to it on radio in the back alcove, shared dinners, and sometimes, after therapy sessions, they disappeared alone, on the town, restaurants, or so they said, for daddy-daughter quality time. "I never knew what they did. We never talked about it."

"Are you saying it's possible?"

"What? That my dad's a perv, that he took naked pictures of his own daughter or helped someone else take them? I—I—don't know. I don't know the man." She hit the counter with a fist and then slammed it again and again before crying into her shoulder. "He never wanted me. It was Cathy he loved—" Kim's mouth dribbled with tears. Stana motioned me away while consoling Kim, hugging her to her shoulders.

I asked if I could look around, see what I might dig up.

Neither of them heard me. They continued talking quietly, while I moved to the back of the store. Nick was involved. I was sure of it. The big rhubarb at the Gardens the other day, what with his tumbling dice roll across the desk and random punches and all, had an overdetermined artifice to it. It was all too fucking orchestrated for the reporters.

I shook my head, staring into the hardwood floors, searching for answers in the swirling grooves of wood grain. The floor needed to be refinished. Bubble gum was stuck in some of the knotted wood.

In back was a little room separated from the main space by a green curtain on a small white curtain rod. I pushed the curtain back, surveying the room for photographic equipment. There wasn't any.

There was however a stack of *Guns & Ammo* magazines against a small desk; a cot pushed up against cinder blocks with two flat pillows that needed to be punched up; a hot plate surrounded with several empty pea-soup cans, an ashtray packed with a pyre of ashen cigarettes; Bee Hive hockey photos and Export "A" calendars on the wall; and an old Crosley radio. I turned it on. The Leafs were already down 1-0. Habs forward Claude Provost, whom I admired and modeled my own game after, had scored. And the Leafs appeared tired, McClelland said.

We were all tired. I turned the radio down.

Shit, I figured the Leafs would have a little more giddy-up. Come on. Following game one, Montreal coach Toe Blake had said, "We expect to win four games, any four. But there's no doubt about it, the Leafs are not playing like they did last year." That should be bulletinboard material, man. I shook my head and wished I could still lace them up for the blue and white.

Across from the radio was an openly displayed toilet. The porcelain was rust-stained with age. On the toilet's tank was a stack of books, mainly murder mysteries. A black pipe ran next to the toilet, up on through to the ceiling. The ceiling was exposed too—a drop hadn't been put in. Slats of wood, copper water pipes, and electrical lines bracketed the beams hovering above me, separating this room and space from the living space above.

Next to the Crosley was a small array of allsorts candy, an English blend made of sugar, coconut, fruit flavorings, gelatin, and of course aniseed jelly licorice. Square pieces, blocky layers, were stacked three high. Hard dotted nubs stood alone. Two pieces that resembled very small sidewall tires with fat axles in their centers had bites taken out of them. I called Lambertino's home. "Hey, Sal, I can't talk long. Do me a favor." I asked him to check into the bank accounts of Nick, Kim, and Cathy Stabulas.

If any of them were doing anything underhanded or were involved in blackmail kickbacks or porn rackets their accounts would show it. I couldn't access that info. He could. "Just a hunch." I rolled a piece of licorice between my fingers. "A pretty big hunch. I want to see if certain deposits in a high-dollar range have been made." I told him it had to do with one girl gone missing, the murder of another girl 99 days ago, and dirty pictures of underage girls and the Voice of Canada possibly being blackmailed. Oh, and licorice.

"Licorice, huh?"

"Yeah. And what can you tell me about the connection between Cathy and Sarah, the murdered girl? They were friends. Any evidence turn up when you collected stuff from the Kerr apartment?"

"I'll check the files in the basement—"

Leeds had a cohort. I was pretty sure it was Nick, but check the money, always follow the money. He swore at me and said he would and now could I please go away, he's watching the fucking hockey game. Some Leafs fan I was. "Sure, sure," I said and hung up.

Stana and Kim were quietly connecting in the next room. She was talking about neglect and feeling invisible and my head was suddenly pounding so I shut off the lights in the alcove, and lay back on the cot, fighting a shake of dizziness, and listened to the game. Ronnie Ellis was flying. So was Big Z, but the rest of the club was plodding, as if they needed to sharpen the blades of their skates. Béliveau scored with about a minute to go in the period, damn him, and it was now 2-0.

In my time with the Leafs, I played a bruising style, hard checking. I didn't worry much about getting on the sheet. I averaged about 16-17 goals a year. My main objective was to stop the other guy from scoring and offer up opportunities for my guys to counterpunch. I was a reactive player. I didn't create on the ice so much as provide the time and space for other guys to create.

Damn, I missed it.

Béliveau. Now there was an innovator, a jazz improvisation guy, who constantly created new riffs with his easy-going skating style and smooth hands around the net. He *was* the deal. And could he pass the puck. Classy and cool like a John

Coltrane.

People always say there's a rivalry between the two cities, the solitudes of Canada: the English Protestant Toronto versus the French Catholic Montreal. That divide does exist, I guess, but I always respected Montreal, their freewheeling style, and how the entire province of Quebec was behind them. The Habs were a subset of the area's religious theology and mythology. And I'd like to think they respected us, the tight checking, center-man floating back, clogging up the middle style of play we harnessed. We were a thrifty and frugal bunch—very English.

The period was over and McClelland promised plenty of fight for the third.

Plenty of fight? Really?

The man with the homburg was a pioneer for the sport, a potential Hall of Famer in the Builders category, and I don't know, I still felt sad over how Stana and I treated him at the Via Rail restaurant. His eyes in that meeting were reduced to little coins and all of the feisty jocularity was gone. To have killed a child is a terrible thing, to live with the guilt every day, and our discussion did not release him of that pain. Instead it made it more pronounced and maybe that's why tonight, he too sounded tired, his promise of "plenty of fight" a mere pipe dream for himself and the club.

You never give up a goal in the last minute of a period and climb back into a game. It's a deal breaker, an unwritten rule from the hockey gods. And you never get over the death of a child. That's just an unwritten rule of life.

The darkness and smell of forgotten soup comforted me, but there was a veil of light, a thin shaft limning my shirt and part of my face. I lay there listening, the voices in the next room, and McClelland's over the radio, his adenoidal timbre giving us all a quick moment-to-moment, tape-to-tape reality that was as reassuring as the hurt that follows love lost.

But the light and its thin lines. I propped up on my elbows and moved in the direction of it. I couldn't reach the main line. It was lilting through the ceiling. I unfolded a metal chair slanted by the stack of magazines and climbed on it, my head filling with dizzy cotton.

I pulled at a piece of wood. It was loose, stuck in place with spots of Silly Putty. I pulled harder. Above me was another bathroom. Of course, the black pipe connected the two—simple plumbing design 101. From the chair, and the open space of missing wood, I could make out the edging of a shower stall against the far wall. Because the light was on in the bathroom above me, I could see the glass doors, and the towels with yellow trim hanging on a rack. From my space I could probably see a woman from her knees to her shoulders—that would be clearly visible.

Cramped and alone in the hidden shadows below, I could see into the shower stall.

10

My head was a black mass of pain behind my eyes. The painkillers were doing next to nothing for me, but I couldn't visit Abramowitz, not yet, no time, so I went skating as a kind of relief, a reset button to clear my head of its concrete clutter.

I enjoy skating, especially corner crossovers as one skate cuts over the other, shaving the curve close, and then tearing back up ice. I usually skate at the Gardens three mornings a week, 6 A.M. I love the snick-snick of my blades, the cool air on my face, and the openness of a white sheet before me, a sense of the infinite within the finite.

Lefty, the Zamboni driver, lets me in—seven years of signing hockey sticks for the cat built me up some goodwill—and nobody knows about the perk but us, but today, after firing off several rounds at the gun range under the police station on Bay, I was skating at a more routine 10 A.M. pace. Smith wasn't here to bawl me out as the Leafs had decided not to return home after Thursday's loss.

Too many distractions, Coach Farrell said to Bledsoe. The club was scrimmaging in Peterborough, Ontario, 85 miles northeast of the city, and they would not be returning until late tomorrow afternoon.

Before lacing up, I called Migano, explaining how I wasn't moving forward on the Davis front. First, he was in Montreal for a game and now he was holed up in Peterborough. I had work to do in Toronto.

"Priorities, Mr. Fuller?" His voice purred like a European car.

I had to find the girl, the one I hoped was in Toronto and still *alive*.

"I get that, but what am I paying you for?" A good-natured confidence permeated his words.

"Nothing apparently."

He laughed at my candor.

Then I told him what McClelland Stuart shared yesterday about the missing $568,000 and who stole the money from whom.

"That's twisted, Hayden. McClelland should just stick to calling hockey games and paying off his gambling debts."

"*He* owes at Coughlins?"

"Do Canadians love donuts? Yeah, he loves the wheel, and don't let him tell you differently, capisce? Always drinks a glass of milk. No booze. Bets black. Anyway, I never stole the money. It was grifted from *me*, or if you like the Bolemac Corporation, and I'm the Bolemac Corporation."

"You and Smith," I corrected.

"Smith? I'm the head kingpin. Smith?—he's an auxiliary member, if that. Get on Spinner and Steinmetz." He thought they were holed up on King Street near the waterfront. Some associates had seen them at a local A&P. "Get their story. When you find them, get me."

I didn't like the sound of that. I get them, and then what?

Steinmetz and Terrien will get got that's what. "Associates? Can you elaborate?"

"You wouldn't want to know or if I told you, you wouldn't believe me. Legit guys. Politicos. Made guys in the non-Italian world, if you know what I mean."

I rubbed the edges of my mouth. "I'll track Davis after tomorrow night's game—"

"You do that."

I skated for another twenty minutes, trying to clear my head of Babe and his indirect threats and Cathy's disappearance and my sinking feeling that her own father was involved and killed her to cover up his twisted sexual preferences. Black licorice, and now the blackness behind my eyes was a light gray.

I skated and skated, seeking that space between conscious thought and involuntary action, the quiet zone of absolute stillness where nothing mattered and I was just mindlessly doing, no longer analyzing or fretting about what was to come next, but skating through pockets of silence.

Then I grabbed a bucket of pucks and my stick and skated to the slot and fired shot after shot: number-one and number-three hole, top shelf: right and left. It was a rhythm, the twine denting, me leaning on the lower part of the stick, gutting out leverage, the stick torquing with each quick wrist shot, faster, faster. I was doing pretty good. A few crossbars and the odd shot high over the net, but I was landing some beauties just under the bar.

I gathered up the pucks and moved from the slot to the left circle, and then the right circle. Same rhythm, same leverage, same dented twine. I was in a flow, the pockets of silence now filling me with grace. A few more pucks sailed over the net, a few more rattled the posts, but I was hitting my spots about seventy-five percent of the time. Flow. It was in me; I was in it.

I sighed, breathing in the Gardens air, and gathered up the pucks one final time and placed the bucket and my stick back in the penalty box, and then skated and skated and skated, pushing away Cathy and Babe and Nick. And the cool blue of the lines, the sharp checkered red of center, and the various circles, some filled in, others not, the boundaries of a game, giving everything a kind of order, and my heart, my strides, were in step, beat, step, beat, with those structures, aligned, and I felt a connectedness to the game, to the past, to this moment, to this time.

I skated with that feeling of assurance, trying to hold onto it, while pushing away an awareness of its very existence and suddenly all the doubt and despair spinning like dirty cotton candy webbed into my conscious space, and once you become aware of the freedom begot of stillness you allow it to be taken away from you by the penal colony of doubt, and those pockets of silence are gone and you have to find them all over again, the next time out, the next crossover, the next breath of air on the ice. And you *do* find stillness. You find it again and again and again.

I needed to find it now.

Cathy's father.

God damn him.

"Hey, superstar! Can we talk?"

It was Sal Lambertino, his voice a no-nonsense slap like a puck whapping around the glass.

I skated over to the boards, leaning in by the players' bench, my gloves slightly sliding down my hands.

"You could still play, couldn't you?" Sal tugged and massaged at the fenced edges of his Hemingway beard. "I saw you going top shelf. Pretty good."

"Thanks." I was pretty sure I could lace them up, even with a year away from the game, but unless Montreal called me I wasn't suiting up for anyone. I didn't respect anybody else. I had it too good for seven years. Why would I want to play for the Rangers?

"Maybe if the Leafs get new management you'll be back in blue and white?"

"Maybe." I laughed. "Any word on Smith?" I blew air between my lips and wiped sweat from my forehead.

"No. He was last seen at some charity event for Toronto's Sick Kids hospital."

"Swell. Nick?"

His account was dirty: $150-deposits a month, regularly, going back at least ten years.

"I knew it. Stuart. He's blackmailing Stuart."

"Leeds's account, the same story. I checked on that one too."

I let out a sharp whistle. Lefty and his Zamboni were now chugging up center ice, leaving a fresh squeegee streak that made the Gardens' overhead lights gleam against the ice like new china plates.

"Licorice? That was your clue, huh?"

"Well, yeah—"

"Well, I'll be damned."

"I think Nick was also present during some of the smokers at the Gardens. I think he was behind the camera."

"Probably. But I tell you, Smith's going to walk." The Leafs legal team is already covering up the story, Sal said, pushing back his stop sign of a hat. "And word on the street is that you guys—Stana and you—exaggerated the facts for your own agendas."

"Bull fucking shit."

"That's poetry. I like that. Bull fucking shit. Nice. And get this, the Old Man is going to take back temporary control of the club until the dust settles."

Not a bad idea. The Old Man has integrity, a leader who can be trusted. He might be in his mid-seventies, but he's mentally sharp and physically active. According to the paper, he plays mixed doubles every day for an hour. "I think Nick's a sick fuck and I think he's behind his daughter's disappearance."

"Blackmail's one thing, but that's something else." Sal looked down at the cuff of his police jacket. One of the buttons was missing. "How the fuck did that happen?" He held up his arm and studied the cuff more intently.

"I think Nick made Cathy pose nude. I think—will you stop looking at your fucking cuffs—"

"I'm sorry. I'm listening."

"Next you'll be picking your teeth with a toothpick—"

"I said I was sorry. Now don't get nasty. I mean picking your teeth in front of someone, that's gauche—and to suggest that I would ever do such a thing is just plain nasty—" He smiled.

"Sal, fathers aren't supposed to—"

"Incest?"

"Do I need to draw you a damn picture? *Yes*." I wiped the pain from my eyes. Suddenly I couldn't breathe. I bent at the waist, trying to clear my lungs.

Now it was Lambertino's turn to blow air through his lower lip. He removed his hat and scratched his sandy-haired head—it contrasted strangely with the gray of his Hemingway beard. "Wow. If that's true—" He scratched his head again. "I still need evidence—"

Men are pigs. "That's what Cathy wrote in her journal."

"Tell me something I don't already know."

"I think Nick raped her." I blinked my sore eyes. "And I think Nick may have killed Cathy. She was going to talk, tell her story to Stana. You didn't see Nick in the Don Jail. *I did.* A totally different cat. Brutal, all the Old World sheen was gone. The humility topos bit. Gone."

Chase & Sanborn. The coffee ad? The spanking ad?—Cathy wrote about it in her Big Chief tablet. Those were cries for help.

"Lots of inferences. No facts." He shrugged and reached inside his breast pocket, pulling out three or four folded photographs. "Found these in the case file."

It was Cathy inside the log cabin, the one out in Vaughan where Sarah was killed, 100 days ago. I recognized the candles on the table, the bunk beds, the threadbare bedroll, the dinted carpet, and the stovetop fireplace. She was smiling, her head slightly tilted. Sarah was in another photo, standing by the wall, looking out the window as the tall grass bent with wind.

"They were out there together. They both knew this place before she was killed there," I said.

"Yes. Migano owns the land, but he said he thought the cabins were abandoned." Sal shrugged. "He knows nothing about anybody visiting out there."

"A Coughlins rendezvous point?"

"Maybe?" He rubbed his beard. "Migano said the cabins

would be plowed under soon as the land's converted into a new subdivision."

I don't know why I didn't tell him about the little shafts of light emanating from the shower stall above Nick's grocery store *office*. "So what's next? We talk to Nick?"

"If we can find him. Someone paid his bail. And he's missing."

"If he killed Cathy, I'm going to kill him," I said.

"I didn't hear that." Sal's eyes creased.

I didn't know what had come over me. I was no vigilante. I hadn't even fired a gun. Okay, at a target range two, three times a week, but never at an actual person, *except that time out at the cabin and all I did was hit a car radiator and make it hiss. And then we found the girl in a suitcase.*

Last night I dreamed I was in a suitcase. It was roomy, I could breathe and the air smelled of a pungent, sickly sweet odor, naphthalene, and I realized I was a dying moth, chewing on the suitcase's lining.

Firing pucks at a net. That's what I'm good at.

"Got one more little bit of information for you, pal—" Landover Leeds was killed with his own gun.

"His own gun? This is Canada—we have gun control laws. Why did he have his own gun?"

"Who knows? It was registered and everything. Kept it locked in a box in a drawer in his office. How did it get out of the box and he get plugged? You got me." His eyes squinted.

Jesus Christ.

Maybe Nick had something to do with Leeds and the photographs, Sal conceded. And he was probably blackmailing Stuart, but the incest angle and murder. That wouldn't hold up in a court of law without more evidence.

"I'll get the evidence," I said.

WHILE NOSHING a quick lunch (hot dog with cherry peppers, pickles, green olives, and mustard from a street vendor on Spadina), I called Stana from a phone booth to catch her up to speed. It was cold in Toronto, and I tugged at my jacket collar. I told her that Nick was now missing too, and I had a lot of other info to share, but I didn't want to talk over a phone. Could we meet in my office, 45 minutes? She said I was getting paranoid. Nobody was wiretapping us. She was working on a rewrite. Typewriters clacked in the background. She wanted takeout: egg rolls and moo goo gai pan. Forty-five minutes.

"Sure," I said.

Unfortunately, Stana said, Nick Stabulas was *not* the occasional ogler at Landover Leeds's Speed Graphic sessions. At least not with these two models. Laurinda and Dawn didn't recognize Nick's photograph, but Stana was positive that if we could remove the girls' mental block—placed there no doubt by Lanzo the Great—the girls would start talking and point to an even higher executive in the Leafs front office.

I reminded Stana of the licorice we found in the cordoned-off room to Nick's store.

A lot of people like licorice, she said.

Smith, I wondered?

"Why not Bullard, Hayden? What do we really know about him besides a fondness for fondling women's breasts and eating potato chips? He's my prime suspect. He craves attention and Bullard's clearly in Smith's shadows. Smith is brighter, a law-school grad, and the son of the former owner."

Good point, I said. "What else you got? I feel you're building to something big."

Her pencil clipped against the tip of her lips and the edge of the phone's mouthpiece. "$568,000 was put down on that slice of land out in Vaughan today."

"What? I thought the money was missing. Who put it down?"

"Who do you think? Bolemac. Migano and Bullard. Kim handled it for Ogilvie and Beggert. Bullard's the partner, not Smith. They're squeezing Smith *out*."

"Wow. So Migano has his money? What's he need me for then?" In the background typewriters rat-a-tat-tatted like angry machine guns.

"To throw suspicion on Davis? But why?"

"Good work," I said. "The moo goo gai pan is on me."

"That's not all."

"Oh?"

"The zoning for the land? Bolemac got it changed. It's no longer residential, but commercial. They're building on commercial land—"

"Commercial?"

TWENTY MINUTES LATER I was climbing the stairs to my second-floor office two steps at a time, thinking about land in Vaughan, Ontario, and Stana and the takeout I was carrying and game three of the Leafs versus the Habs tomorrow night.

So I didn't notice that my office door was unlocked and two shadowy figures were sitting in my chairs; the one behind my desk had a gun in her hand.

"Hungry," I said, dropping the takeout on my desk blotter.

"So glad you could drop by, Mr. Fuller." It was Lisa Steinmetz. The gun was a pearl-handled .32. Lisa wore a short black jacket, long-armed gloves, and a tight-fitting dress. Her eyes were steady, calm, and darting right through me, the gun pointed at my navel.

"Sorry about this, Hayden." Spinner's tight curled hair looked like iron filings. He wore an open sport coat and a wrinkled off-white shirt. He raised his hands. "The whole gun thing ain't my bag. This was Lisa's idea." He apologized with his eyes.

"Uh-huh."

"I mean, you were always good to me, during all my call-ups. You're top drawer, man. Top drawer." And then he waved a hand at me, fingers fluttering as if he were a traffic cop wanting to get cars flowing again on Queen Street. "However, I must ask for your gun. You carry one, right? Side holstered?"

"Right. What happened to 'this whole gun thing ain't my bag,' baby?"

He shrugged and looked over at Lisa.

She told me to cool it, not with her eyes, but with two or three F-bombs.

Spinner looked slighter between the shoulders than he did when he played with the Leafs. Maybe I was used to seeing him in Cooper hockey pads, but I think he had lost weight. I handed him the snub-nosed, handle first.

"We got some info to sell—" Lisa leaned forward. The dim light in my office gave off a ghostly appearance as if Lisa were emerging from a foggy world more suited for silent film stars like Lon Chaney. The halting rhythms of her voice were also gone. Question marks no longer ended each sentence. And her hair color was now Lucille Ball red. A disguise no doubt.

"Can I sit down?" I pointed at a hard, wood chair, the only other one in the room.

Spinner said sure, sure, and tucked my gun away in his belt. I flipped the chair around so that I could rest my hands and chin over the back of it. I pulled down on my porkpie. "It's your deal. Deal."

They wanted $1,000, in exchange for giving me some info. "I don't have that kind of money—"

"$500?"

They were desperate and no doubt needed to get out of town. "Who did you guys double-cross and who's trying to kill you?"

Lisa sat up more firmly. Maybe she was anxious to speak and maybe her butt was just sore—all of the chairs in my office were hard: keeps conversations short and moving along, no need to linger. I knew a fella once, Molson's exec, who held all his office meetings in a hallway, for brevity's sake. People don't talk as long when they're standing.

Lisa's face was troubled, pulled down by the weight of anxiety: cheeks, despite the blush, were heavy and drawn; lower lip, the red of a fire wagon, dropped like a sheet; and the mascara around her eyes was too thick, giving her a 1920s vamp reckoning.

"I can do $500," I said. "But it better be good. The info."

"It is. It's about Cathy Stabulas—" Spinner studied his fingers. "We've seen her." He paused and smiled, enjoying his moment. "She's alive."

"Where is she?"

"Where's the money?" Lisa's gun waving wasn't quite as level as I'd like it to be.

"Can you maybe put that down?"

"No."

I shrugged. She was direct at least.

"Go ahead. Eat. You guys must be hungry."

They reached for the stained bag and helped themselves. I asked permission to dial Stana for the money. Lisa said yes with the gun. I filled Stana in on the situation without mentioning Lisa's .32, and Stana said she'd dig up the cash, the newspaper had a pot of change for stoolies and other "incidentals" and since she was getting a big story out of all this, the *Telegram* could put up a large percentage and I could pay Stana back the remaining percentage whenever I got more solvent and above water. I think I had about two yards in my account. Fifteen minutes. She'd be here. "Oh, and bring more Chinese food," I said.

Twenty-five minutes then, she said.

"You got sweet and sour?" Spinner asked.

"Goes right to your hips." I laughed. "I never eat that shit. I got hot mustard—"

"Hot mustard? Come on, man. That's candy ass." He reached for a packet. "Well all right, if that's all you've got."

"Sweet and sour?" I requested from Stana, and then hung up.

Lisa wiped clips of egg roll from her lower lip.

"Okay. What do we do in the meantime while we're waiting? I like pinochle."

Spinner shook his head. "You were never that funny, Kodak Kid. Don't try to entertain us. We get the money, you get the info, we're out. Let's keep things light."

"Sure."

Spinner crossed one leg over another, like one of the Doublemint girls. It wasn't the casual lower leg, just above the ankle, pushed over the knee pose struck by most hockey players. "I suppose you have questions?" He placed a hand under his chin.

"I have a lot of questions. Who did you steal the money for, the $568,000?"

Spinner let out a deep sigh. "I guess $500 in coin entitles you to some answers." He smiled again and they admitted to taking the money, Spinner and Lisa, but he wouldn't name names. Leeds was the middleman. The fence. In twenty-four hours they were supposed to get a cut, ten percent, but when they arrived Leeds was dead.

Outside the sun was hidden in clouds and the sky a gray canvas curtain.

"I called you—that night from Leeds's office. I called you." I glanced over at Lisa, the barrel of the gun glinting arcs of light from my desk lamp. "You were already home. You couldn't have seen him dead—"

"I arrived. Just me. After you left, before the cops arrived—" Spinner was now sweating. He coughed and refolded his legs, left now over right.

"Were you the one outside the window?" I had thought it was a girl. I didn't tell him that part. "The one in the rain?"

"It was raining," he said, "but I don't remember noticing you at no window. I was gone pretty fast—"

"Did you kill him?"

"No. Of course not." He dried his forehead and then his eyelids and loosened his shirt collar. His white shirt could sure be pressed. It looked like a wrinkled paper bag. Even Spinner's upper lip was wet, resembling a perforated mustache. "*You* reported to the press that it was a woman you saw running away in the shadows of light. So it couldn't have been me you saw—"

Right, I did report that. Right. Christ with these headaches I get, sometimes I forget who I told what to. And right
about now my head was a drowning hornet's nest. "Starzz?" I
rubbed the edges of my mouth. "How does she fit in?" Could
she have been the shoeless woman I saw running in pen-
cil-streaks of rain that night?

"Nobody knows who she is—" Lisa noshed on a second
egg roll. "She wears a mask and she'll do anything, I mean
anything, any fantasy."

"The management's been building up expectations, cause
Starzz hasn't done her thing in a few months. Folks can't wait
for her return," Spinner said. He mentioned something about
S&M and a ball and a whip.

"Maybe three months, she's been gone. Visiting the Orient for, get this, 'new techniques.' That's Coughlins' spin on
things," Lisa added.

"Kim Stabulas? She Starzz?" She had been to Coughlins.

"Is she in the Orient? Weren't you listening—?"

"Can't be Kim," Terrien said. "She's too classy."

"Oh, she's classy now." Lisa let out a short groan.

"So much for that character reference, huh?" I said, wagging a thumb at Lisa. "What about Cathy? Is Cathy Starzz?"

"Cathy?" Terrien shook his head. "No, no. Too sweet."

Lisa blew even heavier air between her lips. "Sweet?"

I turned to her. "You've been jealous of Cathy all along—"

She said nothing.

"You got her into Coughlins to, to, to destroy her—" I said.
"Yes."

Terrien looked again at his fingers, and the arc of light
from my desk lamp seemed to have a frosty glow. Lisa glanced

away at the blotter, absently taking in the words in front of her, the fingers of her left hand, tap tapping against my various appointments, the gun shaking even more noticeably in her other hand.

Leeds, the guidance counselor, had talked Lisa into the therapy sessions and following his "Worship the Cock" introductions exposed her to Coughlins. There she met some pretty interesting men, hockey players, and some even slept with her—recognizing her value, making her feel important.

Then one night, she took an orange pill and Leeds performed a relaxation exercise in which Lisa imagined herself on an island in the Caribbean. She just floated in the waters, feeling the sun on her shoulders, nose, the part in her hair, and then, she was naked, freely expressing herself for two men and their camera. She never knew how she got there. She was just there, like she were hypnotized or something.

"Or something? And yet you have some trace memories about it?"

"I know. I don't think I'm supposed to it's like a—a—"

"A world off its axis? Your head full of dirty cotton candy?"

"Yes." Leeds was the ringleader, talking her through whatever paces he had her perform. He spoke very kindly. But there was another man. "Nick Stabulas."

"Nick. Nick was there—" I let out a sharp whistle and snapped my fingers. "I knew it."

"Yes." How dare he, she said. The sonuvabitch. How dare he. He knew that Lisa was Cathy's friend and how could her father be involved in something like this, just standing there, watching, as Leeds took several photographs.

"Did he speak in an English accent and smell of licorice?"

"I don't remember any accent, but the licorice, now that

you mention it—"

"He had no idea that you'd remember. He was no longer the voyeur hiding in the closet, watching through slats, or lingering in shadows, peeking in windows. Instead—" I shook my head and looked at the splashes of dirt on my shoes. They resembled falling stars with teardrop ends.

Apparently, the Tangerine Room parlor trick of relaxation waves didn't quite work on Lisa. "It was a regular placebo with me, I guess." She smiled awkwardly, proud at herself for knowing such a word. "So I wanted to get even—"

"But not with Smith, just Nick. Smith's the real ringleader, isn't he? He's the one you stole the money for? It was Migano's money and you stole it for Smith. Leeds was the go-between. Migano found out and had him whacked. Starzz works for Migano." I breathed heavily, my lower lip giving out.

She shrugged. "You're way ahead of me."

"Starzz works for Migano. She killed for Migano. Got the money back for Migano." *Powder burns. A woman getting close. Maybe she even did a lap dance for the king of photography. She asked to see his gun and guns go off as guns will—*

All this Davis stuff was a smokescreen to send me off on yet another wild detour. This case was full of lies, mean side streets of deception: Migano in his maniacal quest for payback; Kim in her denial of ever visiting or knowing of Coughlins and the Bolemac Corporation; McClelland and his cover-ups over a prior connection to Leeds; Lisa and her dated naked portrait of Cathy, tossing unwarranted suspicions on Danny Davis; Lisa (again) and her alleged friendship with Cathy clouded over by jealousy and revenge; Davis himself, screwing other men's wives; and Nick Stabulas, playing the role of the loyal, desperate father who truly harbors in his heart an unhealthy desire for his daughters.

"Don't you see? Migano has *his* money. Stana told me. He put a deposit down on the land in Vaughan, and he has been running me around, distracting me. Migano's going to kill you—" I said.

Spinner fidgeted with his shirt collar once again.

"Yes. It *was* Smith we were working for." He was never at the photo shoots; however, he did want the money, *Migano's money*. She nodded and her eyes misted. Smith wasn't in on the land deal at all. It was Bullard. Cal Bullard. He was making his move, independent big-time operator, independent of Smith, partnering with Migano and Bolemac for the land grab. Mr. Potato Chips was looking to be in a different kind of chips.

"And Smith was jealous?"

She nodded. He wanted to wreck their partnership.

How could a lard-ass flunky like Bullard be in on something so big that would place his financial standing above me? I can't have that. That was Smith's line of reasoning. Another lie: their partnership, their running of Maple Leaf Gardens wasn't on as solid a footing as their smiles and Royal hand waves to us plebes would suggest. Phonies.

"Smith thought Bullard was a total ass, especially after a late night cocktail session in which the general partner tried to sell the Big Z to Chicago for a cool million," Terrien said.

"Yeah, I know the story," I said. "Everybody knows the story."

"Yes. But after that event, Bullard was told to keep his nose of out of hockey decisions. Stick to concessions and watered down sodas and salty popcorn." Terrien shrugged. "That punishment made Bullard want to get even, to one-up Smith.

Thus the land grab—" Terrien shrugged again. "And Smith hates being one-upped."

So Smith took the money—because he knew Migano was short—and he was hoping to either destroy their partnership or buy his way into the operation. Become a trio instead of a duo—that's what Smith wanted. Right?

Spinner nodded this time.

McClelland Stuart had the story only half right. Yes, Migano was strapped. The $568,000 was crucial to his keeping an equal hold on the company. Smith stole from his own Gardens' safe to wreck Migano. "What a needy fuck," I said. And I got to thinking again about the shift in zoning from residential to commercial. What was Migano really up to?

"Yes. But am I any different?" Lisa shrugged, placing the gun down in front of her. She had felt betrayed by Leeds and Nick. They had destroyed any vestiges of innocence she had and she struck back, luring Cathy there. "Revenge." She shrugged. "It's the oldest motivation isn't it? Goes back to Cain and Abel. It was just three or four times, I took her. That's all. The third time, I got her to take an orange pill and Leeds did his relaxation hypnosis bit on me and Cathy and Cathy took all her clothes off." Her lips became a thin line. "I eventually stole one of the photos from Leeds and mailed it to Nick."

"So what does Leeds do with his private collection of junk—blackmail—?"

"He rents them out, rented them out, to people who are into that—" She followed the lines in the ceiling and studied shadows in a far corner. "He had quite a collection, I hear."

"What about Sarah Kerr? Did Leeds rent out her photos too? She was underage. Fourteen, fifteen?"

"Sarah Kerr? I don't recognize the name—"

"A friend of Cathy's?"

"Nothing. Sorry." After the fourth or fifth time, Cathy quit going to Coughlins. She never knew about the nude photo session. No memory. "I told her about a lot of shit that went on, but I couldn't do that to her." She touched the tip of her chin and breathed.

"I see—"

But Lisa did make Cathy her confidant, telling her tales of what happened at Coughlins, the fucking in stretch limos, the $20,000 poker nights, the brawls over a dart game, and Starzz, the girl in the Mardi-Gras mask who would do it all. "How was I supposed to know Cathy wrote it all down?"

"What?"

"The debaucheries—all of it. In one of her Big Chief tablets." Cathy was planning to blow the whistle on the whole outfit to Stana, when they took her away.

"When they? Who's *they*?"

"I know." She paused. "When we see the money, I'll tell you—"

"*I*?" asked Terrien.

"*We*," Lisa corrected. "When *we* see the money."

"Did Cathy ever see Starzz 'perform' at the club?"

"Yes. Twice, I think."

"Why didn't they kill Cathy?"

She shrugged. "You got me. They chose to hide her instead."

"Where is she?"

"When I get the money—"

Quick, hurried steps were on the stairs behind me. Heavy, not as nimble as Stana usually is, but she was weighed down by bags of Chinese food, a lot of Chinese food, I suppose.

I turned to the frosted-glass door and they barged in, Fortunado and Leighton. They wore overcoats, gloves, and scarves covering part of their faces. The bigger guy, Leighton, was now holding the gun. Fortunado had been demoted. Leighton's eyes were narrow, his face determined. The gun gleamed in the arc of office light.

Lisa reached for the .32 but two quick shots hit her in the chest. She stuttered once or twice, fluttered back and then flopped on my desk, her eyes vacant. Blood was at the corners of her lips, the gun motionless in front of her.

My ears hurt from the gun blasts and I looked over at Spinner who held his fingers up before his eyes, hoping to disappear into some sort of Zen nothingness or stop another volley of bullets with his bare hands. Superman, he wasn't. My gun was still trapped against the belt of his pants.

It was all so damn quick—Lisa alive and now dead—like hammering a nail, and I couldn't think, no words, no actions, and suddenly I wanted to scream at Spinner, where's the girl, where is she, tell me, before they kill you, you dumbass, and maybe I said something or other to that effect, I don't know, but a gun flashed across my mouth, I felt blood and tin between my teeth, and then I dropped into a black pool. It was cold.

11

A glow of light skimmed over my eyes as the world went from dull red to darkness and back to dull red again. I tried to open my eyes against the pendulum splash of light and dark. I threw up in my mouth. It wasn't pleasant.

"What's that, Crumpled Suit?" I recognized the gravel crunch of Lou-doo's burr.

I spit out chunks of hot dog and olives and soda and looked for the moving light and found a bare bulb on a wire, hanging from a garage ceiling. The garage was brown, dusky. Corkboard and power tools draped one of the walls. The floor was coated with a giant plastic shower curtain. I was tied to a chair, my hands tight behind me. The bulb wasn't moving. It was as still as the '65 GTO parked to the right of me. I was the one moving, not really, but in my head, I was moving, all twisted up and dented.

I closed my eyes, but that only made those pendulum splashes of red and canvas black return.

I tasted tin, and traced my tongue across my teeth. One of them was sharp and chipped, another one was missing. I could taste the hole, the blood, the hole, and it hurt and my head hurt, but not as bad my eyes hurt when I shut them or as awful as the gurgle sounded, bubbling up to my left.

Strapped to an even bigger chair and tied down with heavier ropes was Spinner or what was left of him. His head hung over the chair's back and he gurgled some more, blood puffing out of his lips like a weak chewing gum bubble. The bubble got bigger and then popped and then there was another smaller bubble and another small pop.

His right eye was dislodged from the orbital bone and hanging on the side of his face. I don't know what it saw if anything. His breathing was very shallow and I didn't think he had enough left to make it.

"You okay?" A low, distant voice floated my way like heavy clouds.

And then the clouded voice broke up into the even-steady purr of Migano. He smelled of Old Spice and his hair looked great as always. "Sorry if my boys roughed you up." He smiled. "But I like you. That's why you're still alive." He pressed his lips together. "My apologies also about the girl. I don't like to hurt women, as you know. But she gave Leighton no choice."

I shrugged, the room still moving like a crazy teeter-totter. My head felt wedged in a vice grip and I threw up again, all over my suit and tie. It was a cheap tie. Zellers. I apologized for the mess.

"Hey," Migano motioned to Lou-doo. "Get him some water. Untie the ropes."

Fortunado nodded, touching the rear of the car, removing a pigeon-spot of schmutz with a chamois. Leighton was eating a sub sandwich. It was fat and I could see at least four types of cheese and even more slabs of meat. I wasn't hungry.

Fortunado ambled over to the water cooler next to the GTO, blue with chunky mag wheels on the back. I loved that car. I wish I could drive out of this fucking place in that love-ly car. The cooler gurgled, bizarrely out of rhythm with the gurgles bubbling forth from Spinner. His mouth was dotted with spots of blood. The bubbles got smaller, less dynamic in shape. By contrast, the bubbles gurgling in the cooler were huge spots on the glass.

"What are you going to do to me." It wasn't a question.

"You're a smart guy. You didn't see any of this. We already cleaned up your office. These bodies will be buried somewhere, somewhere with a poetic touch." He smiled and laughed lightly. "I like poetry."

"I'm sorry if I can't join you in the gaiety, but I'll throw up again if I laugh—" Between a window and the closed garage door was a green Coleman lantern. It was probably plastic and fueled with a small bulb and wouldn't start much of a fire. Where's a good Molotov cocktail when a fella needs it? That *was* a direct question.

"You better have a dentist look at those teeth—" He shook his head apologetically. "Molotov cocktail. You're funny, sha-mus." He smiled. "Leighton, did you have to hit him so hard?"

He shrugged and waited to swallow. "There was a gun in the room. I had to act. And he carries heat."

"But not today." Migano pointed at my empty holster.

Not today. Last I saw of the gun it was adding panache to Spinner's fashion statement.

Dull red flashed throughout the room and my head, once again, was a drowning hornet's nest, buzz buzzing inside, and I couldn't shake the sound away. "Why kill him, why? He's nothing to you. You have your money."

"Oh, you know about that." He smiled again. "Yes, I have my money. All $568,000. But he disrespected me." He pointed in the direction of a gurgling Terrien. "And for that—" He shrugged. "Justice. Poetry. Now where to put the bodies?" He tapped his chin twice and raised an eyebrow. "Yes, of course. That's where."

"He's just small-time. You're bigger than this, man."

"When people hurt me, I hurt back. Capisce?"

I looked into his eyes and then the corkboard and a hammer and a power saw. I didn't know if I had the strength to access any of these to fight my way out of here.

"You, you haven't hurt me. You're all right, Fuller. I like you. Now Davis, that guy I don't dig. Him, I'd still like to whack. Just on principle. You don't fuck other men's wives."

Migano sure had a lot of rules. I wondered if anyone ever called him Ten Commandments Migano. Or Babe "Vengeance is Mine" Migano. Or—

"You're babbling," he said.

I didn't realize I had been talking out loud.

"At least you didn't call me King Herod Migano." He smiled like a movie star.

Lou-doo handed out a paper cup of water. It slipped off the lip, onto my hand, and it tasted cool and fresh and was the best water I'd ever tasted and the freshest and I wanted more of that damn water. I even drank the spot off my hand. So I asked, please sir, can I have more? And I got more. It was even better on the second go-around.

"Right, we're good here, right? You're not going to say a word about this to your reporter friend?"

I nodded and threw up again. I shouldn't have moved my head with such vigor.

"Clean him up." He held up his hands.

One of the guys took a quick chamois to my face. Me and

the GTO—best buddies, equals, brothers in schmutz.

"It was Smith all along, wasn't it?"

Migano smiled and looked toward Spinner.

I noticed for the first time that Spinner was naked in the chair and his feet inside a large aluminum basin. They had subjected Spinner to some kind of water torture involving electric shock and a car battery, in an effort to try to discover that Smith had hired him to steal Babe's money.

"Fucking fruit," Fortunado said. "Goddamn gaylord."

"Hey, be respectful." Migano held up a hand. "The man is dying. Don't let the last words he hears be our derision."

Fortunado nodded and looked at some dirt under a fingernail. Leighton's hands were occupied with his football of a sandwich.

The room was spinning again, red and then black, a side-to-side spin. I felt lost in one of Migano's Coney Island fun houses.

"I don't care which way a man swings. I don't care. Does it matter?"

"No," I said.

Migano said he had an uncle who was a fag and nobody made fun of his uncle or else the Babe himself and his Louisville Slugger would knock him to shit. "He was a good man. Responsible. That's all that matters." He paused and looked over at Spinner. "This guy was a good man, too. A pretty good little hockey player."

I nodded. "When they gave him half a chance." I don't know how it is I remember stats but I do: twenty-seven career games, five goals, and nine assists. Feisty in the corners for a little guy. Let that be his epitaph.

Migano patted Spinner affectionately on the shoulder. His

breathing was shallower, rippled tissue paper. "But he stole. From me. Or tried to steal from me. You don't do that." He smiled. "He got in with the wrong people. Smith."

"Right." I nodded with my eyes.

"I got another surprise." He held up his left hand. All of the fingers were covered in rings. Spinner was Starzz. "He owned up to it while my boys interrogated him. He was Starzz. Look at the film again. A guy in drag lap dancing all over Leeds, making him hard."

How did Migano know about the lap dancing? The papers said nothing about that. The press's words were *sordid behavior and goings-on at the Gardens.*

"Starzz killed Leeds. Shot him with his own gun, close range." Apparently Leeds knew the killer, trusted the killer. Leeds liked Starzz. Leeds liked men in drag.

I closed my eyes and thought about the figure running between slats of rain and conical light. The shoulders were a little heavy and the flats I found in the closet *were* big. Spinner *was* Starzz. *He was outside the window, dressed as a woman. One big masquerade.*

I think I said this latter point out loud again.

"Masquerade?" Lou-doo picked at more schmutz, a spackle on the side mirror.

"Why were they in your office?" Migano pushed.

"They were going to tell me where Cathy was—for $500."

"Did you pay them?"

"I didn't get a chance to."

"Did you find out where Cathy is?"

"Again, I didn't get a chance to." I looked over at Cool Athol. He shrugged twice. Fortunado's face was motionless as he rubbed off a third spot, this one by the GTO's rocker panel.

"Try Rosedale," Migano said. "Terrien said something about Rosedale." He shrugged. "Don't ever say I never tried to help you." He smiled again.

Rosedale was an affluent neighborhood in downtown Toronto full of old money and a bunch of ex-United Empire Loyalist types who enjoyed British theatre, tea and crumpets, and worshipped the Queen. They lived in ivy-walled houses with big bay windows and a pleasant view of Whitney Park across the way. Smith had a house in Rosedale, so did his lawyers and his father, The Old Man.

"Don't try to kill Smith," I said. He's a connected guy, not in the Italian sense of the word made, but a made guy nonetheless, and they'll come after you, old money, secret-handshake society fuckers.

He touched an eyebrow with an index finger and nodded thanks.

There was a gasp of a gurgle from Terrien, a bubble splat, and then no more bubbles.

"Is he?" asked Leighton, munching his sandwich, a leaf of prosciutto draping out of the back end. He wiped a spot of mustard off his lower lip.

Migano placed a finger by the side of Terrien's neck. He waited. "He is now."

Leighton took another bite.

"I drive the car this time," Lou-doo said.

I looked around the room but didn't see any shovels.

Migano leaned over and kissed the top of Terrien's head. "Goodnight, Sweet Prince," he said.

—

THERE WAS WATER everywhere. Up to my ankles, past the cuffs of my pants. I sloshed along hardwood and water gushed from a filter fan or maybe it was an air conditioning unit or perhaps the back end of a dryer that was propped next to the stove. It bled in waves and sparkled like blue and white ticker-tape confetti.

Nick Stabulas pushed a broom along the floor as if it were a hockey stick and the water a puck he wanted to sweep into the corner of the kitchen. Whatever he was doing it wasn't working, and he pressed his lips together in a determined grimace. Nick had less hair than I remembered and his eyebrows were gone. "Help me here, Hayden."

I was standing in the water but I couldn't seem to move. My left foot felt like it was on a placemat in a bathtub and if I turned and stepped I'd fall off the world's edge. My shoulders were sore from holding my pose for so long.

Water continued pushing through the wall and Cathy, her red hair pasted to her forehead, her nightie tied up tight to her neck, was screaming to shut the water off.

"I can't," Nick said. "We need the water. We need it." He was by a toilet that didn't have any stall doors and water rippled from the top of the bowl all over the floor and onto his shoes, white, low-cut canvas sneakers. The water wasn't clean.

"Shut it off, Hayden," Cathy said to me.

It never occurred to me that she could shut off the water.

She shouted again and then her red hair turned white blonde and the face filled with the sharp angles of Sarah Kerr's.

I slid and sloshed toward the wall, wondering how does one shut off water. "Maybe we should listen to your dad."

"Shut it off, please, please, please," said the muffled voice, a suitcase mumble.

"No, I need it," Nick repeated.

I FLUTTERED MY EYES and they felt coated with soggy cereal. I rubbed out the gunk and flashed my eyes again and adjusted to the bright sun filtering through the curtains. I was on a queen-size bed, functional sheets, a puffed-up pillow under my head. The gray dresser came with an attached mirror. A compact, tubes of lipstick, and a heavy upright purse crowded the mirror. The purse had huge rings the size of those circling Saturn. I was in Stana's apartment.

I groaned. My teeth still hurt. I felt the hole in my mouth with my tongue and wondered how I got here. My tongue was sore too. I must have bit it when I got pistol-whipped. I don't remember much of what happened after Spinner died.

A shadow filled the door's threshold. It was Stana, hooking an earring into her left ear and fluffing up her hair after having just showered and touching it up with hairspray. "I was starting to worry about you." She adjusted the clasp on her watch. "I can make you an egg sandwich? Carnation Instant Breakfast?"

"Sure."

She smiled and handed me some pills. Painkillers. She had her wisdom teeth pulled two years ago, and these were the remainders. She had also set up an appointment for me with a dentist for Monday. I'd have to see Abramowitz too.

"What day is today?"

"Saturday."

I tumbled to the side of the bed and slid into my pants. The room was too bright and I asked her to close the curtains.

"They are closed," she said.

"Can you close them tighter—" I was dizzy and leaned forward, hands on thighs to anchor me. "How did I get here?" I rubbed my mouth, smelled my hand. Geez, my breath was awful.

"Babe Migano." I was rather incoherent last night, and then passed out upright in the doorway standing between Leighton and Fortunado.

"How do they know where you live?" My head was cluttered up with dirty cotton candy, only now it felt like it was spun Plaster of Paris.

"I'm in the phone book, silly." She shrugged, hooking in another earring. "And I guess they know we're kind of an item."

I nodded, pushing my arms into my soiled shirt. It didn't smell any better than my breath. I took the shirt off and tossed it on a chair. I'd go with the T-shirt look, me and Brando and James Dean.

"Coffee?"

"Sure."

She left for the kitchen and I wobbled to my feet and stumbled into my shoes. Rosedale, Migano said. Rosedale. I had to get to Rosedale. Smith's house also had construction done by Bolemac and no doubt there was a sliding panel in a study somewhere and hopefully Cathy behind that panel. Rosedale.

I wandered to the kitchen, bumping the dresser on my way out, my steps surprisingly light. An egg was frying and the instant coffee warmed my hands. I took a sip and struggled to swallow. I was a mess. And I didn't know what to believe anymore. I looked at my fingers. "You know, I was just wondering—Migano—right?"

"Right." Her eyes narrowed slightly as her hands gripped a

coffee mug. Steam curled off the lip in backward S's.

"How did he know where Lisa and Spinner were?" Migano's men had come to my office. I thought it odd that it wasn't Stana with the Chinese food. Instead, it was Lou-doo and Cool Athol.

"I guess they had been tailing Spinner and Lisa from King Street. Remember you said someone saw them at an A&P on King. Followed them to your office—"

"No. Spinner was a skittish cat. He was too careful." I shoved my hands in my pockets. "I called you. I told you to bring the money—"

"Yes. That was yesterday—"

"Don't humor me—the money. You see. That's where you slipped up, Stana." I leaned against a chair in the kitchen to anchor me and blinked my eyes, hoping to regain feeling in my face. "You forgot the money."

"Forgot?" There was just one S curling now, slow and steamy.

"I called you, told you to bring the money. You called Migano." There was no anger in my voice. It was just flat and dead, the way I felt . . . inside. "You called Migano."

"That's—that's—a" She plunked her cup of coffee on the Formica table. "You're starting to really piss me off. You know what—"

"Oh, am I? I'm pissing you off?" I pointed to the bedroom. "Go get your bag, your purse. The one that looks like a milk crate. If there's $500 in it, I'll eat my words. I'll apologize."

"I'm not going to get my purse. These accusations are—"

"Unwarranted? You never went to the bank. You called Migano and his boys showed up instead of you. Get your purse. Get the $500—"

"Do you realize what you're accusing me of—you—I love you—"

"Get it. Two more people dead, because of a phone call." I kind of liked Terrien. He was a little guy, feisty, honest. "Show me the money." I rubbed my face again. Even my eyes felt numb.

"I already took the money back. There's no money in the purse—"

"It's Saturday. The banks aren't open." I slammed a chair against the table and headed through the kitchen and to her apartment door. "Did you think they'd kill me too? What did you think would happen?"

"I didn't *think* they'd kill you—"

"That's right, you didn't think. You were just protecting yourself and the next story you had to write. I'm just a *character* in one of your goddamn stories."

"Hayden—"

"Save it." It was cold outside but the sun was a burning egg and maybe it would get to be a better day.

I TOOK THE TTC to my office, and once I climbed the stairs to the second floor, I realized that I didn't remember a thing about the ride over on the subway. Who sat next to me? What books were people reading? Were they reading books? What was that conversation about between the young couple—her hugging his shoulders—across from me? Were they even talking?

I stumbled to the hard sink. It was next to my hat rack. I splashed my face with cold water and used the hat rack to steady me. Damn I didn't have my porkpie. I must've left it at Stana's. I stuck my head under the sink and the water ran and ran and ran. It was cold and felt good.

My .38 was lying atop my desk. That was real polite of Lou-doo and Athol to leave me some artillery. It hadn't done Spinner any good, but maybe it could come in handy for yours truly. I visited the cop shop's indoor pistol shooting range twice a week, sporting both earplugs and over-the-head earmuffs, scoring nines and tens on the target's rings. I sighed and struggled opening the top desk drawer. It was stuck. But I finally shook it loose, grabbed some extra shells, and noticed that the chair behind me was dotted with two faint starbursts of blood. They couldn't clean it all away.

I breathed heavily. Rosedale.

The phone rang. Seven, eight, ten times.

It rang again. The receiver had smudges all over it. I'd clean it later.

Eight, nine, ten.

101 days ago, Sarah Kerr's body was found in a suitcase.

I left the office, my shoulders not as heavy, my mouth hurting like hell.

NICK STABULAS WASN'T at his grocery store. Hadn't been seen since his bail. Kim wasn't there either. A neighborhood girl was manning the place. Because of my sore teeth, I passed up on buying some popcorn with the damn jolly circus elephant on the box.

Smith wasn't home either. I called and called. Moments later, I was tearing up the steps of the Gardens, looking for Pal Cal's bunker. I knocked on the door. It wasn't gentle.

"You trying to break my collectibles," Pal Cal said, with a big smile on his face, as he opened the door. "Oh, it's you." He wore a red robe, tied loosely at his generous waist. Wisps of chest hair poked out from the robe's pleated fabric. It was a bad look.

"Where's Smith?" He wasn't answering calls, he's not in his office, and Lefty, the Zamboni driver, said Smith's usually here by noon on game day.

"Probably out golfing, who knows?" Bullard shrugged. His face was craggy, and the lines around his mouth gave him the look of a marionette. He wasn't eating potato chips. There wasn't a fleck anywhere.

"Hockey season's not over. He wouldn't be golfing. God damn it. This is game day. Where is he?"

He held up a hand. It was covered with three Stanley Cup rings. "I'm not his keeper."

"Migano's going to kill him, because he double-crossed the cat. He's going—"

Bullard blinked his eyes and took a step back. "Migano's not my concern—"

"Stop it. I know you're the brains behind Bolemac—he's your partner. Migano's your partner. You guys squeezed Smith out. I get it—"

"Well thanks." He crossed his arms and beamed, the robe bunching up even more by his portly waist. "It's nice to get recognized once in a while. Everyone thinks I'm some kind of clown, a buffoon. No, I'm smart. I have business savvy."

"You and Migano are buying up land in Vaughan. Building a city. Whatever. Smith hated that, being excluded, wanted in. You didn't let him in, right? Are you going to let me in your office?"

"Well, you see?" He shrugged, the corners of his mouth rising. A female voice behind him giggled. Through the space between his arm and hip, I saw Laurinda reclined along the top of a wet bar. Her legs crossed. She was topless. Flecks of chips were all over her breasts and belly.

"I'm kind of busy right now." Pal Cal smiled.

"Right." I should have known. I let out a sharp sigh. "You don't care what happens to Smith, do you?"

"Not really." He shrugged. He was ready to make the break from his partner and find his own independence.

"He stole from Migano and Migano's going to deep six him," I said.

"You need comp tickets for tonight's game?" Bullard laughed, looked over his shoulder and gave a gentle flutter of the fingers at Laurinda. His jowls shook as the door closed, separating me from his bunker house of fun.

I WAS AT ROSEDALE in less than ten minutes and parked out front of Smith's palace. In terms of size, it appeared only slightly smaller than Maple Leafs Gardens.

Maple trees lined the pathway to the front door and vines and lush greenery covered the house's second-floor cathedral-style windows and arches like an inviting beard. The high windows were wide expressive eyes looking upon the curved driveway and the interloper below.

I shoved my hands in my pockets, glanced around and ran. Bits of stones and small sticks snapped and clicked as I reached the front door. The sun dropped below a line of big trees and Smith's place was awash in shadows. By contrast, his Rolls glinted in the glare. I pushed the doorbell. Nothing.

I waited. Tried the door. It opened.

It hadn't been closed all the way.

I wondered if this was all a trap and feared whether a fancy alarm system would be blaring in less than thirty seconds—I certainly didn't know what three-digit code to punch in to deactivate the system—and the police could be wailing up the driveway any moment now. Swell.

I walked quickly past hard-edged furniture, a thick armoire, and crossed cutlasses above a shelf and some kind of African spear and giant mask in a far corner by a spittoon. I called Smith's name and looked about a room with an L-shaped couch and shag rugs. The line of the sun caused my watch to glow and bounce light on the ceiling. There was nothing on the ceiling, of course, but the bounce effect and sudden spot of glare made me spot another lens of light, caught by the sun at the foot of one of the couch's legs.

It was Smith's Lombardis. They were resting awkwardly on the side of their frames. One of the temple pieces was twisted and there was blood along the grooves of the hinge. Smith was probably smacked with an open hand or the barrel of a pistol.

Shit.

I placed the glasses in my coat pocket and lifted my snubnosed .38 from its side holster. I hurried past an open foyer area, with more couches, chairs, shag rugs, and portraits of the Leafs from the 1940s, including Syl Apps, Teeder Kennedy, and Harry Watson.

I hustled down a flight of short stairs to what was clearly an entertainment center. Three televisions were positioned high on the wall for simultaneous access to major area stations: CBC, CTV, and CHCH out of Hamilton.

The closest wall of the foyer was awash in terrariums, green speckled plants that looked like obscure species of octopus or artichokes. They rested in a desert setting or among smooth stones or dark moss and it was a strange mix—colors and shapes and climates that just didn't fit. There might have even been some orchids in the wall art, but I don't know, the whole shebang just seemed to be trying too damn hard. Cover my walls with art prints: Renoir, Matisse, even Rothko with his all black or white or red canvases. These glass gardens were like an ungroomed dog. I wanted to throw a stick and have all the terrariums chase after it and exit the room.

A roulette wheel was to my left, another straight ahead. A craps table was to my right and on the wet bar were a few eight-sided revolving poker chip racks. A bottle of scotch was next to them. Empty.

Migano? I guess a lot of fellas drink scotch.

I breathed quickly, hoping a secret alarm wasn't covertly sounding somewhere, exposing me. The sliding panel in Smith's Gardens office was behind a bookshelf. This room had no bookshelves. There wasn't a discarded Steinbeck anywhere.

I sighed.

Was Cathy still here? Was Smith dead?

I circled the roulette tables and found a switch on the farthest one. I toggled it back, and suddenly the wall across from the terrariums slid open, and sharp light cut a blocky path in front of me. I tightened my grip on my gun.

And in the glare, I saw the silhouette of a woman.

12

She walked into the light, red and white flannel shirt, blue jeans, and tennis shoes: an Ivory Soap kind of purity. She had a strong, proud chin.

"Stana? What are you doing here?"

I holstered my gun.

"Your hat." She held out my porkpie. Her eyes were full of sadness, pulled down to resemble the tails of wasps.

I said nothing.

She played with the thin necklace around her neck. The ankh appeared upside down.

I pushed the porkpie back on my head and wondered again what the hell she was doing here.

She had heard me mention Rosedale several times in my sleep the other night and figured this was the next place I'd look for Cathy so she headed here, hoping we'd cross paths, and she could explain about, about—

"Letting Lisa and Spinner die—?"

"I didn't know he was going to—"

"Come on, Stana, don't be so disingenuous. What did you think was going to happen? They were going to play a wicked game of pinochle? Please. Don't bullshit me—"

"No, I—I—was scared—and I certainly wouldn't have sent you to your death—I—"

"I don't want to hear it. I'm tired. I want to find Cathy."

I quickly surveyed the room. Nothing. No perfume; no *East of Eden*; no jazz records. But it was loaded with more offbeat details. The floor was dull concrete; the walls cinder blocks on one side, wood paneling on the other. But what really got me were the accoutrements: eight or nine machine guns draped the wall, black flags on a different kind of golf course, black flags probably lifted from the Old Man's militia. They were vintage Tommys and AK-47s, with round cartridges and banana-curved. There was also hand grenades from Canadian pineapples to German potato mashers, tear-gas shells, and tear-gas masks. On a short shelf were stacks of money, positioned sideways. On a longer shelf were rolls and rolls of 8mm film in plastic cans.

There was a white space on the wall where a machine gun had once been. A missing AK-47?

"She's not here." Stana shrugged. "But—" She stepped aside and with a sweeping gesture announced, behind her, our guest, Mr. Steven Smith, President of the Leafs. A blue and white towel was firmly placed in his mouth. "Oh, and this note was pinned to a lapel."

Took you long enough.

Migano. Who else? What a genius. He didn't have to kill Smith, just truss him all up for us to find tied to a chair, and let us explore his secret lair and discover even more damage, the crucial chunks of evidence to nail his secret-handshake-society ass.

Smith didn't look so hot. His face had sharp cut lines and a shallow gouge by his forehead. There was a welt the size of a small potato where an eyebrow should be.

I moved toward the rolls and rolls of film.

AK-47. That's what was fired in our direction, 101 days ago, the day Sarah Kerr was killed.

Smith shook in the chair, his arms vibrating rapidly, his eyes straining. He was mumbling something that vaguely echoed Marlon Brando's bop speech, "you got to put something down," in *The Wild One.*

"Just stay the way you are, Mr. Smith. It's a good look for you."

His eyes darkened and both of his chalky eyebrows arched like angry cats as he rattled the chair. I thought he was going to pile-drive a hole into the floor.

I pried the towel from Smith's thin lips. "Who'd you loan the AK-47 to, Mr. People?"

"Fuck you."

"I reapplied the towel and turned to Stana. "Give me a hand here, will ya? Let's check these out." I pointed at the film cans and slowly twisted off a lid.

It didn't have the polish of good stag material or the charm of France's cinema vérité movement, but it was incriminating footage nonetheless, footage many of the subjects would rather see burned or buried.

As I slowly unfurled roll upon roll, I unearthed offbeat images of women grinding on men's laps, prominent men playing poker, spinning the roulette wheel, tossing dice, or pinning the pasty on a naked woman wearing a haggard donkey mask. One of the donkey's eyes was missing.

Members of parliament were present, and hockey legends like a forty-goal scorer for Detroit and our own Danny Davis with a naked red-headed girl grinding away on his lap while another naked girl, big and blond, towels off with Davis's tie, shimmying about like a low-rent Chubby Checker.

No, it wasn't state of the art. The camera was stationary and the subjects often moved in and out of the frame, blurring lines between the seen and unseen, but this was incendiary stuff.

"Look at the background." Stana pointed at the corrugated curtains, the wet bar and the apparent blue and white chrome. The film was in black and white but this was clearly Smith's secret hideaway, the party room beyond the sliding bookshelf at the Gardens. "How you doing, Mr. People?" I smiled in Smith's direction.

He and the chair slowly fell sideways and his feet kicked the air like a scuttling crab.

"Blackmail, no doubt?" Stana shook her head with disapproval.

"No doubt."

What we discovered in Leeds's locker matched up with this. It was a direct connect. Steven Smith, the Bell and Howell auteur, was the maestro, making these movies for his own twisted purposes: to exploit, to scare, to intimidate.

Smith mumbled and Stana laughed.

"So how did you get here exactly, Stana? Migano? Did he drive you here? Let you in?"

Yes, she called Migano, asking for the three-number passcode to disarm the alarm. She deliberately left the door open, for me.

"Oh." I nodded. "And how did you find this secret lair?"

She played with a collared corner to her red-and-white checkered shirt and rubbed under her nose with the back of a hand. "Migano told me where the switch is—"

"Migano again. Always with the Migano—"

"I want to explain about that, about—" She chewed on the collar corner's tip.

"I don't want to hear—" *Did one of Migano's men, Athol, kill Sarah?*

"You say you don't want to hear about it, but you do—"

I sighed dismissively.

There was no underage porn among our findings: no moving images of Leeds's therapy girls, no Lisa Steinmetz at sixteen or seventeen.

However, with foot upon foot of the grainy images we did find, Smith could get what he wants when he wants. A zoning law changed so he can build or add to his empire: *no problem, Mr. Smith. Just don't show my movie.* A politician to back whatever side project would benefit the Leafs' Czar: no problem, Mr. Smith. Just don't show my movie. A Leafs hockey player who deserves a pay raise but is denied by upper management: *no problem, Mr. Smith. Just don't show my movie.*

Favors. That's what all these subjects on film owed him: favors. He was king of the cinema.

I dialed the cop shop and was patched right into Sal Lambertino. "What's the score of the game?"

"It hasn't started yet, asshole. Not for another six hours." He laughed.

"I know, I know. Just yanking your chain. But you're not going to believe this. Smith was getting beat up by some punks, they bloodied his glasses—I got the specs in my pocket—no, no he's okay—no, no, he can't talk right now, but you'll want to talk to him. After the hooligans fled I just happened to stumble onto Smith's secret lair. Like the one in the Gardens, and well, we hit the mother lode here, pal, the *Gone with the*

Wind of evidence. One crime committed after another. All caught on film. Bring the vice squad."

Sal knew the Rosedale address, and I imagined him subtly scratching at his fence of a Hemingway beard. Would this find hold up since I didn't have a warrant?

"What warrant? I'm not a peace officer, Sal. Smitty was in trouble. I had reasonable and probable grounds to enter his domicile and to rescue him from the hooligans—no, they got away, no—can I help it if I happened to stumble upon this cache of smut?"

He said he'd get a judge's order fast, a warrant to haul in all of this and Smith's bony ass.

"Try to get that judge who is a Habs fan," I said.

That just cracked him up.

I hung up and turned to Smitty. "Well, Mr. People. Help's on its way."

Smith swore with his eyes, while his feet kept scuttling the air.

Stana elbowed me in the side and gently nudged additional 8mm film into my fingers. McClelland Stuart, in his homburg, drank milk in a big chair while a curvy girl rubbed her breasts up against his face, and then drank his milk for him.

Damn.

And then after twenty or so minutes of unfurling additional film, I found footage of what I probably already knew but didn't want to have confirmed.

There was a woman with white blonde hair, her bare back to the camera, her shoulders angled. Tan lines were noticeable between the spaces where her bra should be and wasn't.

She turned slowly toward the camera. A Mardi-Gras mask was firmly in place as she walked closer and closer, placing her in a saucy medium close-up shot, hands on hips.

Her breasts were small, perky, not quite fully developed. There was a mole between them.

Suddenly I knew which girl was the elusive Starzz.

HOURS LATER, Kim must have still been out showing houses because I wasn't able to reach her about Cathy. Nick wasn't back at the store and his whereabouts were still unknown. Smith was in a holding tank downtown and the CBC was trying to figure out whether or not to break the subject on air tonight. Migano must have been laughing in his ski lodge at how this had all played out for his soon-to-be-ex-auxiliary partner. Stana was with me at Mainly Drew's, drinking a single Guinness. I was knocking back my second tonic water—probably not a good idea given the hole in my mouth.

"Okay, I'm ready to listen—" I cupped my hands together and turned sideways in the booth. "Shoot."

The hockey game was on the wall above me. The Leafs had some pop, especially Davis, who had missed a glorious chance from the slot. The puck hopped over his stick. Seconds later he missed another opportunity by the side of the net.

"You make it sound as if I'm in the goldfish room—*shoot*."

"Goldfish room?"

"You know with the bright lights and the cops standing around, hands on hips as their cigarette smoke twists toward the ceiling fans—"

"That's only in the movies. I'm not as cool as the cats in the movies. This is real and there's two people dead." I held up two crooked fingers for emphasis. "I stood by helplessly as both of them died. And I feel sick about it—"

Strangely, however, my head was actually doing much better: no dizziness, no foggy patches of memory, no feeling like I'm about to throw up in my mouth.

"God damn it." I pointed at the TV. Béliveau again on a screen shot—fuck. Bower had no chance, 1-0 Habs.

Stana nodded absently. She wasn't covering this game. She felt a greater need to come to terms with me. We had been lovers and now we're just friends. I had told her that we could never go back to being lovers again. A line had been crossed.

Even worse, there was no way to get Migano for the killings. We knew that. What evidence did we have? The bodies would never be found. And if they were, I'd be dead.

She twisted her shoulders and absently stirred her drink even though it wasn't the type that needed stirring. I wanted to yank the straw from her but opted to play this moment with blue-note cool, laid back like a John Coltrane tenor sax riff.

Stana paused, collecting her thoughts, two slender fingers caressing the side of her face. She wore a violet dress, stamped with red-shaped designs that could easily have passed for a hanging series of shoe insoles. The dress was high-necked, covering the clavicles, and the sleeves rested just above the elbows. She had four bracelets on her left wrist. They didn't seem to make a sound when she gestured. "Migano and I—" Her hand left her face and tapped the top of her glass.

"Yes?"

"Had a fling last year after you and me were done—"

"You and Babe Migano?"

"Yes."

I couldn't believe this. She had an affair with one of the

kingpins, perhaps *the* biggest kingpin, in Toronto's organized crime world. Sure, he oozed style, élan, and cool. And yes, at least he had respect for women, unlike Smith and Bullard, but bottom line he was a kingpin.

Migano, with his connections to the Leafs, had hinted at getting Stana greater access to the players and perhaps even featuring her as the host for a new series he was creating with yet another pot of money he was shifting around.

Toronto After Dark would feature the Oscar Peterson Trio and air on an indie UHF channel. It would be all about hockey, player profiles, their lifestyles, and Stana would interview Leafs greats past and present, their wives and girlfriends. Their discussions would cover everything from politics to cooking to great books to read.

"You fell for that? Come on, Stana."

She played with her hands, the bracelets soundlessly spinning. "I was at a loss after you were gone—I—"

"Don't put this on me—" Yes I didn't return her calls and letters, but Migano the gangster? And then I thought about what Kim said days ago, *a woman doesn't care how a man makes his money, just how he makes love.* She was in love with him too. Everybody loved Migano. "You just wanted to get ahead and this was another one of your pragmatic moves, like running the story about Small Bear, his wife, and Davis," I said.

"I thought you forgave me for that—"

I looked at my fingers. "You're an opportunist—"

She turned sharply and leaned against the table, her shoulders throwing her forward. "*Smith* photographed me and Migano, making love in the CEO's office. The camera was running, the one behind the two-way glass. I had no idea."

"You were at Coughlins?"

"No. It was a date. Migano took me to Smith's office to discuss business and one thing led—"

Didn't I see? She and Migano were *victims*, subjects to be ruled by King Smith's blackmail threats. Only this time Migano got proactive. He learned the alarm code to Smith's Rosedale residence, broke in, and after hours of searching the film's library, found the damaging 8mm evidence. He probably also lifted a few other gems, ones he could use for leverage against the CEO and president, maybe even a gritty little ditty featuring Starzz dancing on Leeds's lap. Maybe an AK-47 to boot.

"You did *it* in Smith's office?"

"I didn't *do it*. I made love. Yes."

"How was he? I bet Babe was real good—"

"Well—" She looked away.

"Right."

And once Migano got the film back he decided to go after the blackmailer through indirect means.

"Very indirect," I said. "What did Migano want from you in return for this film he stole?"

"My allegiances, my help, a favor." She couldn't look at me.

"How long have you been in his pocket?"

"*Pocket*? That sounds so dirty—"

"Well, it is dirty—he said he had someone inside—'Aces.'" *His words, not mine.*

"A while," she cut me off.

"How long?"

"Months," she admitted.

How much information about this case was Migano feeding me through Stana? What about the toupee and the note hidden under the cheesecloth? "That was a set-up, too easy, too convenient, wasn't it? That note, the combination numbers, everything, and you knew it and directed me to planted evidence at Hart House."

I snapped my fingers. "Of course. You knew Leeds was dead before we even went over there. You checked in with Migano while I was interviewing Kim and then drove alone in the Galaxie to Leeds's office, checked his corpse, and planted evidence. Then returned in plenty of time before I got done with Kim."

She looked through my shoulder.

"Who did Migano say killed Leeds? And don't tell me Terrien. That's just another smokescreen—" *Another lie, another cheap amusement.*

She played with the lip of her glass and tears slowly splattered on the tabletop. "Kim. He said, Kim. But don't quote me, that's—"

"*Off the record?*"

"Don't be like that—"

"Decorum? Now. Please." Kim was too cool during our interview to have just killed a man. But maybe she did do it, and that's why she made all those damn overtures at me, to distract herself. I sighed sharply. "The stuff in that locker wasn't even Leeds's—right?"

"Not the 8mm film, no," she said. "That was Smith's. But the photographs were Leeds's." She shrugged and didn't touch the tears of her eyes. It was an arresting tableau, one I didn't feel at liberty to fix.

"Apples and oranges, huh? The apples are Leeds's photos. The oranges are Smith's films, and Bullard's not as stupid as everybody thinks. The two *aren't* connected. Apples and fucking oranges." I threw my hands up with disgust.

"I can't look at you when we talk about this—"

"You better look at me. You didn't have to look at Lisa and Spinner as they died. Lisa went over very fast. Two shots, like hammering a nail. Dead." I snapped my fingers.

"Please—"

"Spinner took a lot longer to die. Blood bubbles kept popping from his mouth and his eye was out of its orbital bone—"

She covered her mouth with her hands and her eyes crowded together.

I never thought I'd tell her what I had seen in that garage, but I wasn't feeling like Hayden Fuller anymore. I was somebody else. "Well, Stana, all of this—us, the case, Lisa and Spinner, Smith and his films—is fucking messy. Look at me—"

Her eyes were red-rimmed, the mascara unbalanced star-pointed smears.

"And then there was Cathy. She was about to spill the whole thing. The works about Coughlins, her father, maybe even Babe Migano. But then she found out you were in cahoots with the Babe and she couldn't trust you and she got real scared. Would you turn her over to the Babe? Would he kill her? Rather than give you an exclusive she had to go hide. She's in exile because of you—"

"That's not true."

"Bullshit." I grabbed her by the chin, my voice calm, but my face itching like I had on a mask with a dirty string rubbing at the back of my head, around my ears, and a third face was emerging, one part avenging angel and another all hellhound. "He called in the favor, right? Give me Cathy. And she caught wind. Maybe from Kim—she knows Babe. Heard him talk. Warned her sister. Loves her sister despite the pain of her father's love for the one and not the other. Loves her sister even more than she loves Migano, who she has a thing with."

"No."

"Come on, the truth. He wanted you to give her up."

"I wouldn't do that—"

"Sure you wouldn't." I tapped my fingertips together. "Babe did say give me Lisa and Spinner, didn't he? I'm curious. How did he ask? Was his voice a polite carnal purr of a European car?"

I let go of her chin.

"You son of a bitch," she mumbled, her mouth full of tears. He just wanted to talk to Lisa and Spinner. "I didn't think he'd kill them. Maybe rough them up a little—he wanted information, he wanted to know—"

"He also wanted to *talk* to Cathy didn't he? Goddamn it, tell me the truth. No fucking lies."

"Yes."

"He wanted to hurt them, hurt them all—that's all—there was nothing else behind his motivations. Nothing." I waved her and her explanations away with a quick hand flip and we didn't say anything for five or so minutes.

I couldn't even follow the damn hockey game. My face was aflame, my eyes cinders.

I wondered how I could ever have loved her.

Another five minutes passed.

Rosedale. We didn't nail Smith the first time with the evidence Migano planted in Leeds's locker, but the second go-around sure did the trick. The second tip explains everything—Migano's desires to vaporize Smith from the goddamn planet. Cathy was *never* at Rosedale. Another false lead. *Another cheap amusement.*

She tapped her glass of Guinness. I looked into my glass of tonic water, the bubbles flat.

From a phone booth, I called Kim again. No answer. Nick: nothing. Before the end of the second period, Small Bear tied up the game on a wrist shot that slithered through Lorne "Gump" Worsley's chest protector.

When I returned to the table, Stana was gone. I finished my tonic water and decided it was time to honor the dead.

THE RIDE TO VAUGHAN on Highway 400 North, the old Toronto-Barrie run, took me just over an hour. I had the windows wide open, and the air was crisp and cool and reminded me of flying kites with my dad.

We never did a whole lot together, my father and me. He was often sleeping the hard rest of the drunk on a couch or hitting my mother, but every now and then he took me to a hockey game or helped fly a red kite at Wilket Creek Park, letting out more and more string as the kite rose and flapped, and appeared to hang still in the sky like a spot of mercury, a wobbly iris.

For a second, the glare off the overhanging streetlights blazed streamers on the windshield that reminded me of my kite tail, swimming with sky.

After inching down a long skinny road that turned from pavement to gravel to dirt, I was at the site, the huge acreage of land that Bullard and Migano had bought up. I shut off the lights and walked and walked and walked.

I saw thin spots of cabins, like discarded dice, in the distance. Sarah and the suitcase. 101 days ago.

There were sentries of CAT machines and bulldozers parked next to the cabins. The discarded dice were to be demolished, forgotten.

The sky was full of silver: the stars and moon creating pockets of silence for me to slide into. A red flag marked one corner of the property. The expanse between me and where black sky touched ground was a hard disc. I couldn't see any other flags.

Migano said he was going to do something poetic. What would be more poetic than to bury the bodies on this hallowed place where his dream would be built?

I walked further, my hands in my pockets, my head no longer hurting, my eyes on the stars, and I spoke, mumbled, some words, incoherent but a mashed-up narrative nonetheless. About Lisa, I lamented how she had been given a tough break, an abusive father, another man, the father of a friend, who betrayed and manipulated her, and how that hurt made her want to hurt back, and that there was a sadness to her, a sadness that nobody, except maybe Spinner, really wanted to extinguish. She was forgotten, but not for me.

And then I said an epitaph for Spinner, how he was a guy underestimated by many and deserved better than he got and I think he was good for Lisa. I could see it in their eyes—I think they really cared about each other. Gay or not, he loved her.

And I stood there under the stars. Breathed and understood.

I wanted to curse the heavens and not cry, but I did cry, for them, myself, for Stana. For all of us.

It was an act of mourning.

And then I heard it. Chains click-click-clicking as wheels

slowly climbed the sky, and then voices, thousands of voices screaming—joy and pain—as wheels, hundreds of them, thudded and pounded wooden tracks.

And a giant wheel, and another, and another, spinning not together, but in different arcs, to my right, to my left, full of bright lights glowing slowly, as cars twisted, and more joyous voices rained down.

And below the Ferris wheels, people on the boardwalk, eating cotton candy, talking, kissing, running, lost in funhouses, barrels spinning, floors turning faster and faster, as crowded folks fall from the human roulette wheel and huddle and bunch and grip together like a charm bracelet of bodies.

And somewhere a kid with a red kite enjoys all of this, standing back from the midway's attractions, drinking a cola. Afterward he tosses balls at wood bottles and thinks this bazaar, this wondrous place that Babe Migano has built, this is indeed Canada's Bazaar, and it is indeed pretty glorious.

13

It didn't take long to get back into the city. Most of the traffic was going the other way after the Leafs' overtime win over Montreal. I had listened to what was left of the game on the radio. Davis scored the tying goal midway through the third—the crowd had been booing him all night. Maybe they were upset over the point-blank chances the ex-scoring champ had missed, or maybe they had caught wind of Stana's ongoing investigation and how he was about to be named as a frequent guest at Coughlins. In less than an hour, I'd have even more of a story for Stana.

I wish her well. I mean that. I'm not being ironic. Well, not that ironic.

I dry swallowed another painkiller.

The gang was all there at Kim's apartment. Cool Athol and Lou-doo filled the door behind me, arms folded with command presence. Lou's hair, liquid napalm, had enough pomade to burn a town. Athol wore his Oliver Hardy bowler and his hands were on his hips, flaring his jacket so that I could see that he had a side-holster too. His eyes flitted about like hovering dragonflies.

Babe Migano wore a dark suit, a jaunty pink rose in the

lapel, and he slowly sipped scotch. "Salut." He raised the shot glass. "Nice job on Smith."

"Thanks, but right now I have bigger fish to fry." I tipped my porkpie.

I smiled, my legs, shoulders and arms loose like a pool hustler ready to pocket a tricky combination shot. The headaches were gone. The room quieted. A clock that looked like a cat's face stuttered, eyes moving left, right.

Kim pulled her legs closer to her chin. She was sitting in her big comfy chair. I didn't smell Chanel. She twisted hair behind one of her ears and sighed.

"All right, you ready for the big finish?" I planted myself in front of a coffee table and rubbed hands together. I smiled my lupine lopsided grin, the same smart-ass leer that's riding on my private investigator's license.

"How about those Leafs, huh?" Lou-doo interrupted, a clumsy attempt to loosen the tension his boss and his girlfriend were feeling. "Keon in overtime. That guy's money."

I nodded. McClelland's radio play-by-play had suggested that Big Z's forecheck forced J. C. Tremblay to cough up the puck, and then Keon corralled the pass, broke in on Worsley, and beat the Gumper stick-side with a backhand. Programs splashed down as the home crowd let out a pent-up cheer of relief. The Leafs were back in the series.

"Money," Lou-doo repeated.

"Shut up, Lou." Migano smiled at me. Even his pink rose appeared to be smiling. "It's your floor, shamus." He looked at his watch. "But I do want to catch Peterson's final set at the White Heat, so pick up the pace."

"Sure, anything for jazz." I smiled back. "It took me a long time to figure this case. What with all the lies and double-crosses." I held up a finger. "There was one constant. Love, people helping and covering up for others out of love. With every case, I ask that central question. Where's the love? Why was Cathy abducted and who did it? Simple, huh?" I laughed. "But it wasn't that simple. Cathy wasn't abducted."

I rubbed the edges of my mouth. Kim tucked her knees in tighter. She *did* look wonderful in Capris. Giant hoop earrings caught the light and enunciated the flash line along her lower jaw.

"Cathy found out that Stana is on your payroll, Babe. So she couldn't trust her. The story she was about to break about Coughlins and all the shenanigans going on at the Gardens, forget about it. She feared the story would never break and she'd wind up a corpse buried out on that big subdivision you're building an amusement park on."

That got a response. Migano leaned forward and Athol's hand moved closer to his pistol. "Leeds was the key. He wasn't killed by Terrien. That kid couldn't have harmed anyone." I lifted Kim's chin and smiled. "*You* know where Cathy is." I walked to the stonewall and thumbed the lip of the ledge.

Kim no longer looked at me. She was worrying the inside of her mouth.

"Look, Landover was killed by someone he knew. There were powder burns on his chest. Close range." I shoved my hands in my pockets. "For some reason, Babe, you thought Kim did it. Why? Because she told you she did."

"What?" Babe was no longer looking at his smiling flower.

"Stana told me, although she swears that comment's off the record." I shrugged. "You love Kim, Babe, and when she told you what she allegedly did you tried to cover for her. You sent Stana over there to plant evidence. The toupee and the hidden 'key' to a locker full of smut. And let's not forget the trumped-up Terrien angle. The fucking shoes."

Babe looked back at the flower in his lapel and smiled slightly. "What about the girl you saw in the street without shoes on?"

"Oh, Stana told you about that. Your ace, huh?" My lips formed a tight line. "I saw a girl all right, but she *was* wearing shoes. I expected her not to be so I projected—"

"Bullshit," Athol said, eyes narrowing.

I turned and slapped hands over the front of my shirt. "What color's my tie?"

"Huh?" Migano's face creased like an avant-garde painting.

"Answer it."

"Black like the skinny one you wore for our first meeting." The tents around his shoulders puffed up again.

"That's right," Lou-doo said. "Black like the Ace of Spades."

"He's not wearing a tie," Cool Athol said, his fingers gracing the gun's checkered grip.

The way his eyes danced around every area code but this one, I figured the cat wasn't taking in anything, but I was wrong. I made a note not to underestimate him.

"Right." I pointed at Athol, revealing my open-collared tieless look. Cool Athol was on his game. "But two of you seemed to think there was one there. Our eyes play tricks all the time—that night I saw what I wanted to see." I started laughing and I couldn't quite stay on top of it. Maybe I wasn't quite the relaxed pool shark that I thought I was. "It wasn't Kim that killed Leeds. It wasn't Terrien either dressed up as Starzz. What a reach that is. Starzz was Sarah. The first girl killed, 101 days ago. I've seen the film. The mole on her chest.

Cathy was Sarah's friend, and Nick was involved with Sarah. It's all hunches of course, but detectives go on instincts. The night of Sarah's murder she had been raped. Someone's going to pay for that." I touched stone ridges, feeling for a toggle switch. "Cathy tried to protect Sarah. Sarah ends up dead. Nobody's seen Starzz in three months. The Orient? Really?" I laughed. "With her friend murdered, Cathy wants to get even, spill the whole Coughlins story to Stana, but Kim loves her sister and warns her about you Babe and the reporter on your payroll. So what does Cathy do? Goes underground." I looked over at Kim. "Right?"

Kim nodded at her knees.

Athol took a step forward.

"As a matter of fact, Kim loves her sister so much that she's willing to take the rap for her." I started laughing again. It wasn't how I wanted to play this.

Kim rushed from her seat, as if she were going to hit me, and then changed her mind. She stood before me, her lower lip wobbling. "I'm glad you didn't hit me, or else I'd have to hipcheck you into that chair." I smiled. "Sorry, I'm an ex-hockey player. Some habits die hard."

She smiled slightly. She didn't want to, but she did. She sat back down.

"Cathy's hiding is really a kind of voluntary seclusion, courtesy of Kim. Kim's no warden, she gives her sister the freedom to come and go as she pleases. One night, Cathy goes and visits Leeds, convinces him, for old times' sake, to open his gun box, and he lets her even play with the gun for a while, and guns go off as guns do—"

"My sister never killed anyone—"

"This time she did. You convinced Babe that you did it to

get back the $568,000, but it was Cathy."

"How about that Keon," Lou-doo mumbled with glee.

"Shut up, Lou," Babe said, his voice low, easy.

"She did it for Sarah. She knew about Leeds, the Tangerine Room, the therapy sessions—"

Someone had to pay for Sarah and her death, 101 days ago.

"Boss, you want me to shut this guy up." Athol's fingers tightened along his gun's checkered grip. His eyes hovered over me, then back to his boss, and then the shag rug and maybe parts of downtown Toronto. He had a hard time staying in the vicinity. I wasn't even sure he was in the 416 area code.

"No, no. Let him rave. I admire his chutzpah. That's a Jewish word fellas, for balls."

"More or less," I said with a shrug. "But women can have chutzpah too." I turned to Lou-doo. "How about that Keon."

He nodded proudly. "Keon's money, man." And he wasn't just talking figuratively. Apparently Fortunado put down $200 on the game and Keon's goal helped put Lou-doo in the coin, big time. "I couldn't believe the odds I was getting," he said.

"I'm happy for you."

Lou-doo smiled like a ten-year-old.

Cool Athol's fingers twitched, awaiting instructions.

I studied Kim and her Capris. "The powder burns." I took a breath. "It was someone Leeds knew who he thought he had control over. . . . You got a glass of water?"

Migano poured me one from a pitcher crowded with ice.

Next, the bathroom at Stabulas's Grocery and the dislodged piece of wood, and the light streaming in from above. "Nick had a fetish for underage girls, looking at them, wanting them. He was involved with Leeds in their sick habit and somehow Cathy had become a victim of this porn ring. And let's not forget the dash of hypnosis right out of a fucking Buck Rogers serial. When did it start—the rape?"

Kim glanced at Babe, and hurried her look away. Athol's eyes hovered about me, and then over ten different locations before returning to yours truly.

"When I was twelve." She sat at the edge of her puffy chair, hands level, her voice a flatline. Nick would come into the room Kim shared with her sister and place a hand over Kim's mouth and say she was beautiful.

"He never touched Cathy?"

Her voice maintained a flatline. No. Never. But Nick made the Irish twin listen. Cathy was ordered to turn the other way and face the wall, but she heard it all. "For years my sister has been sexually inactive, a *saint* because of this."

"And then when you got too old, he wanted Sarah, didn't he? He wanted younger girls. She was Starzz at fifteen."

"Yes."

"Cathy knew about this too. That was another secret she was about to reveal, but you tried to talk her out of it." It would blow the lid off the whole thing. Starzz, Sarah, Coughlins, repeated rapes. "What would it do with your standing at Ogilvie and Beggert? What would it do to your relationship with Babe? He believed in the purity of women. What would he think of a woman who had been thus sullied?"

Kim's eyes watered and she covered her face.

"You take too many chances," Babe said.

"If I didn't take chances, I wouldn't be here now." I shrugged sluggishly. "Cathy loved you too. She wanted to make amends. Tell her story as an act of healing. Help her sister."

Babe moved closer to Kim.

"I didn't think Babe could live with what had happened to me—"

"I can." Babe kissed Kim, caressing her shoulders, holding her.

"And that brings me back to Cathy. The stuff in the drawer wasn't hers. It was Sarah's." Cathy, according to Mrs. Kerr, had gone back to the apartment after the police confiscated a bunch of possessions. Cathy found the hidden stash of S&M material and locked it in her drawer to protect her friend, or maybe use later as evidence.

Kim nodded.

I sat down, rubbed the corners of my mouth.

My shoes were lined with black dirt, Canada's Bazaar. "The first time I was here, I smelled Chanel No. 5. A pleasant enough smell, Kim. I thought it was yours. I shouldn't have." I stood up, pushed back my porkpie, and returned to the stone wall, the one displaying the color television and expensive ivory art carvings by Eskimos. "Bolemac did construction at the Gardens, at Smith's, and here. Two of the three had secret compartments, sliding walls, hidden lairs." I blew air slowly between my lips and felt along the wall's edgings, fingers slithering for a switch. "Third time a charm?"

Embedded in one of the crease lines of stone was a button. I pushed it. The wall silently shifted from left to right.

There on a plush couch sat Cathy, her red hair brimming with backlight, and Steinbeck's *The Grapes of Wrath* on the long, low coffee table in front of her. I waved. It was a weird gesture. I was kind of at a loss for words, but I was so glad to see her and the crumbling rocks returned to my stomach but in a good way.

Her lips were pinched tight, her shoulders tense and upright.

But despite the bodily tension, she smiled back with her whole face and eyes.

Next to her on the couch was the reason for Cathy's stiffness—Nick Stabulas. He wore green work pants, suspenders and a V-neck T-shirt. He was coring an apple with a rather large knife. He did not look at me or smile in any way.

Of course he'd be hiding here. Mr. Exploitation. Where else would he be but desperately using his daughters to get by? A master manipulator, Nick had no qualms over calling in a favor from daughters he had abused repeatedly.

I stepped into the lair and tipped my head to Cathy. "Did you hear everything? Do I need to say anything again?"

"You don't need to say anything again."

And then I heard it, the American pronunciation, the *gen* as in Jen instead of the Canadian strong "gain" on the second syllable. "You were the one who tipped me? 101 days ago about Sarah."

She nodded, hands on thighs. She wore white pants with the zipper in the back, a black scarf around her neck, and a bright shirt full of pastel-colored circles. It gave her an upbeat tempo. I hoped that mood would win the day.

"Am I right? About the past events—am I? You weren't really a prisoner here. You were free to come and go. And one night, you killed Leeds. I don't really give a damn about that. He was an asshole. Exploited you and Sarah, got you both into the porn ring, but Sarah liked it, didn't she?"

Cathy looked away.

"She felt empowered. The mousy girl, the willowy one full

of sexual allure. Sex was a drug for her."

"I tried to get her free of it," Cathy said.

"She needed to be free of her mom." I shook my head. "Leeds was the lowest of the low and deserved to get got. I'm not turning you in, Cathy." I guess, in a way, Migano and me had some things in common. We liked women.

Cathy nodded again, her eyes brushed with happiness.

I stared at Nick and his cocky, self-assured leer, as he rotated the apple with the large knife sticking in it around his thumb and forefinger as if it were the world spinning on an axis that he controlled.

"And what about me?"

"You, Mr. Fucko. You're not so lucky. Why'd you kill Sarah?"

"What?" Kim said.

"I didn't," Nick said.

"Sure you didn't. Did you wait around the woods and watch me and the police standing about like schmucks as an empty motor boat broke across the ice?"

"You can't prove it."

"What did Sarah ever do to you?"

"She laughed at me, said I had too many hang-ups. Nobody laughs at me."

Kim let out a short gasp.

The spin of the apple was slow and Nick's eyebrows meshed again into a long machete blade. "So she allowed me to punish her." He smiled an angry leer. "What are you going to do about it, tough guy?"

I had seen that anger before, when he slapped Kim around.

"Well, since you asked." I gestured and rubbed the back of my neck. "Take you in. Arrest you. Throw away the fucking key." I shrugged, pulling back my jacket, revealing the snub-nose at my side.

"I don't think so," he said.

"I don't get you. You killed Sarah. You—"

"Spare me the speeches. Willowy? That's tough. Maybe I was feeling empowered when I killed her, huh?" His head sunk into his raised shoulders and combined with his mood gave off the gloaming of an unrepentant toad. He wasn't placing blame on anyone. No victim card. He owned up to his evil—he was just a badass fucko. Iago of the Year Award Winner, 1965.

I held up my hands as if to say okay and wondered how many people were in on his and Leeds's little photograph racket.

"A lot. You'd be surprised. What with the blackmail kick-backs from Stuart, and the sales to middle-school boys, enough to keep my storefront in business."

"Well don't brag about it. I was just asking out of polite-ness—"

"Look, there were older men too. Middle-aged men. Just as some men prefer veal instead of steak, other men prefer—"

"Shut up—" The gun was now in my hands, leveled at him.

"I made some nice money." He leered, oblivious to right and wrong. "It was good. Fun."

"Let's go." I waved with my gun.

"I don't think so."

"Think again. You have no hold on anyone anymore." I wiped the edges of my mouth again. "Isn't that right, Babe?"

He looked into his pink rose and then squeezed the tops of Kim's shoulders. "That's right."

"If you take me in, I'll talk." Nick's cool don't-give-a-damn demeanor wasn't cracking. He was just laying out his case, but the Old World accent, the one filled with traces of humility, was so far gone as to have been part of another lifetime. Now, he sounded like any other Anglo punk.

"You're finished, creep."

"I'm finished, when *I* say I'm finished." He looked at his fingers. "Look, I'll tell them about Coughlins, about the Gardens, about Babe's tie-in with the deaths of Lisa and Spinner—" His eyes were lean, his face a still mask: his cheeks, his lips, barely twitching as he spoke.

Athol pulled his gun and aimed it at the back of my head.

"I'll tell how Smith tried to create sex scandals with people in power. How Bullard was involved with an underage escort girl, Starzz, a.k.a. Sarah Kerr. What will that do to your land deal, Babe?" He smiled darkly. "Bolemac. You're tied in to all of this. Don't forget what I know."

I let out a sharp whistle and turned around. Athol's eyes were hovering in the direction of Montreal, Cambridge, and Barrie, anywhere but on this room, and me, this moment in Toronto. He was an unsteady mess. "Athol, put the gun away. Babe—" I breathed deeply.

"I'll tell them Cathy killed Leeds." Nick's smile grew bigger, like a big wobbly bubble.

"I can't have that," Kim said. "Him talking about my sister that way. They'll lock her up."

"I can't have that either. You got to keep harmony with your woman," Babe said. "Athol, take the fuck out."

"Which one, boss? Who do you want taken out?" Athol's eyes and gun flashed between me and Nick and Montreal and Saskatchewan.

"Oh, for chrissakes," Migano said, but it was too late by

then.

In the indecision of the interim, Nick had seized Cathy in a rock-hard headlock and yanked her towards him. The sharp-edged knife was still in the goddamn apple on the coffee table. Instead, by Cathy's temple was a much more dangerous weapon, a Smith & Wesson .38. Where did the gun come from? I was spending too much time following the spin of the knife to be looking for a gun.

"I'm getting out of here." Nick tugged Cathy closer, his finger whitening on the gun's trigger guard. "I got nothing to lose. If I go, she goes." He shrugged, his jaw and chin jutted forward.

"Don't, Babe," Kim pleaded. "Let him go. Just let him go—please, please, please."

"Boss?" Athol's gun was poised like a sharp flag.

"You better kill me, Dad," Cathy intervened, "because I won't lie for you. No free passes. Give yourself up. I'm telling everyone what you did—what you did to my sister, to me, to Lisa—and Sarah, who I loved as a second sister." She couldn't look at him. "And I'm not saying a word against Babe. Because of my sister." She could only look at Babe. Her voice was a husky whisper. She didn't smoke but the timbre sounded as if she did.

"What about your love for your father, huh? Where's all that love?"

"I lost that sometime ago." She took a deep breath. "I'm going to tell my story. With truth comes healing." This time she was looking at him.

"Where did you read that? From a fortune cookie at Sai Woo's?" Nick clamped a forearm under Cathy's chin, silencing her. The leer deepened. "I'm getting out of this room—"

"You might want to stand up then." I leveled my gun at him. "Give yourself a fair shake."

"What?"

Athol's gun was now trained on me. So too Lou-doo's.

"Boss—" Lou-doo's usual gravel was now replaced with wet mud. "Boss—"

"Be money, Lou," I said. "Just be money. I got this." I wanted to catch Nick off guard so I threw quirky tidbits his way. I told him how hockey nets were four-by-six and right now, with you seated like that, Nick, your head is about four feet off the ground, top-shelf. I practiced top-shelf shots all my life and this was a top-shelf moment.

"This isn't a goddamn hockey game."

No, but the focus and commitment I brought to hockey I bring to everything I do. At the police station, twice a week, I take target practice, headshots, Nick.

He smiled. "You shoot me, my reflexes kill the girl."

"No. A bullet in the right place and the assailant goes down like spaghetti, loose limbed, one dead marionette. Let go of Cathy. I'm counting to three."

"You were never that good. Top-shelf, my ass."

"I really think you should stand up. I won't have as good a chance with you standing—it evens up the odds—"

He refused.

"Boss—" Lou-doo asked.

"Boss?" Athol seconded.

"Babe, stop him, stop them—" Kim screamed.

"I always said the kid had chutzpah." Babe's voice was bold and confident. "Let Hayden skate with this. Play it out, kid—"

Athol and Lou sighed and I sensed they were lowering their guns behind me. And I slid back between pockets of silence, calm, relaxed, the infinite space becoming finite. I feared nothing.

"One."

Nick's fingers moved from the trigger guard to the trigger.

"I scored 107 goals," I said.

"Most of them were low and to the stick side. I watched you play."

He wouldn't let the girl go. He knew what he was doing. Nobody in prison likes a guy who rapes twelve-year-olds.

Short eyes, they call such perpetrators.

"You were never that good," he challenged.

"I did all right."

He laughed. "You're no Bobby Hull."

"No."

Cathy's eyes didn't widen with fear. Sure her mouth parted slightly, but she remained calm, she had skated into those pockets of silence with me. So had Kim. She was no longer screaming. I heard her breath catch, like right after a referee's whistle, before play starts up again.

Nothing was breaking my flow, the pain, everything, was gone. My shoulders, arms, and legs: loose. "Let Cathy go."

"Prove it, hotshot."

Cathy nodded with her eyes, *do it*.

"Two."

"Prove it. I don't think you're that good. You were never that good. A marginal player at best, a third-line guy."

"Drop the gun—"

His hardened trigger finger was white phosphorous. "Prove it. Prove it, you motherfucker, prove it, you candy-ass."

And I did, right under the bar.

BONUS MATERIAL

TORONTO, 1965:
CHEAP AMUSEMENTS' BEAT

A FOURTH FACE
CHAPTER 1

Toronto, 1965

Cheap Amusements' Beat

A Memoir

In the late 1940s my Aunt Louise went on a date with a Toronto Maple Leaf.

Louise was a real character, a gifted storyteller. She'd go to Buffalo for a weekend and come back with an American accent that would last for a week.  Anyway, she had written Cal Gardner, care of the Gardens, telling him how much she and her family loved the Leafs, talking them up to their customers, and Gardner arrived one inky winter night to Louise and her parents' home, in the West End above their mom-and-pop variety store. Cal and Louise went to Bassel's for a burger and some after-dinner dancing.

Before they left, my Dedo Chris took their photograph to hang next to the Export "A" Leafs calendar in his store.

I have two such calendars hanging in my basement, one from 1951–52 celebrating the '51 Cup team with Bill Barilko, and another from 1963–64, celebrating perhaps the greatest Leaf team, the 1962–63 Cup-winning squad.

For an immigrant family Cal Gardner's visit to a store on Old Weston Road was a major iconic moment, a daughter of Macedonians going on a date with a hockey player. Canadian acculturation. Dedo, Louise, and the rest didn't get that whole symbol thing back then, let alone "acculturation," but for my grandparents who spoke little English, this must have been something, one of the "Blue and White" and their daughter.

The Petroves had arrived.

Hockey was the backdrop to everything when I was a kid. Dad diagrammed plays with the salt and pepper shakers across the dinner table, told me to quit playing with one hand on my stick ("Use both!"), and often said to neighbors, friends, "You can come over, but it's Saturday. The hockey game will be on." The hockey game will be on. No apologies. We'll be watching—and talking—hockey.

HOCKEY AND TORONTO. Sports writers often describe Toronto as the center of the hockey universe. Our hockey team is one of the original franchises, over 100 years old, winner of 13 Cups. Toronto houses both the Hockey Hall of Fame and *The Hockey News*. NHL meetings are conducted there and in New York.

Hockey is part of the city's infrastructure and immigrant fabric.

And Toronto is a city of immigrants.

My grandparents, born between 1899–1907, arrived in TO in the 1910s. Both of their marriages were arranged. My Dedo George was a baker and eventually operated his own diner. My Dedo Chris ran a grocery store. Babo Vangie and Babo Sophie raised children and helped with their husbands' businesses, working long hours. I'm third generation, the product of immigrants, Macedonian Roma.

I stand on their shoulders.

Throughout my childhood, the 1960s and 1970s, the bigger the game, chances were we'd be watching it at Dedo's. After all, he had a 26-inch Solid State, color TV. Back home we were still watching games on our humble 14-inch Zenith, black and white.

My cousins, uncles, aunts—our conversations often began with talk of the Leafs and the game's stars: Jean Béliveau of the Habs, Frank Mahovlich of the Leafs, and Bobby Orr, of the Big Bad Bruins. Orr was the greatest player I've ever seen with his end-to-end rushes, quick acceleration into the offensive zone, and razor-like passes.

Dedo Chris was a Leafs fan, but he also had a soft spot for the Chicago Blackhawks. You see, Tommy Ivan, their GM and braintrust, hailed from the same village in Macedonia as my dedo.

When I was seventeen I attended my cousin Chris's wedding and confessed to him that I wanted to be a writer of crime fiction, like Raymond Chandler. My cousin (who was named after my dedo) grew up playing hockey on backyard rinks; as a teenager he had a tryout with the Oshawa Generals, and was close friends with Bruce Boudreau (who later played for the Leafs and coached a bevy of pro teams including the Minnesota Wild). So Chris's advice shouldn't have surprised me: "Write about hockey."

And I guess after all these years I finally did just that, combining my appreciation for the city of Toronto, my ethnic roots, and admiration for literary fiction with a love for hardboiled mysteries. Thanks, Chris.

ORIGINALLY, I had planned to use the legendary family story of the "hockey date" as the backdrop to *Cheap Amusements*. Cathy Stabulas, the novel's "missing girl," had years ago gone on a date with Hayden Fuller. This subtext would give the novel some high-octane personal dynamics. Hayden's emotional commitment would be right there for me as a writer. In acting, we call such backstory choices the "hot ones." This was very hot.

Too hot.

I wrote the first draft fast and loose like Eddie Felson shooting pool. Don't think. Follow, feel the impulses. And then I took a step back and realized this backstory premise was a total phony. I didn't know Hayden well enough to pull off his psychological journey. The "interior" moments to his inner quest were forced and not as meaningful as they ought to be.

In a subsequent draft, I dropped the biographical connection (keeping the mom-and-pop variety store as a setting, however) and developed the Sarah Kerr subplot: a prior case, ninety-some days before, in which a young high school girl goes missing, only to be found crumpled up in a suitcase, two bullets behind an ear. Hayden suffers residual guilt in failing to find that girl alive. It was his first big case. He lost her. This provided the right emotional motivation and psychological momentum for his latest case involving Cathy.

A chance for redemption.

The first book in a series, I assume, is a feeling-out process. Who is this character I'm writing? He's me, but not me. Where do we intersect, differ? Having recently finished a sequel—*A Fourth Face*—and the loose plotting (bound to change once I start writing) for a third Fuller yarn—*November Rain*—I think I can now take that inner journey of the original inspiration for *Cheap Amusements*.

I wasn't ready then.

I am now.

THE VOICE for Hayden I found quickly.

I didn't fully know him yet, but I felt his presence, his sensibilities.

The voice was just there—a rare gift, when a character and a writer's personality blend to form a tone: in this case, comic irreverence with an empathetic core.

Hayden cares passionately for people but has an outside-looking-in quality that hollers back to my child-like and teenage self. I didn't know what "othering" was, but I was often made to feel that my Canadian identity in the Anglo suburbs was suspect.

On my crescent, the sky was often a powder blue, the air full of outdoor grilling or the brisk smell of autumn and winter. My sweaters, from a habit of chewing the ends of sleeves, often reminded me of breakfast porridge as I darted behind thin trees and played war games.

So many of the conversations in getting-to-know-you sessions with neighborhood kids, and later on the schoolyards, went like this: "So, Tracey, where you from? You don't look Irish." My original surname was Traicheff. My parents changed it when I was in third grade so that things would go "easier for me than for them." Anyway, "Toronto," I'd say. "I'm from Toronto. I was born at St. Michael's." "But your people, Tracey? Where you from?" "I'm Canadian." "Yeah, yeah, but you're not from here." "Macedonia." "Where's that?" "Near

Yugoslavia. Greece." "Oh, so you like olives?"

I echoed this feeling of cultural liminality (being a part of Canada but apart from it too) in *Cheap Amusements*, as the young Hayden is asked similar questions about his Jewish roots. "Where you from?" "Toronto. I was born in Toronto." "But where are your people from?" "Russia." "Oh, so you're a commie kike?" "Yup, I'm a commie kike. L'chaim." Fuller, like me, was born with a different surname. His smart-ass quips mask our combined hurt. But Hayden is much more comfortable, prouder of his Jewish identity than I was in being Macedonian.

Toronto may have been a city for immigrants, but I didn't find it very welcoming in the pre-multicultural 1960s.

The suburbs of my childhood were largely Anglo, Scottish, and Irish with names like Tomlinson, Ogilvie, Campbell, and Brown populating the road hockey matches we played well after the streetlights came on. By the 1970s a new influx of immigrants arrived to Canada, not from Eastern Europe but elsewhere. When my dedo and babo sold their variety store it was to a Pakistani family. The public school I attended in the '60s and '70s is now predominantly populated by Asians, many refugees from Hong Kong following the loss of British rule in 1999.

Maybe that's why I set *Cheap Amusements* in 1965. I'm still working out the hurt of not feeling at home in my own country. Sure, I like 1960s fashions (the look of *The Green Hornet*, *Honey West*, and the *Dick Van Dyke Show* establishing a kind of a post-Kennedy era jazz cool), and the Original-Six NHL, a time when Canada was in hockey ascendancy as the world's top powerhouse. I like having to use phone booths to make phone calls. I like muscle cars. Hayden drives a 1963 Ford

Galaxie like the black-and-whites on an old cop show. I also love jazz: the hard bop of Sonny Clark, John Coltrane, Miles Davis, Dexter Gordon, and Hank Mobley.

Jazz is the music, the rhythmic strum I hear when I think of TO. The year 1965 represents the cusp of change, the transition between the Eisenhower era's square-jawed heroes and the long-haired cats of the post-Tet Offensive. Hayden is between these two worlds. He sports a 1950s buzzcut and wears a porkpie; he appears old-fashioned in a rapidly changing world (the permissive society of the '60s with its go-go boots, anti-war protests, sexual experimentation, and hallucinogenic drugs), but his politics are left-leaning, his heart progressive, always supportive of underdogs and the rights of individuals to be themselves. He isn't quick to judge.

That year, 1965, is also important to me as a writer because I'm still trying to come to terms with what I couldn't understand then. Yes, I knew then that with my hooded eyes, large nose, and generous lips I couldn't possibly pass for the Anglo mainstream, but I sure wanted to. And much later as someone who enjoys acting, I knew I would never get the Fast Eddie Felson roles. I was no Paul Newman, no romantic lead. Zero Mostel. That's me.

I identified with Jews because they appeared comfortable in their liminality. *Mad* magazine and Lenny Bruce poked holes at Anglo puffery of entitlement and privilege. In my teens and twenties, I admired the pop art of Jack Kirby, the writing of Bernard Malamud (*The Assistant* is set in a mom-and-pop variety store). Jews had cultural capital, chutzpah. I wanted a piece of that.

—

IN THE SEVENTH GRADE Darryl was a real cool cat. Jewish, he embodied chutzpah, walking with his shoulders back, his eyes never darting away, holding onto yours with respect. There was a calm stillness to him, of planting his feet and knowing who he is.

I wanted to know how he became.

At twelve, he was the youngest blackbelt in Canada, and he took no shit from nobody. Every morning in Canadian schools, we sang "O Canada," "God Save the Queen" and recited the Lord's Prayer. During this time, Darryl always left the room. Quietly. But he *left* the room. That prayer wasn't a part of his rituals.

I wanted to bring some of Darryl's pride and confidence and sense of self-worth and dignity to Hayden Fuller, who remembers the signs of his childhood dotting the shorelines of Balmy Beach: "No Dogs or Jews Allowed." But he's not going to let any such sign stop him from touching sand. No sir.

So Darryl, you probably don't remember me. I was the goofball making with the wisecracks and flashing ironic peace signs at kids, but there's a bit of you in my private eye.

Thank you.

AS A WRITER of literary fiction I'm attracted to voice: sequential events, narrative choices, modulated through a particular point of view, attitude.

My attitude is one of respect for my story's characters and living comfortably with uncertainty.

In Raymond Chandler's Marlowe novels, he piles up details, forcing readers to sift out which ones are meaningful from the extraneous dross.

This isn't my approach.

I opt for free-indirect discourse, sliding from direct dialogue into summary mode, filtered through Hayden's sensibilities. This choice has two results: one, I avoid committing to an all-too-common practice of genre fiction reading like converted screenplays; and two, the filtering of scene work into a mode of telling creates doubt in the reality presented. What is summarized isn't "exactly" what happened or was said. This uncertainty permeates the world of *Cheap Amusements*, and I suppose it originates out of the uncertainty I felt growing up in Toronto, a kid who didn't quite fit in. The world felt like a mystery to decode.

And I didn't have a decoder ring.

THE BLUE OF TORONTO is a color of sky I've never seen anywhere else. I guess because I hail from there I romanticize this sky, but every time I return home, I'm drawn into that powder blue, like slipping into a pair of comfortable faded jeans.

And the Toronto of my childhood is like a pulsing jazz score: the gray action of Front Street with its hotdog vendors; the pulse of Union Station with departing and arriving travelers, men in dark felt hats and women in dresses and heels; the minor-key melody to the campus of the University of Toronto with its hard Anglican lines and film noir moldy moodiness; the bright bop trumpets of people dining at checkered tables at George's Spaghetti House, eating escargots, as Leaf rearguard Bobby Baun sips a beer along a narrow bar.

The biggest landmark was found on Carlton Street. Maple Leaf Gardens. Here the beat was an Art Blakey drum solo, pulsing with the breaths of thousands watching the Leafs. We, Dad and I, sat up in the grays, hazy spent cigarette swirls twisting above us.

For years, Dad told the following story: "I take my kid to his first game and you know what he says? Gee, Dad. It's in color."

I was four years old in 1965. I figured my heroes would be skating in a black-and-white world. After all, that's how they appeared on television.

Anyway, the soda at the Gardens was always watered down. The popcorn too salty so you'd drink more of the expensive thin-flavored pop, but the Eskimo Pies were my fave. The chocolate would faintly coat the inside of your hand, like scratches of dirt from a sacred garden, and one time, after looking at photos of the past Leaf Stanley Cup championship teams in the lobby, Dad and I made the long climb to our seats in the grays, hands touching, dirt smeared between our palms, a moment of communion.

IN 1965, my mother wrote Frank Mahovlich, the Big M, #27, a letter.

Frank was our hero. He was a Croatian Canadian, the closest player to a Macedonian in the NHL. With his lopsided grin, he was shy, humble. When he scored we felt it. When he was booed we felt it. One night, Brian McFarlane, CBC's color commentator, said something to the effect that Mahovlich was just standing around out there, it was time he did something.

Because he was so big, his easy-going loping stride made it seem like he was lazy. Anyway, McFarlane and the press believed everything Coach "Punch" Imlach said about Mahovlich (things like "Hockey is a streetcar named desire and Mahovolich hasn't caught it"—Coach never could pronounce Frank's surname right, often adding an extra syllable or changing the *ah* sound of the "o" to a short stubby "a"), and what they passed onto the fans was accepted uncritically by most. Leaf fans ragged their gifted winger. The last time we won the Cup: 1967. Mahovlich was booed when the players were introduced at a victory celebration at City Hall. Frank was sensitive. He felt the enormity of being perceived as an underachiever . . . and had a series of nervous breakdowns in the 1960s.

During one such breakdown, Mom wrote him a letter care of Wellesley General.

In it, she said we all felt he was picked on because he wasn't English-white. She also told him what he meant for us, the children of immigrants, and how we loved his game, his speed, and felt, like us, he was undervalued and underappreciated.

Frank wrote Mom back. Several handwritten pages.

Mom never shared that letter with me. She summarized its contents, but the specifics of the letter, its words, were for her, something she always cherished and kept in a cedar chest.

Today Mahovlich is revered as one of the all-time greats of the game. In 2016, *The Hockey News* ranked him #26 on their list of The One Hundred Greatest of the Last One Hundred Years. On the Leafs Top 100 Greats of all time, he ranks #9.

The past is forgotten, forgiven.

But I remember.

From Cal Gardner to Frank Mahovlich, hockey has always been a part of my family history, my life, in and out of Toronto.

These memories, influences, exist within me, planets orbiting about, planets I visit and walk around for my writing.

And Hayden Fuller, ex-hockey player turned private eye, is a jazzy amalgam of all this.

A Fourth Face

They think I did it."

His voice was buried shells on a beach, thin creases, full of sand. I didn't recognize it at first.

I squeezed my eyes in an effort to open them more fully. They were caked with cereal crust and the shadowy figure before me was a series of rocks floating by the side of my bed. I propped myself up on my elbows.

Thin traces of moon lit his shoulders and the tips of his chin and hawk nose.

"Bobby?"

He opened his mouth without speaking. The clock-hands on the nightstand glowed 3:40 or 8:17. It had to be 3:40—it was too dark to be morning. My face was hot but my forehead was cool and the ceiling fan twisted with a slight rattle.

Anyway, I hadn't been sleeping well. My therapist says I got shit to work out. That's how she talks, "shit to work out." The Sixties is a progressive time.

I have this reoccurring dream: I'm trapped in a musty suitcase, full of moths, my father's bourbon-soaked voice yelling, "get out, get out." I'm never sure, in the dream, if he's imploring me to fight and free myself from the suitcase or to extricate myself from his life. Get out!

"I saw her. A plastic bag." Bobby dropped his forehead into his shoulder, his voice taking on more sand. "I didn't do it—"

The rattle of the ceiling fan was louder than I expected it to be. It was as if some of the sand had slipped inside its bearings.

Bobby Ehle was an ex-Leaf defenseman, and tonight his face was full of little scratches like he had fallen down an ivy trellis or some such damn thing. There were deeper marks around his Adam's apple and along the tops of his hands. His hockey story: At the start of the 1964 season, after being a seven-year pro, three-time Stanley Cup champ, and second-team all-star the prior season, he retires, leaving training camp in Peterborough, Ontario, having had it with my ex-coach Hugh "Two-Fisted" Farrell, a regular resident philosopher. "Hockey's a game of emotion, Ehle. It's a streetcar named desire, and I don't think you've ever caught it."

Two Fists sure loved that line. He said it to Big Z, me, Billy Harris. He should get it registered. You know with the *R* and the circle?

I think Gordie Howe has one next to his name. Really.

You can look it up.

I'm kidding. Who the hell would do such a thing? He's known as Mr. Hockey, but he's not full of himself, and Bobby was known as the Pest, the Intimidator, and the ever-so-pithy moniker Little Shit. The latter was only uttered behind opposing team's locker room doors, a shared space that the press had limited access to.

I guess Bobby eventually caught a different streetcar than the one Coach was riding. I don't know what he'd been doing the last year or so. One time, I saw him in back of the Gardens, near Church Street, smoking a cigarette, signing autographs. It looked like the last place he wanted to be, but there he was, shoulders hunched, chin on chest.

As I adjusted to the shadow light, the marks on Bobby's hands became more apparent. The skin around the fingernails was nicked up, gouged, and flecked with dried blood.

And his voice. It wasn't the same. The fast rat-a-tat-tat he had as a player was now full of beach sand and much slower than I remembered.

The real reason Bobby walked away from hockey? He was depressed. His wife Nancy had cheated on him with a plastic surgeon, Cliff Airedale, a tall angular guy with a baggy ass and a hitch in his walk, a guy who should carry a tennis racket wherever he goes, a guy who thinks a goatee makes him Beat Generation cool.

I took the pictures of their "interludes" with a Leica and fast film so I know how baggy his ass is.

Bobby had hired me. It was my first "case." Before snapping covert pix of Nancy and Cliff, I took mainly photos of the fellas' girlfriends and wives, sexy snapshots to keep in a cedar chest or the far recesses of a desk drawer. The Bobby case helped pay for my new hi-fi. Unfortunately, the dividends didn't outweigh the full cost. The story of the affair broke when my girlfriend at the time, Stana Younger, reported it in the pages of the *Toronto Telegram*, and I wound up drummed out of the NHL for "moral turpitude." Bobby played the rest of that season without me, and then hung up the skates after a few weeks of training camp, summer 1964.

It was now a year later. Summer, 1965. July. Nancy Ehle had returned to being Nancy Drouin. And I had the feeling Bobby wanted to hire me again. Something about the sand in his voice.

"Plastic bag?"

"Yeah. It was on her face." He grinned a troubled cork-screw leer, like he couldn't get things to add up in his head. He always had that look as a player, in practices, during games, while playing cards on long train rides. It was a look inhabiting a vacant parking lot and at the same time an intense stare filled up with crammed cars, stories he couldn't share. Now the voice was heavily medicated.

"She's dead?"

He nodded. Slowly.

"And you—saw her?"

"I was following her." He looked away. A scar, the chunk of a golf divot, was a small river creasing his lower lip, and the skin around his eyes were puffy leeches, the face of a boxer. Bobby was tough but he was dirty. He led our team in penalty minutes every year, scrapping with the likes of a Lou Fortunado, and one night at Madison Square Garden, Lou-doo tried to tomahawk Bobby's hair from his scalp with sharp clutching hands and razor-like forearms, and Bobby knocked him cold with an overhand haymaker, but he didn't take off his gloves. You don't fight with your gloves. Hockey code. But Fortunado *had* treated Bobby's hair as if it were an unwarranted accessory, and Bobby just lost it. Did he do the same thing with Nancy? Did he hit her with the same out-of-control intensity?

"You had a restraining order." I reminded him of what I read in the dailies, Stana Younger's column. Every goddamn day. "You're supposed to be nowhere near her—" He had been previously arrested, including sixty days ago, but Nancy dropped the charges.

She did that on more than one occasion.

"I know, I know." He shrugged, his left ankle turned awkwardly. "I wanted another chance—" He rubbed at deeper scratches on his left cheek. There were sharp, parallel lines, three tines on a fork. He scrubbed his tan-colored hair, trying to remember something.

"She's not your wife anymore—"

"I know, I know. I got the memo, okay?" His brown eyes filled with remnants of a corkscrew leer. "To be honest with you, I don't know how I got to her apartment. I was just there." He leaned his forehead into a flat hand and steadied himself. "And I saw her—"

There were lots of things he couldn't remember anymore. Too many concussions. "Who was number-15. On the Leafs?" he asked. "Fifteen?"

For some reason it was important to know this, now.

"Billy Harris," I said. Our fourth-line center.

"Four?"

"Red Kelly." Our best back-checker, next to Keon. Shut down Béliveau.

"Seventeen?"

"Me." I smiled, my face hurting a little. "Hayden Fuller." Drummed out of the league for a "hobby."

"Right, right." He remembered his "D" partner, Bobby Baun, and our goalie Johnny Bower, and the Captain, Benjamin Small Bear, but their faces, and highlights from various games, like the overtime winner he scored in '61, were all disappearing, shallow puddles lifting up from a hot sidewalk.

I don't know if it was because I only had two hours of sleep, but suddenly the whole room was full of sand, in my eyes, behind my eyes, in my mouth, in my head, on my skin.

It swirled about like a dust storm. It stuck everywhere. I felt like I was in Oklahoma, 1934.

"What's with the scratches?"

He shrugged. "Barroom scuffle? Habs fan?" The joke wasn't getting any play. Maybe the timing was off. He delivered the line two beats too slow.

"Look at your hands. The scratches around your neck. Someone was fighting back. Desperately." One of the fingernails on his left hand was torn off.

I was now circling him. "Why were you following her?" My knees hurt a little.

"I wasn't *following* her."

"You just said you were."

"I misspoke. I was just. There. Like. There."

"What, suddenly you're Tinkerbell now, floating through keyholes, magically appearing in people's apartments? C'mon, Bobby, level with me."

"I don't remember."

"Did you kill her?"

"No." He shrugged.

The ceiling fan needed an adjustment or two.

"I was worried about her, I guess, so I wanted to see. Her."

"Worried. What do you mean?"

"Airedale's bunch. She's mixed up with them."

Well, she had been sleeping with him, the guy in need of a tennis racket.

That ended a while ago. They were still friends, Bobby said. Imagine that guy being. Your. Friend? "I've seen them at his clinic. Guys with gloves on their hands."

"Gangsters?"

What was Bobby doing at the Queen Street clinic?

He couldn't remember the name of the clinic. Neither could I.

"Hitmen," he said, nodding. Slowly. "That's the kind of guys who wear gloves." He raised his shoulders. "Did you hear about that publishing house in Montreal, the one that publishes literary novels that nobody reads?"

Literary. When did he learn that word? In his playing days all Bobby ever read were comic books and racing forms. He really liked Hawkman. Said they had similar beaks.

"Yeah." I read the story. A fire burned down half the building, delaying the release of several titles, including a new collection of poems by Leonard Cohen.

"Nancy overhead Airedale's crowd vaguely. Talking about. It. Taking sideways credit."

"Uh-huh."

"Nothing specific."

"Right."

"And then there was that English paper in Montreal—"

"*The Citizen*?"

"Yeah."

A small bomb was found in the lobby with a threatening note attached, something about those who tell the stories having the power. The bomb squad rushed in and uncovered three or four faux wires, discovering it was nothing but a smoke bomb, a variation on a mild teargas canister.

"Same outfit?"

"Maybe."

My stomach was full of cold rocks but everything else about me was gritted with sweat and sand. I needed a shower.

"Believe me, Hayden. I never hit her. *Ever.*" He reached into his shirt pocket and dry swallowed some pills. A lot of pills.

And those hands. A fingernail missing.

"That's not what the papers said." I was still circling. "The scratches? Those are fresh—" The lower part of my back was on fire. I leaned left, right, stretching. Maybe I needed a new bed.

Stana last week ran a three-part feature, an exclusive story with Nancy Drouin, detailing Bobby's depressed moods as a player, his melancholic outbursts, his intense jealousies whenever Nancy talked to another man. He'd punch her again and again and yell, "Don't you ever disrespect me. You hear what I said. Don't you ever—"

"We'd scuffle a little. In the past. That's all."

"What about tonight?"

"A little." He pushed a hand against his forehead. "I think. I'm not. Sure. God, I think. My head hurts—"

"You remember 'scuffling'?"

"I think so."

"Your head? That's what the pills are for?"

"Yeah." *Like I was telling you, Hayden, concussions.* He'd had a lot of fights in the pros, and sat out a dozen or so games each season with excruciating pain, black dogs barking about in his head. One time, the pain was so bad that before a game Bobby was lying on the locker room floor, his head resting against the cool concrete.

Coach stepped over him as he rattled on about desire.

The ceiling fan whirred like a helicopter. I was still circling. "C'mon Bobby—the truth—"

"I was just there. And the plastic. Bag."

"You were just there? Scuffling." I wondered if he'd take a lie detector.

"Hell, yeah. Lie detector. Fuck. Yeah. Wrestling. That's all. Scuffling. I never, ever, punched her. I pushed her sometimes when she got a little crazy, slapped her back when she slapped me, but I never punched her. You got to believe me." The whirring got louder.

I looked up at the ceiling fan. "What the fuck's with that?" I wasn't very good at fixing things. Toasters, lamps, light switches, forget about it. My pop never passed on basic electrical skills, or carpentry or masonry, nothing. I was good at making phone calls.

It wasn't the goddamn fan, he said. "Helicopter." *That really cracked him up. You think a fan can get that noisy, Hayden? He was still laughing, crumpling over. Maybe it was helping with his headaches.*

"In my backyard? A *fucking* helicopter?"

He was heading to Oslo, Sweden. Oslo's in Norway, I told him, and he said he always sucked at geography, but the place in Sweden sounds like Oslo, it has an "o" in it anyway, a lot of o's, but for now the helicopter was taking him somewhere up north, bush country, and from there he was going to make his way to Sweden to coach hockey. "They want us Canadians over there. They say Terrien's there too."

Brian Spinner Terrien was buried in a plot of land about to become an amusement park. But only I and a handful of people knew that. Stana knew.

"Sweden. They have extradition, Bobby—"

"This will all blow over by then."

He'd be in *Oslo, Sweden* in less than twenty-four hours.

"I'm hiring you to find out who killed her. The real killer." He shook his head again. "A plastic bag, man." He popped another pill, and the laughter stopped, a match puffed out.

Was she seeing anybody?

No. He nodded. "Well, maybe Terry."

"Who's Terry?"

"Some fucko she met at the clinic. Terry Quinton."

I wrote it down on a yellow pad by my nightstand, next to the clock, and my .38, in its holster, loaded.

Bobby's shoulders suddenly shook. *Nancy's death eyes, man, were shiny coins. Bright and much bigger than they should have been.* He absently touched one of the tines on his cheek.

"I don't know if I can take these headaches much longer. Sometimes I figure—"

I handed him a glass of water.

"I loved her."

I bit my lower lip.

Blades whirred.

My mind drifted to the suitcase and my father, yelling.

Shit, I don't know how the helicopter even landed in my backyard without waking the whole fucking neighborhood. I live in the suburbs, a kind of Toronto Levittown, where every fourth house is the same. Fortunately, some of the houses around me haven't been finished yet. The house to my left needed sheet rock added to the upstairs frames, and the two houses to my right were on bald brown dirt, awaiting the additions of mats of grass. But my yard was a different story. A helicopter sat like a huge black dragonfly filling up space, kicking up puffs of dust. I hadn't mowed in weeks. It looked like South Vietnam out there.

I could make out some markings on the copter, KEY. It was black and white and the front windows tinted. Who was the pilot? Bobby couldn't even drive a car, well, not well. He was the worst, taking his hands off the wheel, frequently, to make whatever point he was bloviating about. He was no Richard Petty. "Who's flying the bird?"

"Was I really a second-team all-star my final year?"

"Yeah."

He nodded, his lips pushed together, and he looked away, his voice dropping. "A friend. Flying the insect." He handed me five-hundred dollars. Slowly. They were crumpled and resembled fat worms. "That's all I've got." His face was boyish, bashful, as if he were afraid of being in trouble. "Don't be mad at me."

"I'm not mad. Who's flying the bird?"

"You look mad."

"I'm just trying to figure things out."

"That's just for starters. The money? What do you call it?"

"A retainer?" It was more than generous. My fee was forty a day and expenses.

"Yeah, that. Retainer. Will you look into this?" He crushed a hiccup in a big shoulder. "Help me?"

"I got to tell you, Bobby. It doesn't look so good. The evidence, I mean?"

I'll take a lie detector. In Sweden. Send it to you. He wanted so much for me to believe in him. *He was like a little kid.* "You're really not mad at me, right?"

"No, Bobby."

"You sound mad."

"Jesus Christ. I said I wasn't. I'm not. The bird?"

He reached for his pills. They were tiny bird bones in his big hands. "I didn't do it." He dry swallowed.

Maybe it was the headaches. I get them too. Maybe that's why I decided to help him. "How will I get in touch?"

"You won't. I will." He took down my number. Here and at my office, near Yonge and Bloor.

"Okay." Look, I told him, I had to play this cautiously. Not make a big ruckus. I was trying to get back into the NHL. The Montreal Canadiens had invited me to their summer tryout camp; GM Sam Pollock had even visited my house and we talked about art; he too was a big fan of the Original Seven and A. J. Casson, but NHL President Clarence Campbell didn't care much for Pollock or Montreal or Casson for that matter (the Philistine) and blocked my ability to play anywhere in the NHL next season. However, Soupy said if I continued to keep my nose clean he'd reevaluate my chances for reinstatement later this summer.

"The Habs?"

"Yeah."

Bobby shook his head. Slowly. "I'd love to have played. For the Habs." He was from Laval, a Montreal suburb.

My getting banned from the league wasn't quite on the level of the 1955 Rocket Richard case or any reason to riot, but the Montreal fans sure were kicking up a great big noisy fuss saying the NHL was once again pitting itself against the French Canadian team and everything French Canadian. I guess I had become a bit of a celeb for solving the Stabulas, missing girl case. Got good press notices. Even Stana wrote me up a two-page spread in the *Tely*.

Got some good business out of it too: a woman whose cat, yes Felix, had gone missing, and a fella who thought his wife was cheating on him. She was. With another woman.

Bobby had read the *Telegram* spread. That's why he was here. He liked how I operated.

I reminded him that I didn't even know how to fix light

switches.

"Bilingualism in Canada has always been about being French and having to learn English," Bobby reminded me. "It's never the other way around." He shrugged. "You speak French?"

"*Un petit peu.*"

"*Je me Souviens?* That's the name of the outfit that Nancy knew about and runs with Airedale's crowd. Was. Running. Or Airedale was. Taking credit for? Shit, I'm not sure. *Je me— no.* That's not quite the name. Something like that."

I remember. Bobby couldn't remember much of anything.

The floor creaked as Bobby ambled to a dresser and looked at himself in the mirror. He wiped his tired eyes and didn't like what he saw. And then he traced his face in the glass with his fingers, or hand, at least that's what it looked like from where I stood in the angular lights of the moon. He was writing words on his face, trying to erase his face with words, but there were no words on the mirror. Nothing.

Just his face: vulnerable, sad. That's something, my therapist argues that I struggle with, being more present in my feelings. I was supposed to be taking a rest cure. On my last case, I had killed a man, a miserable fuck who raped young girls and exploited women, and everyone felt like *I needed time alone, to heal.* My therapist said I wasn't dealing honestly with my emotions, my past, my relationship with my father (why is it always about the father?), and I needed to truly listen to that voice of discontent that tells us all is not good, but I wasn't hearing any such voice, not even late at night when I couldn't sleep. "Vulnerability is the key," she said, *let go of things and admit what hurts.*

Maybe I needed a new therapist.

And what was there to admit anyway?

I guess I should tell her about my reoccurring dream, the one with the damn suitcase. She's into Jung and dreams.

"Yeah, I read about that too," Bobby said. Slowly. "You blew him away. Head shot. He got got. Got what he deserved. Abusing women. That guy was a real lowlife."

I don't know if he saw the possible connection to himself.

Irony is not a strong point with hockey players.

For Jane Austen, whom Stana adores, yes. But hockey players, as a general rule, not so much.

Bobby was definitely bigger than I remembered, his pants hitched under his round, hard belly, his belt a notch too tight. Certain meds can slow you down and pack on the pounds, I guess.

"The scratches, Bobby? From Nancy? Before you killed her?"

"Look, Hayden. You're my friend. Would I ask a friend for this kind of favor, if I wasn't speaking the truth?"

"You would if you were desperate."

He moved from the mirror, his face disappearing into the shadows of moonlight. "I *am* desperate, damn it. After Stana's articles, who's going to believe that I didn't do it?" He hitched up his pants and returned to the mirror. Maybe he saw other faces there that I couldn't see.

"Hey, she's just doing her job," I said.

"I'm sorry. You're. Right. I forgot you two had a thing."

Not anymore, not after her tie-ins with Babe Migano. But the two-page spread in the Tely was nice.

"Look into Airedale, the doc, he's running some kind of racket and I think he killed her."

"What kind of racket?"

"Maybe that publishing house. I don't. Know. Nancy hint-ed at some things—Cassel for chrissakes." He shrugged, looked at his fingers, and smiled his perpetual corkscrew leer.

"Drugs?"

And then he mumbled something about blue pills.

"What kind of pills?"

The ones he was popping were white. I noticed. Tiny bird bones.

"Damn." He screamed, his voice a short burst from a .45. His head wasn't working right, goddamn it. He couldn't re-member the name. But blue was the color of the pills, and at least some of his migraines were blue. Like. The. Pills.

"You said something about Cassel, Lenny Cassel, Detroit kingpin? Did Nancy tell Stana about Cassel and his possible involvement with Airdeale?" *It was probably her next big sto-ry, knowing Stana. I'd have to see her again and get the skinny to follow the thread.*

Maybe I'll return the photos. I have a couple of nude art photos, okay five or six, I took of her back in '62, when I was learning my craft, and we had a thing going. I still look at them, occasionally.

"Yeah. Damn straight. Lenny Cassel. Detroit mobster."

He was a sick, scary fuck. A slight man, thin in the shoul-ders, but the eyes, burning snakes. Lenny had disappeared three, four weeks ago after a witness testified to the feds that she had seen him kill a prominent politician and reporter in a black, shadowy alley. He used a machete. Chopped the shit out of them and tossed chunks of limbs into green trash bags. Lenny thought he was alone but a restaurant owner, tossing a different kind of refuse into the trash, saw the mur-ders. Lenny has been hiding since. Reports had him spotted in three American cities and two in Canada. Nancy saw Lenny at Airedale's clinic.

"You're sure?" Maybe he was involved in some kind of drug front. The blue pills.

"Maybe. Nancy. Told. Me. She saw him."

I nodded.

"I used to go to Cliff's clinic. He does some kind of hydrotherapy. Water treatments and electric shock."

"And blue pills."

"Yeah. The pills helped. For. A. While." They calmed him down, relaxed his headaches.

"I thought Airedale was a plastic surgeon?"

"He's a doctor, ain't he? Has his hands in a lot of, let's say, projects." Airedale's clinic specialized in out-patient procedures, the removal of moles, etc., and also electric shock and hydrotherapy for depression. He's got a ton of famous clients, including actors, that guy on that TV western with the spotted dog—and the sidekick who wears a top hat? Always says cheerio?"

"Uh-huh." *Bonanza*–wannabe that show. "I thought you hated Cliff."

"I do." But Nancy had gone there. "You know he worked on her nose? Yeah. Took the bump out of it—"

"I see—"

"And that's when I saw all those men with gloves on. Something's going on there and Cassel's involved."

"Could Cassel have placed a plastic bag over a woman's head?"

After all, he had hacked two people to death with a machete. What could he do for an encore?

"Anything's possible with that cat." He smiled his corkscrew leer. "Nancy talked to Stana. Told her things. See the reporter."

Stana. I wasn't looking forward to the idea of seeing her. Maybe I should wear new shoes.

The blades whirred louder.

Stana. My stomach still had this empty space in it, like a hole, over what had happened before, my last case.

Stana. In a way I did want to see, if, as my therapist suggests I was really being honest with myself, and my complicated feelings toward Stana, new shoes or old shoes.

Bobby waved goodbye and before I knew it, the slow walking Ehle was under snapping blades, the yellow moon a slice of lemon.

He never did give me the name of the damn pilot.

And then the nose of the dragonfly came back towards the earth, up, down, and lumbered, over fences, houses, and I wondered if it would ever stay above the horizon line.

On to Oslo; Sweden that is.

Jesus Christ, that just cracked me up.

Watch for
A Fourth Face
Summer 2017

GRANT TRACEY is the author of nearly fifty short stories and four collections of fiction, including *Final Stanzas*, published by Twelve Winters Press in 2015. He teaches courses in creative writing and film at the University of Northern Iowa, and he has been the fiction editor of the *North American Review* for over fifteen years. He was the recipient of an Iowa Regents Award for Faculty Excellence in 2013. In addition to his writing, editing and teaching, Grant has acted in more than twenty community theater productions. *Cheap Amusements* is his first novel.

Final Stanzas

stories by

Grant Tracey

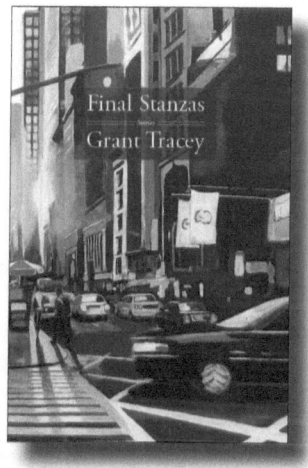

Available in print, digital &
a unique audio edition from
Twelve Winters Press

'With the compelling force of cinema, these stories pull us
across geographical and emotional borders into the deepest
recesses of the heart. It's a fine and moving collection.'
　　　　　—Steven Schwartz, author of *Little Raw Souls*

'Certain works of fiction require you to devour them in
one sitting. . . . *Final Stanzas* falls into that category.'
　　　　　　—Kelsie Plesac, *Blotterature*